DANGEROUS

BOOK SIX

Delusion

DELUCA
BROTHERS

RHONDA BREWER

Dedication

This book is dedicated to all the authors out there who have helped me in my writing journey. There isn't a better community of people.

Acknowledgements

There are so many people to thank for making this book possible, I could almost write another book on that alone. A simple thank you never seems enough to convey my gratitude but I will try to do that the best I can.

The first thank you goes to a few amazing ladies who help with editing and errors. Michelle Eriksen, Abbie Zanders, and Amabel Daniels are amazing women and dear friends. I want to thank them for their constant support and keen eye. To my dedicated betas and dear friends, Jackie Dawe Ford, Nancy Arnold-Holloway, and Karie Deegan, thank you so much for the support and encouragement. Also, a special thanks to the many authors who have become both friends and mentors. Last but certainly not least, to my readers. You are the reason that I can continue to do this.

A very special thank you to my husband, Danny who gives me the inspiration for the romantic heroes I write and encourages me every day. To my two children Laura and Colin, both of you show me everyday how proud you are and how much you love me. To my beautiful granddaughter, Emma. You may not be old enough to read yet, but your smile gives me inspiration to keep going. To my dad, James, I thank you for loving and supporting me every day.

I love all of you.

Chapter 1

Lora Norris dropped the last box on the floor in the small kitchen and sighed. Her life was such a mess. Forced to move to a small town where she didn't know a soul, didn't have a job or even know where to find one. Finding employment was priority because her nest egg wouldn't last forever. All she knew was she had to find something before it ran out. After all, she had a four-year-old daughter to support.

After Lora's father died, the family home was sold because her mom found it difficult to live in the house without the man she loved. That was when Lora suggested her mom live with her and Molly. Things were ok for about three weeks, but then the notes started.

The letters were cheesy at first, sweet poems and declarations of love from a secret admirer. Thinking it was the guy she was dating at the time being silly, she shrugged them off, but then things got disturbing.

With the mysterious delivery of strange gifts, photos, and drawings, Lora was forced to move three times, but within a few weeks of each move it would all start again. The police couldn't seem to figure out where it was all coming from, or they just didn't care.

Lora hated the constant state of concern or paranoia she felt. If it weren't for her mother, her former boss, and her mother's best friend, Lora would have packed everything and left Newfoundland to get away from all of it.

"That's the last of it." Lora turned to see her normally stylishly dressed boss place Molly's table next to the kitchen door.

"How am I ever going to thank you for helping me with all this?" Lora plopped down on one of the kitchen chairs and sighed.

"First of all, I offered. No thank you necessary. Second, the only thing I did was rent a truck under my name so that crazy creep wouldn't find out." Dallas Ball was not only her boss, but her best friend.

They met when Dallas interviewed Lora for an Interior Designer position for her firm. They hit it off right away, and Dallas hired Lora on the spot.

Lora worked at Ball Interior Design for more than six years, and she loved her job as well as her clients. That ended when Lora walked into Dallas' office the previous week and quit.

Appalled by the decision, Dallas demanded to know what was going on. Lora explained and admitted that all the previous moves were not because the apartments were unfit. Lora broke down and told her about the letters, cards and disturbing gifts. Since that day, Dallas referred to the person as the *crazy creep.*

Considering some of the gifts, Dallas wasn't wrong, but Lora was scared. She'd heard so much about stalkers and what they could do if they didn't get what they wanted. She'd taken to never going anywhere alone and only going out when she had to.

"Mommy, I got a bed in my room by the window," Molly shouted excitedly as she scurried into the kitchen.

"That's a window seat, Molly." Lora lifted her little girl onto her lap. "We can sit there and read stories, or you can watch for bunnies in the backyard."

"Bunnies," Molly squealed and jumped down from Lora's lap. "I'm gonna go see if I can see them now."

Lora and Dallas laughed as Molly bolted out of the kitchen. All the moving didn't seem to affect her daughter, which was a huge relief. The last thing Lora wanted was for her daughter to be scared.

"I can't believe Daphne doesn't use this house." Lora's mother entered the kitchen. "It's precious."

Daphne Hobbs was her mother's best friend and was one of a small group to know where Lora moved. Daphne offered the house to Lora when the letters continued after the third move.

"It's a beautiful place and the garden's incredible. Molly will beat herself out for sure running around out there." Dallas meant Molly would have so much room to play she'd be exhausted by the end of the day.

The house was a small bungalow with a covered deck around the front and left of the house. The front door opened into a small foyer which led into a large bright living room. The large eat-in kitchen was off to the left, and the four bedrooms were at the back of the house.

"The only thing I need now is to find a job." Lora sighed.

"I told you not to worry about that." Her mother chastised her.

"Sheila Norris, you can't expect your daughter to sit home and not work." Leave it to Dallas to read Lora's mind.

"I didn't say that, but at least give it a couple of weeks to see if the police can find the man." Her mother sat down and reached across the table to grab Lora's hand. "We may not have to stay here very long."

"That's what I'm worried about, Mom." Her stalker found her three times already. There was nothing to say he wouldn't do it again.

"Honey, Daphne assured me she hasn't mentioned us staying here to anyone, and all our mail goes straight to Dallas." Her mother squeezed her hand.

"That's right, and if I can't get out here to bring it to you, then I'll courier it." Dallas took Lora's other hand.

"Thank you both so much." Lora's vision blurred as she tried to hold back the tears.

"I'm glad to be out of the city." Tears formed in her mother's eyes. "Your father would've loved this place."

Her father taught high school Math and Science. Samuel Norris or Mr. Sam as his students called him, loved being a teacher, but his first love was coaching basketball and baseball. He spent a lot of time in the school gym and most times could be found there preparing game strategies. It was where the janitor found her dad after he'd suffered a massive stroke. Her father just turned fifty-three. Not only had Lora and her family been shocked by his sudden death, but the students were devastated.

Three weeks later Lora received the first note, and things got worse from there. It appeared the stalker knew every move Lora made, which was why she didn't have a whole lot of faith he wouldn't find her again.

"Well, I'm here to work not to sit around on my ass and chat." Dallas plopped a box on the kitchen table and pulled it open.

After making a considerable dent in the unpacking, Dallas left a couple of hours later. She told Lora to call at least once a day and promise to let her know if they needed anything.

"I swear, if I find out you're in need of something and you don't tell me, I'll drive out here just to kick you in the ass." Dallas gave her one last hug.

"I promise you'll be the first to know if I need anything." Lora smiled and watched her friend walk toward the U-Haul truck.

To see someone like Dallas climb behind the wheel of the large vehicle was odd. Even in her jeans and t-shirt, she was the definition of femininity, but she knew how to handle the big moving truck.

Not seeing Dallas every day would be odd and she'd miss her job. Lora had always lived in the central part of the city so moving to a small town was a significant change. It wasn't the same as Toronto or Montreal, but still, everything was close, and she'd miss the coffee shop across from her office building.

Most of all, she'd miss her volunteer work at the high school where her father taught. The principal, Clyde Spencer, told her he was sad Lora wouldn't be able to continue, probably because it meant he needed to take over her job with organizing the duties for the people who donated their time to help at the school.

Her father's assistant coach had hugged her and asked her to keep in touch. Some of the students that Lora took under her wing when she'd started were extremely upset that she wouldn't be back the following year.

Between the girls from the drama club, Clyde's son Sterling, the janitor's son, as well as the boys from both the basketball and baseball teams, Lora received more hugs and saw more tears then she'd ever expected to see.

No one knew why she had to leave, but to keep herself and Molly safe, she had to disappear until the police found the stalker. There hadn't been any comments in the letters directed at Molly, except he indicated he, Lora, and Molly were a family that nobody would tear apart.

That terrified her, but it forced her to tell her brother who got more than a little pissed because she kept it from him. Even when she explained she didn't want him to be distracted at work, he was still upset, but as a pilot, Ethan couldn't afford to be distracted while on duty. He needed complete focus on what he was doing.

The next morning Lora made her way to the grocery store. Daphne told her that Harbor Street contained stores where most locals shopped. It was the only street in Hopedale with a traffic light as well, and Lora chuckled when she walked along the road.

A couple of restaurants, bars, a movie theater, a pharmacy and a beauty salon called Snippy Gals, lined one side of the road. Hopedale Harbour was on the other side, and the dock was lined with large fishing boats unloading their catch.

Lora and her mom picked up most of what they needed before they moved, but she wanted to see if any job possibilities existed. Since most of the businesses in the town were in one area, it made it much easier to search out the employment situation. She figured if she asked around, someone might give her a lead.

"Hi." the teenager behind the register in the small grocery store smiled.

"Hello." Lora loaded the few items onto the moving belt.

"Did you find everything you needed?" The girl was way too perky, and Lora almost choked when she saw the name *Sunshine* on the girl's tag. No wonder the girl was so cheery.

"Yes, I did. Thank you." Lora waited as Sunshine rang in her items and the young teenage boy at the end bagged everything.

The clanging of tin drew her attention to the entrance, mostly because the bell startled her. Two tall, very handsome police officers sauntered in with one laughing at something the other said.

"Hi, Sunny." One waved and winked at the young girl.

"Hey, Nick." Sunshine didn't even glance at the man as she continued her task.

"How's school, Dillon?" Nick asked the boy bagging the groceries.

"Good, so far. Just doing general studies this semester. I won't apply for the Police Studies until next year." The boy gave a huge smile.

"Good for you. Give us a shout if you need any help with anything." Nick grinned and followed the other officer down one of the isles.

"I will. Thanks, Nick." Dillon nodded.

Lora tried to appear inconspicuous as her eyes followed the two men until they were out of sight. Something about a man in uniform always turned her head.

"They're so cute." Sunshine sighed when they'd got out of hearing range.

"Yes, very handsome." Lora smiled.

"Yeah, too old for me though." Sunshine giggled.

"Maybe a little," Lora said with amusement.

"You look about the right age." Sunshine rested her elbows on the counter as Lora pulled out a couple of bills to pay for her purchases.

"Are you the local matchmaker?" Lora grinned.

"Nope, that would be Aunt Cora?" Lora spun at the sound of the deep voice behind her. "I could tell you about her over a drink."

"Umm. What?" She glanced up into sky blue eyes.

He wasn't the man who spoke to Sunshine and Dillon, and something told her this one was a bit of a Casanova. The arrogant grin and his relaxed swagger told her he was confident in his pick-up lines as well.

"A.J., stop hitting on our customers." Sunshine rolled her eyes.

"He can't help it, Sunny. It's a reflex." Lora spun to the sound of the other voice and into another set of blue eyes.

"Okay." Lora turned back, but before she could take her bags, the one Sunshine called A.J. held out his hand.

"I see a beautiful woman; I've got to get to know her. Sergeant A.J. O'Connor and you are?" He winked.

"Umm... Yeah... I'm going." Lora grabbed her bags and walked away.

"Bro, you're losing your touch." Laughter followed her through the door.

There was something about Nick's deep voice that Lora felt through her entire body. As if it made her vibrate with need. Of course, it had been a long, long time since she'd had any sexual contact with anyone other than herself and her vibrating friend.

He's so hot.

"Lora for the love of God. You're not fifteen years old anymore." She mumbled as she loaded her bags into the back of her car.

"I'm sorry about my brother. He really didn't mean to make you uncomfortable." She squeaked at the sound of his voice.

"Holy shit." Lora almost fell into the trunk when she turned around.

"I didn't mean to startle you." Nick stepped back and gave her enough space to compose herself.

"You're like a ninja." Lora laughed nervously and closed the trunk.

"Not really. I just want to apologize for A.J." Nick flicked his head toward his brother.

"Not necessary." Lora eased around him and pulled open her car door.

"I know, but you looked a little spooked." Nick smiled, and Lora forced herself not to sigh.

"It's okay. Thanks though." Lora got into her car and started it as he stood there staring. For a moment, she wasn't sure he would move but he gave a little wave as he walked away.

Lora flopped her head back against the headrest and let out a huge groan. What happened to her smart mouth and quick comebacks? A year ago, she probably would have stood there and joked with the two men. Now she didn't know how to respond to harmless flirtation.

She closed her eyes and took several deep breaths to calm herself. A knock on her car window made her scream and almost jump to the passenger side. She peered up at Sunshine stood next to her car with a bag in her hand.

"I'm sorry. I didn't mean to scare you, but you left your ice cream on the counter." Sunshine passed the bag through the window after Lora lowered it.

"Umm... thanks." Lora took the bag. "By the way, do you know if there are any job openings around town?"

"Not sure, but I'm sure if you hand in some resumes to the owners you might find something." Sunshine shrugged and waved as she made her way back to the grocery store.

Two days later, Lora realized listening to a teenager was not the smartest thing to do. She'd handed out resumes to most of the businesses around town and no longer considered Hopedale as a small town. Stupidly, she decided to walk around in two-inch wedges and her feet felt as if they were on fire.

Lora stopped at a diner called *Jack's Place* for lunch, and to rest her tortured feet. Her level of frustration was through the roof since there wasn't a lot of available employment in the tiny town.

Lora lay the bundle of resumes on the counter as she sat on the nearest stool. She pulled out her phone and proceeded to scroll through the job bank. If there was nothing for her in Hopedale, maybe she could find something in one of the other surrounding towns. She glanced up when she sensed someone staring at her. An attractive older woman with auburn hair and a friendly smile stood behind the counter.

"Can I get you something, ducky?" The woman asked.

"I'd love a black coffee and a turkey sandwich." Lora smiled and glanced back at her phone.

"What kind of work are you looking for?" The woman placed a cup in front of Lora and filled it.

Lora's head snapped up and she stared at the lady. At first, she couldn't understand how she knew, but the woman nodded to the pile of resumes.

"Right now, I'd clean the rocks on the beach if it meant a paycheck." Lora's little joke made the woman laugh.

"I don't know anyone hiring for that, but I need another waitress. I'm Alice, by the way, and the owner of *Jack's Place*. My youngest daughter, Kristy, worked here most days, but she's a nurse and got a temporary job out of town. I do need someone on a full-time basis even when she comes back. My full-time girl moved to Alberta." Alice gave her a great deal of information in three seconds.

To be offered a job without an interview or at least a resume was unorthodox, but she wasn't about to bite the hand that may feed her. Lora didn't want to get off on the wrong foot with Alice and knew she needed to be honest from the start. To do that, she would have to tell her the whole twisted story of why she came to Hopedale.

"Why don't you come back to the office with me and we can have a chat." Alice motioned for her to follow. "I'll get Kit to bring your sandwich into my office and my sister-in-law Cora will take care of the tables until we finish."

Lora glanced at the other woman at the end of the counter. Her blue eyes twinkled, and her lips were turned up into a smile. She didn't look like someone who would be serving in a restaurant or pub. Dressed in a pencil skirt and pink cotton sweater, she was more professional, but she didn't seem to think twice about grabbing the apron. Lora followed Alice through the swinging doors leading to the kitchen and tried not to get too hopeful.

"My background is in interior design, but I needed to leave the firm." Lora blew out a long breath. "To be honest, I've come to Hopedale to get out of St. John's. Mostly to keep my little girl safe." Lora explained when Alice closed the door to the office.

"Oh." Alice's expression didn't change as she motioned for Lora to sit next to the desk.

"It was a suggestion from the police in St. John's." Lora didn't know any other way to explain her situation.

"Are you in trouble?" The genuine concern on the woman's face warmed Lora's heart.

"Someone's been harassing me. Stalking me. The police are investigating. I've moved several times over the last year, but he finds me. It started after my dad died." Lora fully expected Alice to retract her offer because nobody wanted that crap in their lives.

"My husband's the Chief of Police. I could ask him to look into this for you." Alice reached across the desk and took Lora's hand.

"That's not necessary, really. The police were incredible, and it's an open case. I've dealt with the same Investigator since it started." Lora swallowed the lump that formed in her throat at the woman's offer.

"Well, if you need Kurt to talk to him, just ask." Alice squeezed her hand and released it.

"You'd give me a job. Just like that?" Lora didn't want to get her hopes up.

"Honey, my husband, four nephews, the wife of another nephew, and one of my daughters are all police officers. I have another nephew who runs a high-end security firm and they drop in here daily." Alice chuckled.

"I don't have a record, and my former boss would have no issues giving you a reference as to my character. She's a dear friend and one of the very few people who know where I am." Lora bounced in the chair.

"I won't bother your former boss. My nephew's wife can find out what you had for dinner last night." Alice laughed. "She's a computer hooker."

"You mean hacker." Lora giggled.

"My heavens, yes. Sandy would find that hilarious." Alice snorted and stood up.

"I'm sure she would." Lora practically jumped to her feet and had to keep herself from lunging at the woman to hug her.

"You can start on Tuesday." Alice reached out her hand and clasped Lora's.

"Thanks so much, Alice. My name is Lora Norris by the way." Lora pulled out her license and allowed Alice to photocopy it.

"O'Connor's my last name." Alice smiled.

"Your family seems to be everywhere in town," Lora remembered the two men at the grocery store and figured they were probably two of the nephews she'd mentioned.

"We're expanding more and more." Alice walked Lora out to the front of the diner. "Come on I'll show you around."

Lora followed Alice as she gave her the tour around the diner. It reminded Lora of the fifties diners that she saw on one of her mother's favorite television shows. The Newfoundland tartan covered the tables. The accents of the colors of the tartan evident in the red seats, gold and green valances above the window and the brown color of the floor. It was perfectly put together.

Lora met some of the family that afternoon, as well as some other residents of the town. When she finally got back home she was cautiously excited.

Alice's sister-in-law was a little odd, but funny as hell. Lora pressed her lips together to hide the laughter that threatened to escape when Cora announced the love of Lora's life was close. Alice explained that Cora had a reputation as the town Cupid and knew when people belong together. According to Alice, the woman was never wrong.

Small towns certainly had odd beliefs, but this was the strangest she'd ever heard. Cora seemed sensible other than that.

Lora could deal with any unorthodox personalities if it meant a job. She crossed her fingers and prayed that things would be okay, and the police would find her stalker.

He stood outside her apartment and stared at the for-rent sign stuck in the window. She'd moved again and didn't tell him how to get in touch with her. It angered him but not so much that he would not search for her.

After all, he'd found her three times in the last ten months. She had to know she belonged to him and there was nowhere in the city where he couldn't find her.

He reached for the envelope in his jacket pocket and pulled out the photos. One at a time he shuffled through them and studied every curve of her body. Putting the camera inside her bathroom in her first apartment was the best thing he ever did. He got to see every inch of her body.

Although, he didn't need to look at them because the image of her naked body was burned into his brain. The scar across her bikini line from birthing her child didn't take away from her beauty. The two tattoos made him hard at the sight of the ink on her milky skin.

"So, my love, you need to stop leaving me. They can't keep us apart forever. I won't have it. Don't worry, I'll find you." He pulled the collar of his jacket around his neck and walked toward the place where he would bring her as soon as it was time.

Chapter 2

His day of hell finally ended, and Nick O'Connor couldn't be happier. He spent his entire shift up to his neck in coroner reports for the latest of the murdered women. His brother, John, put Nick and three other officers on a task force a little over a month earlier. The team was determined to catch the bastard killing these women and leaving their naked bodies in city parks.

The first woman disappeared just before Christmas, and she was found in Kent's Park nine days later. In a little less than a month, a second woman vanished. Her body was found in Bannerman Park after ten days.

It was over a month before the third woman was reported missing but her remains were discovered in Virginia Park only five days later. Then the latest woman was found in Pippy Park only three days after she disappeared.

The deaths were awful, but the similarity between the victims, his cousins and his brother Keith's wife made him uneasy. They also bared a striking resemblance to the pretty waitress who worked at his aunt Alice's diner. Since the first day he saw her at the grocery store just nine months earlier, she made his heart pound and his pulse race every time she smiled at him.

Nick needed to brighten up his day with a visit to *Jack's Place*. He didn't even go home to change because he didn't want to miss her. She had no idea Nick was there to see her, because Lora Norris only saw him as one of her boss's annoying nephews. No, she wasn't like some women who swooned when he flashed them a smile or a flirty wink. Especially, if he wore his uniform.

Nick wasn't arrogant. Okay, maybe that did make him a little egotistical, but it almost always worked for him. He had a face and body that turned heads, which he used it to his advantage. It was why his older brothers called him and the youngest of the O'Connor brothers man whores.

Nick pulled open the heavy oak door to the entrance and sighed as he entered the coolly air-conditioned foyer. June wasn't usually hot in Newfoundland, but over the last three days, it hit the mid-twenties. Of course, that would seem cold to some people, but it was warmer than usual. It also didn't help at a crime scene with a decomposing body.

Nick pulled off his cap, turned left, and walked into the quaint diner. The right side of the foyer led to the pub, and it didn't open until after the supper rush. His Aunt Alice and Uncle Kurt owned the business, but Alice was the essence of *Jack's Place*. Kurt was the chief of police, which made him more or less a silent owner of the pub.

The combination diner/pub was named after Nick's grandfather, Jack O'Connor. When Alice wanted to open the place, it was Jack that encouraged her to go for it. His grandfather suggested calling it *Jack's Place,* as a joke, but Alice loved the name. On the day it opened, he stood in the entrance with a huge grin on his face, making sure the customers knew the name was his idea. He'd passed away just two years later, but Alice still had a picture of him at the entrance pointing to the pub's sign.

A counter ran the length of the right side of the restaurant with stools for customers to sit and eat. On the left side, several booths that seated four to six people sat next to the large picture windows. Between the counter and the booths were some smaller tables.

Nick scanned the entire room, but to his disappointment, he didn't see Lora. Instead his cousin Kristy stood behind the counter pouring a cup of coffee for her fiancé who sat on a stool next to the entrance.

"I don't want a huge wedding, Kitten." Dean 'Bull' Nash groaned as Kristy set the cup in front of him.

"Honey, my family *is* a huge wedding." Kristy emphasized the word 'is.'

"Your cousins got to stop procreating," Dean grumbled.

"I think it's going to stop with Mike." Nick laughed and straddled the stool next to the large bald man.

"It may, but your brothers' wives are popping them out like Pez dispensers." Dean picked up the cup and sipped his coffee.

"Oh, stop it." Kristy rolled her eyes.

"Tell them to stop. Let's add this up, John has a girl and boy, and they're trying again. So that's two and possibly more. James and Marina have three boys and just found out they're having a girl. That's six. Ian and Sandy have three girls and a boy, but it seems like they're finished. That's what?" Dean glanced at Nick.

"Ten." Nick counted along in amusement.

"Right, ten. Keith and Emily have a boy and another boy on the way. That's twelve. Right?" Dean glanced at Nick again.

"Yep." Nick chuckled.

"Mike and Billie's baby girl isn't due for another few weeks, and they're already talking about having more before the baby is too old." Dean rolled his eyes. "Too old, the kid isn't born yet. Anyway, that's thirteen."

"What's your point, Dean?" Kristy reached out and ran her hand over Dean's bald head.

"My point is…" Dean stopped. "It's …."

"It's what?" Kristy grinned as she continued to caress her soon-to-be husband's head.

It was a little uncomfortable with the way his cousin gazed at Dean. Nick was witnessing some kind of intimate secret between the couple, that was obvious.

"Kitten, stop doing that." The clenched teeth gave it away.

"Yeah, I'm just gonna go over and get my own coffee. I don't want to know what that is all about." Nick pointed to Dean's head, and Kristy laughed when he hopped off the stool.

"Kitten, be prepared when you get home later." Dean growled as Nick walked behind the counter.

He poured himself a cup of steaming coffee and turned to exit behind the counter when he was almost bowled over by the curvy, auburn-haired beauty with the sapphire-blue eyes.

Lora.

"Oh, God. Sorry. I didn't see you there." Lora pulled back as if he'd hit her with his taser.

"It's okay. I probably shouldn't be behind here, but I thought Kristy was the only one here." Nick stepped back so she could squeeze by him.

"I was just in the back…" She stopped. "I need to leave, but I can put in an order if you want something."

"Nope, just coffee." Nick held up the cup and moved to the nearest stool on the end of the counter. "Leaving early?"

He didn't mean anything, but her expression tensed as if he accused her of slacking off on the job. Not that anyone would ever think that because she worked harder than any waitress he'd ever seen.

"Alice said it was okay. I just have some…" Lora snatched her purse from under the counter and scurried around to the other side.

"I was only making conversation. No explanation necessary." Nick held up his hand.

"Okay… well… bye." Lora spun around and practically ran out of the diner.

"You've really got to stop scaring that woman away." Nick rolled his eyes when his younger brother plopped on the stool next to him.

"Fuck off, A.J." Nick wasn't in the mood for Aaron's constant digs about Lora.

Aaron or A.J. as everyone called him, figured out Nick's interest in Lora shortly after Nick stopped going to the bars. She wasn't the real reason he'd stopped, but Nick couldn't convince Aaron of that. Nick had grown tired of the club scene and the revolving door of women. He was ready for something steady.

"Oh relax. Just so you know, she's like that with everyone. I can't even get a smile out of her." Aaron slapped his hand on the bar.

"Kristy, stop harassing Bull. I want a coffee and a blue berry muffin."

"You sit there and hold your breath while I run and get it." Kristy gave Bull a quick kiss and sashayed into the kitchen.

"Nah, I'd like to live a little longer," Aaron called after her.

For the next hour, Nick, Aaron, and Kristy helped serve customers who dropped in for supper. It was amusing that it took three of them to fill in for Lora. His aunt said the woman was like a spin top, and she would refuse to have Alice help when it got busy.

"Well, I'm gonna head home." Nick was still in his uniform and probably shouldn't have been serving people, but he did get some great tips. He tossed them in Lora's tip jar. Aaron and Kristy did the same.

"I'll see you later. I'm heading over to Mike's to help him put up bookshelves in Billie's home office." Aaron cleared away the last of the dishes on the counter. "Mike said she wants to get everything done before the baby comes."

"Oh dear." Alice scurried out from the kitchen.

"What's wrong, Mom?" Kristy asked.

"Lora left in such a hurry she forgot her phone in the kitchen." Alice held up an old smartphone with a cracked screen.

"I'm sure Nicky can drop that off if you give him her address." His Aunt Cora's voice startled him. He hadn't seen her come in, but she walked out of the kitchen and handed a bag to a woman at the counter.

"I can drop it off." Aaron wiggled his eyebrows.

"You'll do no such thing, young man. Go help Mike." Cora pushed Aaron out through the door.

"Here, Nicky. Alice, write down the address for him." Cora took the phone from Alice and placed it in Nick's hand.

"I'm not sure, Cora." Alice hesitated.

"I *am* sure." Cora rested her hand on Alice's arm.

"She may not appreciate me giving out her address." Alice still appeared reluctant.

"Mom, she probably needs her phone." Kristy interjected.

"You're not sending a stranger to her house. Nicky's your nephew and you know he's a good boy." Cora cupped Nick's cheek.

It amused him how at almost thirty-two, his aunt still referred to Nick and his six brothers as boys. Of course, he wouldn't dare correct her which was why he stood with Lora's phone in his hand.

Nick prayed that Cora's insistence on him returning the phone didn't have something to do with her cupid shit. Everyone called her Cora the Cupid, and to his knowledge, she was never wrong. She'd also set her sights on Nick in recent months and told him several times to ask Lora out.

"Fine." Alice wrote down something on a piece of paper and handed it to him.

"This is on my way home anyway." Nick and Aaron moved into a bunkhouse on their older brother Keith's property. Since most of Keith's employees started to buy houses in and around Hopedale, most of the bunkhouses his brother built were empty. Now that Nick and Aaron worked strictly with the Hopedale division of the Newfoundland Police Department, it was more convenient to move back to their hometown.

"She lives on Knob Lane. That's a pretty secluded road," Kristy said.

"It's very close to Nicky too." Cora smiled.

"Yeah, I'm gonna go now." Nick shook his head and held the phone up to Alice. "I'll make sure she gets this before I go home, Aunt Alice." Nick kissed both his aunts on the cheek and gave Kristy a quick hug.

"Behave yourself with her," Alice warned.

"I will." Nick made his way out to the parking lot and got into his cruiser.

Kristy was right about Knob Lane. There were only two houses on the entire stretch of unpaved road. A couple of weeks before, Nick got a call to one of the homes over a possible prowler, but all he found were moose tracks in the mud behind the house.

The elderly man who owned the house lived there as long as Nick could remember. Albert Batten wasn't the most pleasant person in the world, but who would be when you lived alone. As far as Nick knew, the man had no family or friends.

Nick pulled into the driveway that he'd almost missed for the second time. Considering he grew up in Hopedale, he should know the roads better, but with the dense shrubs and trees lining the driveway it was easy to miss. It was barely wide enough to drive through, and branches brushed against the side of the car.

"If this car gets scratched up John will shoot me," Nick grumbled.

John, his oldest brother, and supervisor could be a little OCD when it came to the vehicles. He went through hell to get the six new vehicles for the department and made sure the officers took care of them. If Nick brought the cruiser back with scratches, John would have a meltdown.

The small bungalow appeared well cared for with a flower garden on both sides of the front steps. The scent of freshly cut grass surrounded Nick as he stepped out of the vehicle.

Nick knocked on the door and glanced down twice at the phone in his hand while he patiently waited for an answer. He was about to knock a second time when the door opened slowly.

At first, it appeared to have opened on its own. Then Nick glanced down to see a wide-eyed little girl in a pink sundress staring up at him with a lollipop in her hand.

"Hi," she said.

"Hello." Nick crouched in the same way he did when he talked to his nieces and nephews. He hated when he was a kid and adults would tower over him. It was intimidating.

"I'm Molly." She held out the hand without the candy.

"I'm Nick." He shook the little girl's hand as she glanced around him.

"Is that your police car?" She pointed to the cruiser.

"Yes, it is." Nick smiled.

"You're a policeman?" She tilted her head in the cute way kids did.

"Yes, I am," Nick remembered Lora had a daughter. He'd never been introduced to the little girl but saw her lots of times at the pub.

"That means you're a good guy." The little girl pushed her hair back from her face. "I'm four."

"You're a big girl. Is your mom or dad here?" Nick asked because no adult seemed to have noticed the little girl opened the door.

"I don't have a dad, but Mommy's in the bathroom pooping. I'm supposed to sit by the door, but you knocked." Molly explained, and Nick bit his lip to keep from laughing.

He was pretty sure her mom didn't want everyone to know what she was doing at that moment.

"I see, could you…." Nick stopped when he heard a voice.

"Molly, I told you to stay…" Lora appeared in the open door, and Nick stood up.

"Nick? What are you doing here?" Lora picked Molly up and propped the little girl on her hip.

"Aunt Alice asked me to drop this off to you. You left it in the kitchen." Nick held out the phone, and she groaned.

"No wonder I couldn't find it." Lora's fingers grazed him as she took the phone. It was as if an electric shock ran through his body. Lora must have felt it too because she snatched her hand back with the phone.

"Nick's a policeman, Mommy. That means he's a good guy." Molly pointed to him.

"It's not polite to point, but yes you're right." Lora pushed the little girl's arm down.

"It's the first time I've met your daughter." Nick smiled at the little girl.

"My mom takes care of her when I'm at work." Lora shoved her phone into her back pocket. "Thanks for dropping my phone off. I don't have a land line, so I'd be out of luck if I needed to call someone."

"You're welcome. It was on my way home." Nick didn't want to leave, but Lora didn't appear to want company.

"Well, I've got to get this little one into the bath and bed. Thanks again, Nick." Lora started to close the door.

"No problem. It was nice to meet you, Molly." Nick waved as he made his way down the steps.

"Bye, Nick." The door closed as the little girl stuck the lollipop in her mouth and waved.

He made his way back to his car but stopped when he saw an older woman pull into the driveway. She stopped when she saw Nick and practically ran from her car.

"My God are Lora and Molly okay?" The woman was frantic.

"Yes, ma'am." Nick smiled.

"Then why are you here?" She still didn't seem sure everything was okay.

"Lora left her phone at work, and Aunt Alice asked me to drop it off to her." Nick smiled. "I'm Nick O'Connor."

"Oh dear. I'm sorry for the slight panic. I'm sorry... I saw the police car... and you and...." The woman had her hands pressed to her chest.

"My apologies for worrying you. Lora and Molly are perfectly fine." Nick assured the woman.

"I'm Sheila Norris. Lora's my daughter, and I'm sure you've heard a mother's job is to constantly worry." Sheila calmed and smiled.

There was a strong resemblance between Lora and her mother. The brown hair, sapphire-blue eyes, and bright smile.

"I see where Lora and Molly get their beauty. It's nice to meet you." Nick reached out to shake the woman's hand.

"Oh, aren't you a charmer. Wait? Nick? O'Connor?" Sheila held onto his hand.

"Yes, ma'am." It was a little awkward, but Nick didn't pull his hand away.

"Oh," she said as she squeezed his hand and released it.

"Not sure if that's good or not." Nick chuckled.

"Lora mentioned you. And your brothers of course." Sheila smiled.

"There's a lot of us." Nick opened the door to the cruiser.

"Yes, there are. Thank you for dropping off Lora's phone." Sheila backed up, so Nick could get into the car.

"No trouble. Have a great evening, Mrs. Norris." Nick waved as he carefully turned his car around and headed home.

Lora's mother seemed terrified when she saw him. Almost as if she thought something happened to Lora and Molly. That peaked his curiosity.

Lora didn't seem to be a troublemaker, but he knew things weren't always as they appeared. However, his gut told him, Lora wasn't that type of person. She was shy, but her smile brightened up a room, or at least it did for him. Then it struck him. She wasn't shy with the women. It was only men, and it was more guarded than shy.

He'd seen it many times. His brother James' wife had been in a violent marriage, and it took four years before Marina moved on with his brother. Of course, it wasn't her husband who abused her, it was his twin, but that was a whole fucked up situation that turned out great in the end.

Had Lora been in an abusive relationship? Sheila's reaction was odd, but Molly didn't seem afraid or traumatized.

Kristy seemed to be the closest to Lora from working with her at the diner from time to time. Something was off, and Nick wanted to know what it was. If Lora was in any danger, she needed to know she lived in a town that protected its own. Nick wanted to be the one to show her that.

No. She wasn't right. Another one that was utterly wrong. Even when he put the temporary tattoos and scarred them they still didn't measure up. The constant begging him not to kill them or to let them go irritated his last nerve.

What else was he supposed to do? He'd tried everything to find her, but this time they'd hidden her well. She didn't work at that place anymore, and she never went to the school anymore. Her mother disappeared too, which told him the old woman was involved in hiding his love.

Well he wasn't giving up. Sheila never missed her club night. If he had to stay in the woods outside Daphne's house until Sheila showed up, that was what he would do.

He entered the coffee shop and gasped. He knew it wasn't his love, but she was more like her than anyone he'd ever seen. The little boy with her made him smile. She was a mother too. All he had to do was follow her for a couple of days and then recreate his love. What choice did he have?

Chapter 3

"Molly Leigh Norris, you know better than to open the door to strangers." Lora chastised her little girl after she practically slammed the door in Nick's face.

"He wasn't a stranger, Mommy. You know him, and he's a good guy." Molly pulled the lollipop out of her mouth. "Silly, Mommy. You was pooping, and he kept knocking on the door."

"Molly, *please* tell me you didn't tell Nick why you answered the door instead of Mommy." Lora knew the answer before she asked the question.

"He asked where my mommy was." Molly shrugged, and Lora set the child on the floor.

Great.

Molly told one of the sexiest men Lora ever met she was busy pooping and couldn't answer the door. Well, at least it would stop the way he flirted with her. Not that she didn't find him attractive because the man made her melt with his deep voice, dimpled smile and sky-blue eyes. If she were in a different situation, Nick O'Connor would definitely be on the menu.

She just couldn't take the chance of putting someone else in danger. The phone calls, notes, drawings, and creepy gifts stopped, but Lora still felt the eerie chill on the back of her neck from time to time.

She'd been in Hopedale almost nine months, and it was a wondrous place. The customers were friendly for the most part, and the regulars were mostly the O'Connor's friends or family. They treated her with nothing but kindness and respect. Still, it unnerved her when Nick or Aaron flirted with her. Although the only time Aaron did it was when Nick was nearby. Almost as if he wanted to tease his brother or piss him off.

"Lora, I'm home." She heard her mother's voice from the doorway.

"I'm bathing Molly, Mom," Lora called out as she rinsed the soap from Molly's hair.

Her mother joined a committee in Hopedale that helped with events around the town during the summer. It didn't usually coincide with Lora's hours at work, but Alice was on the same committee and asked if her mother could come to a meeting that day. It was the reason Lora got off early.

Her mom appeared in the doorway with a huge grin. Not that her mother didn't smile but since Lora's dad died her mom seemed mostly sad. Lora tried to talk her into joining a support group, but she'd refused.

"I saw a very handsome police officer in our driveway." She crossed her arms.

"That's Nick." Molly was much too excited about Nick.

"I left my phone at work, and Alice asked him to drop it off. It's her nephew. I'm sure you've met him before." Lora sat back on her heels and glanced up at her mother.

"Nick told me." Her mother raised one of her eyebrows.

"Mom, what's with that face?" Lora's mother wanted Lora to start dating again, but a stalker loomed somewhere, and she wasn't about to involve anyone in that.

Roy Lindon was the last guy she dated. He barely missed driving over a cliff when his brakes wouldn't work on his way home from her house. According to the investigation it appeared that they had been cut, and Roy ran for the hills after that.

"Honey, I see your eyes light up when you talk about him coming into eat, and how he flirts with you." She kneeled next to Lora.

"Mom, a lot of men flirt with waitresses." Lora rolled her eyes.

"But when you tell me about Nick, you smile, and your eyes get that sparkle they lost. I've seen him when I'm there too. He can't take his eyes off you." Her mother cupped Lora's cheek.

"Mom, you're seeing things. Nick has a reputation and can have any woman he wants. Plus, I'm not in a situation to start a relationship with anyone." Lora smiled when Molly poured water over her dolls head to rinse off the bubbles.

"You can't stop living, Lora." Her mom was like a dog with a bone.

"I've been saying that to you for the last month, Mom." Lora hated to turn it around on her mother especially since the woman moved with her to a place neither of them knew.

"As a matter of fact, I've taken your advice. I'm going to a dinner party tomorrow evening with a few friends." Sheila stood up and gave her a smug smile.

"Mom, dinner with your friends before card night, is not a dinner party." Thursday club night was something her mother and five of her mom's friend had been doing as long as Lora could remember.

"I say it is." Sheila spun around and left the bathroom.

"Nana's in denial, Molly." Lora laughed.

"I like Nick, Mommy." Molly stared up at her with her blue eyes a mirror of her own.

"I like you, Molly." Lora kissed the top of her head as she helped her daughter out of the bathtub and wrapped her in a towel.

"You *love* me, Mommy." Molly giggled when Lora tickled her feet after rubbing them dry.

"Yes, I do, sweet girl." Lora lifted her into her arms and made her way to the little girl's room to get her ready for bed. "More than all the water in the ocean."

"I love you more than all the rocks on the beach, Mommy." Molly hugged her.

Molly was the only thing that mattered in her life. She missed dating and sex. Oh, how she missed sex, but none of that was important if Molly was in danger. Which meant, even if she did have a chance with Nick, she couldn't pursue it.

Molly was up at six in the morning, and Lora thanked the lord her mother was a morning person. Lora would get a couple of extra hours sleep before work on Thursdays since she worked until six. That way she would be home in time for her mother to get to card night by eight.

"I can't wait to see the fireworks on Canada Day." Molly bounced excitedly as Lora entered the kitchen.

"It sounds like lots of fun." Lora poured a cup of tea for herself and grabbed a banana out of the basket on the counter.

"I read the town council, fire department and police department barbeque burgers and hotdogs. They make s'mores for the kids later in the evening too." Her mother pointed to the town newsletter on the counter.

"Do you think you can stay up late enough for the fireworks, Molly?" Lora had a strict eight pm bedtime, not because Lora enforced it but because her daughter couldn't stay awake after that.

"I can take a nap that day." Molly's idea of a nap was funny since the little girl only napped when she was sick.

"Good idea." Her mother smiled. "Nana will take a nap that day too so neither of us will be tired."

"Mommy, will you take a nap?" Molly gazed up at her.

"I'll be working, honey." Canada Day was a national holiday, but Lora assumed Alice would still open for the public.

"You should check to see if they open that day. Small towns usually shut everything down for holidays." Her mother was probably right, but she wasn't going to ask.

Two hours later, Lora's feet burned, and a bead of sweat ran down the middle of her back. The lunch rush was the busiest time of the day but the best time for tips. Alice paid her a little more than most waitresses made in the city, but it wasn't the same as what she'd made as an interior designer. The tips gave her that extra money she could poke away for something special.

Lora cleared a booth, but her head snapped up when a shadow moved across the window. One of the ladies who worked at the beauty salon a few buildings down scurried down the sidewalk

40

probably in a hurry to get back to work. Lora still jumped at the dumbest things.

"Can I sit here?" Lora spun around and dropped her cloth to the floor when she heard his voice.

"A.J., did anyone ever tell you not to sneak up on people?" Lora snatched up the cloth.

"If he doesn't sneak up on women they run away." Jess nudged her cousin.

Jess was Alice's middle daughter and a police officer. Kristy told Lora that Jess taught self-defence classes when she wasn't on duty, and she was a black belt in Karate as was her father and a couple of her cousins. Lora was tempted to ask several of the family about the lessons, but it never seemed to be the right time.

"Hi Jess, you want the usual?" Lora smiled as Aaron and Jess slid into the booth she'd just cleared.

"Yeah, turkey sandwich on multigrain with avocado and tomato." Jess tucked her police cap next to her on the bench.

Not that Lora didn't know by now. The girl ate the same sandwich every lunchtime when she was on duty. Alice stated her daughter was the only reason she kept avocado in the restaurant because nobody else ate it.

"What would you like, A.J.?" Lora pulled her notebook out of her apron.

"Your phone number." Aaron winked and glanced over her shoulder.

"That's original." The voice behind her sent a shiver through her body. She knew it was him without even turning around. Nick's smooth voice was sexy, and it was hard for her to keep her reaction hidden.

"Like you haven't used that line a thousand times." Aaron moved in as Nick practically pushed his brother closer to the window.

"Stop hitting on Mom's staff and order." Kristy wrapped her arm around Lora's shoulder. "You do have my permission to give them our special spit seasoning or pour a jug of ice water over that one." Kristy tossed a napkin at Aaron.

"She's not that mean, cuz." Aaron narrowed his eyes at Kristy.

"I can come back if you aren't ready to order." Lora glanced at Aaron and Nick. Her gaze stayed a little longer on Nick than it should have but she couldn't help it.

"If you two don't order I'll do it for you. I'm starved." Jess wiggled her finger back and forth between both men.

"Fuck that. You'll order me some health food shit that'll send my body into shock." Aaron grumbled. "I'll have a hot turkey with fries and gravy."

"I'll have the same." Nick smiled at her.

42

"How do you guys stay in such amazing shape when you eat like that?" A high-pitched voice caused Lora to glance at the woman in the next booth.

"We work out. Hard." Aaron wiggled his eyebrows at the woman making her giggle like a teenager.

Can you say airhead?

Kristy and Jess seemed to have the same train of thought because both girls rolled their eyes at the fake blonde.

"I'm sure you do." The woman ran her long nail between her fake breasts, but it wasn't Aaron she devoured with her eyes.

The woman's eyes locked onto Nick, and Lora wanted to scratch the bitch's eyes out. She could always sit on Nick's lap and make it look as if he was taken. Lora shivered at the thought because she'd give anything to be able to show the man of her dreams just how much she wanted to do with him.

"Yeah, it's really gross actually. Sometimes they fart when they do squats." Jess turned to the blonde. "I hate working out with them."

The blonde gasped, and her *fuck me* face disappeared. Lora bit her lip to keep from laughing out loud at the woman's expression and the way she wobbled as she practically ran out of the diner.

"Thanks a lot, Jess," Aaron grumbled.

"Relax A.J.; her boobs would probably pop if you squeezed them too hard." Kristy laughed as she sat next to her sister.

"On that note, I'm going to put in your orders." Lora walked away with a shake of her head but a smile on her face.

It must be interesting to have a large family. It wasn't something Lora grew up with, because both her parents had no siblings, and she only had Ethan. He was on call for two weeks and then had a week off. Her mother convinced him to stay with them on his next rotation. He was supposed to be back the day before Canada Day.

"Lora, order's up," Kit shouted from the service window.

"Thanks," Lora smiled at the cook as she placed the plates for Aaron, Nick, and Jess on the tray, and was on the way back to the table when she realized she hadn't asked what beverage they wanted.

"Damn. I forgot their drinks." Lora mumbled to herself.

"It's okay, Kristy took care of it." Nick appeared at the counter and grabbed the tray from her hands. "She said you haven't taken a break since you came in. I got this. You take a few minutes to yourself."

"I'm fine, Nick." Lora reached for the tray, but he held it above his head. Nick was over six feet tall which was practically a foot over her five-feet-one-inch. "That's not fair."

"It's great to be tall sometimes." Nick winked and sauntered away with the tray.

Lora's gaze dropped to his ass. Any red-blooded woman would do the same. Especially the way his jeans hugged his firm glutes and hung low on his narrow hips. He was hot in his uniform, but in jeans and T-shirt, Nick O'Connor was the embodiment of sexy.

"It's a great ass, isn't it?" Lora turned at the whispered voice next to her ear.

"Sandy," Lora rolled her eyes. "Do you think you should be sizing up your brother-in-law's butt?"

"I know a sexy ass when I see one, but I was trying to be your inner voice." Sandy grinned.

"My inner voice wouldn't say that." Lora adored the woman.

Sandy was funny, and it was obvious to anyone that met her that she said what was on her mind. She was married to another O'Connor brother, and when they were together, the love they had for each other could be felt by anyone close to them.

"You need to have a chat with that inner voice because if you didn't see that fine ass, there's something wrong." Sandy plopped down on the stool.

"Sizing up one of my brother's asses again, Churchie?" Sandy grinned when she turned around.

Lora didn't understand the nickname at first but when Kristy explained Sandy's maiden name was Churchill it made sense. Sandy also called him Doc, but that was obvious since Ian was a doctor.

"Your ass is the only one that makes me hot, Doc. And your chest, and your abs, and your huge…." Ian covered her mouth with his hand before she continued.

"And that's all I need to hear." Lora backed away from the couple, laughing.

"I don't think Sandy has the filter that keeps people from saying things they shouldn't." Lora laughed at Isabelle's accurate description of Ian's wife.

"Maybe we should all drop that filter sometimes." Lora glanced in Nick's direction.

Isabelle was the oldest of Alice's daughters. She dropped by very little, since she ran her own restaurant a little further up the road. It wasn't like the diner. *A Taste of Hopedale* was one of those restaurants for romantic dates or business meetings. Lora had never been inside, but she'd heard from others that the food was exceptional, and the atmosphere was relaxing.

"Lora, I dropped by to ask if you can do me a favor." Isabelle rested her hands on the bar, clasped together as if she was praying.

"Sure, what can I do for you?" Lora loved to help when she could especially since the family was so accepting of her.

"I know Mom's only opening to family and friends on Canada Day. So, she won't need you to work, but of course, she'll want you and your family to be here, but that won't be until midafternoon." Lora was excited to be off for the holiday because she could spend the day with Molly.

"That sounds great." Lora still hadn't heard the favor.

"Well, one of my servers has a family commitment that morning, and I didn't know my manager booked a group for brunch that day, and I'm short one waitress." Isabelle continued as if she was afraid to ask.

"Are you asking me to fill in for brunch, Isabelle?" Lora smiled.

"Yes. I know you've got a little girl, but it's only a couple of hours. You'll be done in plenty of time to join the party, and I'll pay you double time plus tips." Isabelle hopped up on the stool.

"As long as your mother doesn't mind, I'd be happy to do it. I'd never turn down extra income." Lora wasn't destitute, but her savings had slowly depleted, and she hated not having a nest egg.

If her mom didn't live with her, finances would be a struggle. Her mother wasn't wealthy, but with Lora's dad's life insurance and pension, she was comfortable. She and her mother split the bills, and her mom cared for Molly when Lora worked. Lora never wanted her mother paying for anything, but she could never win an argument with the woman.

"You know, I've got events we cater outside the restaurant sometimes. If you're interested and it doesn't leave Mom short staffed, I think you'd be great." Isabelle seemed excited, but Lora could end up in the city, and she wasn't about to take that chance.

"Thanks for the offer but I wouldn't be able to do it on a regular basis. I want to spend my free time with Molly and my mom." It wasn't a lie.

"If you change your mind let me know, but you can still do Canada Day, right?" Isabelle asked.

"For sure," Lora confirmed.

"Thanks so much. Kristy usually fills in for these things, but my sister's so busy these days I'm lucky if I see her more than an hour a day." Isabelle laughed.

"Hey, I only get to see my brother a week out of each month and that's if I'm lucky. He's a pilot and his schedule's terrible." Lora smiled.

"That sucks." Isabelle glanced back at the table where her sisters and cousins sat. "You know, Nick's a great guy. He can be a pain in the ass, and his flirting bone is almost as big as A.J.'s, but he's got a heart of gold." She turned back to Lora with a smile.

"I know he's a nice guy, but why are *you* telling me this?" Lora had been told the same thing by Alice, Kristy, Sandy, Marina, Cora and practically every female in the O'Connor family.

"He likes you, but he's a little out of his element. You aren't falling all over him." Isabelle laughed.

Lora could feel the heat in her cheeks, and her eyes dropped to where she started to wipe down the counter unconsciously. What was she supposed to say to that? If things were different, she would fall all over the guy. Well, not to that extent. She wasn't that type of woman, but she absolutely would have said yes, the first time he asked her to sit down and have a coffee with him.

"Okay, maybe I shouldn't have said that, because he'd probably kill me. I've come to find that my cousins like to spill their guts to me, but I have no idea why." Isabelle laughed.

"I guess you're like their sister." Lora heard all of the O'Connor brothers say it a lot over the last few months.

"Well, I'm gonna go say a quick hi to that rowdy table before I go back to the restaurant. Talk to you later." Isabelle waved as she made her way to the booth and squeezed in the seat next to Kristy.

Lora missed the fun of a social life. She'd always had lots of friends, and it wasn't out of the ordinary to meet them at a club or restaurant. A couple of times a week she'd meet her friends at the coffee shop across from her old office.

Even after her daughter was born, and Molly's father ran for the hills, she still had somewhat of a social life. Now she was almost afraid of her own shadow. When she saw anyone that didn't appear to be a local, it put her on edge. Lora hadn't been outside Hopedale since she and her mother moved.

It was tough to relax after almost year of walking on egg shells. There were times she wasn't sure the police believed her. Even with the cards and gifts, it felt as if most of them blew her off. It was why Lora tried to ignore it at first, but when a creepy gift showed up in her mailbox, she knew it was more than an average secret admirer. That was when she moved the first time.

For a couple of weeks, she felt secure because with the change of address, and phone number, everything stopped. Then three weeks later a box was delivered to her office. She opened it, and all the blood felt as if it drained from her body. It contained very graphic drawings of couples in various sexual positions. She called the police again, and the officer that arrived on that occasion took it seriously. He promised he would do everything to find the guy, but as usual, it didn't lead anywhere. That sort of thing happened with every move. Everything would be fine for a few weeks, and then it would start all over again.

Now she was in a place where she felt somewhat safe and secure. She hadn't received any creepy presents, drawings, letters or texts. Still, she would find herself taking a quick glance over her shoulder without reason, and if her mom was late, she'd feel panicked until either her mother arrived home or she could get in touch with her.

Lora prayed it was over, and the guy finally gave up. Still, nightmares woke her more frequently than she liked. Hopedale was a great town, but she missed the city sometimes. She didn't think she'd want to live there again, but it would be nice to drive into town and go to a movie or shopping. She just didn't want to bring trouble to the town or the people she'd grown to care about.

Something in the back of her mind told Lora to keep her guard up, and every day she was closer to it beginning all over again. Lora didn't worry about herself, her concern was her mother and daughter. It didn't matter what this guy did to her, but she'd move heaven and earth to keep the people she loved out of danger.

Daddy, please watch over them.

She screamed at him to let her go but he just couldn't. She was the closest he'd ever come to his love. He didn't even have to scar this one because she had the exact scar.

"Please, let me go." She tugged at the restraints keeping her secured to the bed. "I'm a single mother."

"Don't worry, my love. We'll be a family with our little girl." He continued to set up the ink to start the first of the tattoos.

He also had to inject her with the sedative because he wouldn't be able to make the perfect tattoos with her squirming and pulling away from him.

Even though he knew the tattoos would not last on her skin, he'd enjoy the calm feeling of drawing on her milky skin. It was the only thing he'd liked with the others. He figured that once she got used to the beautiful pictures she'd want to make it permanent.

"I have a son. Please." She sobbed, but he knew it wasn't real. She wanted to be with him.

"Lora, I'll make sure our little girl will be here soon." He cupped her cheek, and she tried to pull away. "Don't do that." He growled.

"You have the wrong person, my name is…" He slapped her across the face to keep her from finishing the sentence.

"You are my Lora. My love." He pulled out the needle and jabbed it into her arm.

"No… what is…" A few seconds later her eyes fluttered closed, and he got to work.

Chapter 4

He pushed the barbell off his chest to complete the last repetition of chest presses, and Ian set it back on the rack. It was the last set for Nick for the day. His arms felt like wet noodles as he sat up and stretched them over his head.

"That's it for me today." Nick stood up.

"You seem to be spending a lot of time here at the gym lately." Ian tossed him a bottle of water.

"Just keeping in shape." Nick lied, because the truth was he was sexually frustrated.

"You sure that's it? A.J. said you haven't been dating much lately." Ian raised an eyebrow and grinned.

"A.J. gossips like an old woman," Nick responded after he gulped back the rest of the water.

"Yes, he does, but he's not wrong, is he?" Ian wiped down the barbell and walked around to stand next to Nick.

"It's not like I'm sitting home knitting. Jesus, he's one to talk, he doesn't go out much either, lately." Nick noticed Aaron seemed to have something on his mind but for some reason wasn't voicing it.

"Are my baby brothers finally growing up?" Ian pinched Nick's cheek.

"Fuck off, Asshole," Nick slapped Ian's hand away.

"Maybe it has something to do with a certain cute waitress at the diner." Ian smiled.

"What is with you? I swear the longer all of you are married, the more you want to marry the rest of us off." Nick snatched his hoody from the end of the rack.

"I was referring to A.J.'s interest in Lora." Ian raised an eyebrow.

Nick didn't know what happened, but in a split second, he had Ian pinned against the wall and his fist cocked ready to clock his brother.

"Did I strike a nerve, bro?" Ian covered Nick's fist with his hand.

Ian didn't seem the least bit concerned that he almost got a punch to the face. Probably because Ian could kick Nick's ass without a second thought. Nick could hold his own, but Ian was a black belt in Karate, and the only one that could probably kick his brother's ass, would be Kurt.

"A.J. needs to stay away from her. She's got a kid and doesn't need a bigger one." Nick stepped back and released his older brother.

"If you're interested in her, stop hitting on her as if she's just another conquest, and ask her out." Ian clapped his hand on Nick's shoulder.

"I don't do that shit. Not with her." Nick sighed. "I've never… it's strange… I don't want just one night."

"Looks like cupid hit you right in the chest, bro." Ian slapped his hand against Nick's chest.

"Fuck off, leave Aunt Cora out of this." Nick pushed his hand away and pulled on his hoody.

"She's never wrong," Ian shouted as Nick walked through the door.

Ian was right, but the truth was, Nick was scared. Yes, the second biggest man-whore of the O'Connor brothers was afraid to believe his aunt was right.

His strong attraction to Lora wasn't just physical. Although, it was difficult to get his dick to behave whenever he was close to her. She always smelled like lilacs, and he couldn't even walk close to one of the fucking trees now without getting hard.

The biggest problem was he couldn't stop worrying about her. Every time he walked into the station and glanced at the board that contained all the photos of the murdered women, it made his stomach churn.

Another girl had gone missing the week before, and the similarity between the woman and Lora was uncanny. Her body was found the previous morning in Bowering Park. It only took them four days to find this one, but it meant the bastard was dumping them within in a couple of days of their abduction.

Nick's phone vibrated in his pocket as he got to the bunkhouse. He pulled it out and Cory's number was displayed on the screen.

Cory Fleming was another of the investigators working on the case with him. He was a good friend and a member of the cover band Nick's brothers, John, Aaron, Mike, a lawyer friend Jason and himself, put together. It was fun, and they would play for charity events from time to time. They also played a couple of times a month at his aunt's pub.

"Hey," Nick tapped the speaker as he yanked off his hoodie over his head.

"Hey, I wanted to let you know, the coroner said it's the same fucker. That's five now. It was almost two months since the last one, but I get the feeling the next one will be less." Cory sounded as pissed as Nick felt over the situation.

"Fuck, and let me guess, no evidence?" Nick flopped down on the couch.

"It's only a preliminary report. Don't have anything on nail scrapings or anything yet. Maybe this one got a piece of the sick prick." Cory sighed.

"I'd like to get a piece of this fucker," Nick admitted. "Was this one raped?"

"Nope, just stripped, fake tattoos, but the scar was old. I don't get what this nutjob is doing." Cory wasn't the only one.

The fact these women weren't raped meant either this guy couldn't get it up, or he wasn't getting exactly what he wanted. He'd strangle them to death and leave them naked for someone to find. John had the idea the suspect wanted to humiliate the women, but the question was why?

He stood at the edge of the park where the crime scene tape surrounded the area. It took them less time to find this one. He didn't care, the women were trash. None of them measured up to his love.

There was only one thing to do. He needed to find someone who knew where to locate her. Several people came to mind, but his train of thought got interrupted and he tensed as a police officer walked toward him. He wasn't about to screw things up now. He nodded at the cop.

"What's going on, officer?" He shoved his hands into his pockets.

"Sorry, I can't tell you anything at the moment, but we'd like to make sure this walkway is opened up. I'd appreciate it if you would move along." He glanced at the man's tag. The cocky bastard thought he intimidated him, but he wasn't afraid of a brainless pig.

"Certainly," He forced a smile at Officer Parker.

"Thank you." Parker nodded as he turned around and headed back to the crime scene.

Didn't they ever hear that the suspect always returns to the scene of the crime? Then again, it would be hard for them to pick anyone out with the crowds of people surrounding the place.

He didn't have time to worry about those idiots. He had someone to visit. He was determined to get the information even if it required him to beat it out of her. The thought excited him almost as much as the possibility of finally locating his love.

Chapter 5

Lora couldn't keep herself from continuously glancing in the direction of the front door of the diner. Nick usually showed up at the same time every day, and he was over thirty minutes late.

She'd wiped down the counter so much that it started to shine. There were only two people currently eating in the diner, and she'd wiped down almost every surface of the place at least twice.

It was insane that she was so used to his presence and missed his goofy comments. As crazy as it was, she needed to see him.

"You should probably take a break before the supper rush." Alice took the cloth from her hand.

"It's okay. I'm fine. I'm not exactly run off my feet here at the moment." Lora chuckled.

"True," Alice pushed the swinging door and went into the kitchen.

When the front door opened again Lora spun around to glance in the direction. She pressed her lips together to keep the sigh from escaping. The urge to lick him from head to toe every time she saw him in uniform was ridiculous.

Nick marched right to his usual booth and tossed his cap on the seat. As he plopped down on the bench, he raked his hand through his short brown hair. He'd definitely had a stressful day. Lora could tell from the way his forehead wrinkled, and his jaw clenched.

Lora filled a cup with fresh coffee and brought it to the table where Nick gazed through the large picture window. It was another thing he did when he had a bad day.

"You look like you need this." Lora placed the cup in front of him with three creamers because he liked to put them in himself.

"Yeah. Thanks, Lora," Nick smiled, but it wasn't the usual bright, sexy smile that made her panties wet.

"Something wrong?" She couldn't stop herself from asking, but wanted to take it back when he sighed.

"Just a rough day." Nick opened the creamers and poured them into the cup.

"Sorry," Lora didn't want to pry. If it was work related, he probably couldn't talk about it anyway.

"Don't be. Your pretty smile makes my day a whole lot brighter." Nick winked then dropped his eyes to where his hands wrapped around the cup.

"Would you like to order some…." Lora was cut off by a loud crash from the kitchen.

Before she had a chance to run to the back, Nick was on his feet and through the swinging doors leading to the kitchen. Lora was behind him seconds later. When she entered, she gasped. Nick knelt next to where Alice lay on the floor surrounded by broken glass and a step ladder on top of her.

"Alice, my God. What happened? Are you okay?" Lora stepped over the broken dishes to help Nick lift the ladder that tipped over on top of Alice.

"I fell off the ladder trying to get dishes from the shelf." Alice tried to get up but cringed.

"Aunt Alice, we need to call an ambulance." Nick pulled out his phone and glanced at Lora.

"Don't you dare, Nicky. I can get up. Just give me a second." Alice groaned when she tried to move again, but it was clear she couldn't get up on her own.

"Alice, you may have broken something. I'm calling for help." Lora didn't pay attention to her boss's refusal to call for assistance.

"Aunt Alice, you don't have a choice. Now lay still until the ambulance gets here." Nick's voice was sweet but firm.

Lora grew up in the city, and at first, didn't realize how fast news spread in a small town. She found out how quickly about three weeks after she'd moved there. Before the ambulance pulled up in front of Jack's Place, several of the O'Connor family crowded inside the diner, but one person made Lora smile. Kurt O'Connor, Alice's husband.

"Baby, are you okay? That's it. You're hiring someone to take over all this heavy stuff in the back." Kurt held her hand as she lay on the floor.

"Kurt, nobody besides Kit will be working in my kitchen unless they're one of the family." Alice pointed her finger at her husband.

Kit Courtney, the cook, was in his late forties and always had a funny joke whenever Lora went back to get something. He took the day off to take his wife to an appointment. It was the reason Alice was in the kitchen alone, and why she now lay on the floor

"You could have killed yourself, and you know what? I'd be lost without you, baby." Kurt cupped his wife's cheek in his big hands.

Lora had to back away or risk someone seeing the tears in her eyes.

"They're still so much in love." Lora glanced over her shoulder at one of the wives of the O'Connor brothers.

Lora didn't see Marina often. James' wife worked in St. John's and would only come in once or twice a week. Lora was usually on the way home or leaving by the time the pretty woman dropped in. Like the rest of the family, Marina always had a friendly smile. Then again who wouldn't smile being married to one of the sexy O'Connor brothers? Although, Nick was the only one to peak Lora's interest.

"It's so sweet. My mom and dad were like that as well." The memory of her father and how he treated her mom brought tears to her eyes. To her dad, his wife was a queen.

"Are you okay?" Marina must have noticed, because she took Lora's arm and guided her out of the group of people gathered around the kitchen entrance.

"Yeah, I just got a fright." Lora forced a smile.

"Lora, I hate to ask you this, but could you please make sure there's a note put on the door to let everyone know the diner and pub will be closed for the remainder of the day?" Kurt asked as he followed the paramedics and his wife through the door.

"You take care of Alice, and I'll make sure things are taken care of here." Lora smiled at the man as everyone filed out through the door behind them.

"You'll be paid for the whole day. I'll see to that," Kurt shouted as the door closed.

Lora realized she was the only one left in the diner. She glanced toward the kitchen where the door had been braced open to make it easier for the paramedics to get to Alice. It was the best place to start before heading home. The mess of broken plates on the floor had to be cleared before she could even begin cleaning.

Lora grabbed a piece of paper from the printer and scribbled a note to attach to the outside of the door. After grabbing a tack and hammer from the small toolbox under the counter, Lora attached the note to the wooden door and then went to work.

She was about halfway finished in the kitchen when she heard a thump on the main floor. Lora flinched when she realized she hadn't locked the door.

"Damn it." She mumbled to herself and walked slowly out of the kitchen.

Lora glanced around but there wasn't anyone in sight, and the pub doors were still closed. She shook her head and hurried to lock the door. It was the first time she was alone in the diner, and it was eerily quiet. Lora flicked on the radio and turned it up to kill the silence.

As she backed out of the kitchen, mopping the floor, her favorite song started blaring through the speaker. *Brokenhearted* by *Karmin*, always made her think of Nick, probably because as much as she tried to deny it, she wanted the sexy cop, and to hear him call her baby would make her day. She started to sing and dance along to the song as she continued her task.

With the kitchen finished, she turned around to drop the mop in the bucket and almost tripped over her own feet. Nick stood next to the counter with a sexy grin. Lora didn't know whether to scream or pray for the floor to open up and swallow her. She flicked off the radio and pressed her lips together.

"Great floor show. Do you do requests?" He rested his forearms on the counter and leaned forward.

"How long have you been here?" Lora sighed.

"Long enough. Uncle Kurt asked me to give you a hand closing up. I ran home, changed and came back right away. You were in the kitchen, so I went ahead and did the washrooms." Nick tilted his head still with the amused grin on his biteable lips.

"And you couldn't let me know you were here, why?" Lora put her hands on her hips and scowled at him.

"I thought Uncle Kurt told you I'd be back to help." Nick grabbed the mop and squeezed out the water. "I'll dump this and do the front of the store."

"I can do that." Lora sighed.

"Nope, you get to run off the cash register and toss it in the safe." Nick headed to the cleaning closet to refill the bucket. "By the way Karaoke night at the pub is Thursday."

Lora could feel the heat rising in her cheeks, but the moment he bent over to push the lever on the bucket her cheeks weren't the only thing hot. When she realized she was staring, she whirled around and practically ran to the register.

Lora added the receipts, sealed them inside the deposit envelope and dropped it into the safe. On the way to the main floor, she grabbed her purse and heard the faint sound of music.

At first, she thought it was the radio, but quickly realized it was coming from the pub. She flicked off all the lights in the diner and strolled to the entrance of the pub.

There were no customers, since it wasn't opened that day, but Nick sat on the stage strumming a guitar and softly singing. Lora recognized the song right away. *Chris Young* was one of her favorites, but the way Nick sang *Who I am With You*, hypnotized her.

He was part of a cover band with some of his brothers, but she'd never heard them play. If they were all as great as Nick, she was missing out. It was as if she couldn't tear her eyes away and he appeared entirely lost in the song. Lora rested her head against the door jamb and listened.

"He's good, isn't he?" The voice surprised her, and she jumped forward, knocking one of the tables.

Nick stopped playing and spun around. He glanced at her and then noticed the other person in the doorway.

"Sorry, I thought you heard me come in behind you." James grinned sheepishly.

"No. I swear, all of you are a bunch of ninjas." Lora straightened the tables and tried not to look directly at Nick. "Umm… how did you get in?"

Lora knew she'd locked the main door and would have seen him come in through the pub entrance.

"I pick locks." James narrowed his eyes and grinned.

"What?" Lora stared at the handsome man because there was no way he would have done such a thing.

"Just kidding." James jangled keys in front of him. "Aunt Alice realized you didn't have the keys to lock up. She asked me to get the spare set at my parent's house." He held out the keys to her.

"Oh, thanks." Lora took them.

"Is that one of the new songs you guys are putting in the lineup?" James sauntered toward Nick.

"I was just playing with it. It's a Chris Young song." Nick shoved his phone into his pocket.

"Sounded great." That was an understatement because it sounded incredible.

"Yeah, we're going to play it on Canada Day at the beach." Nick glanced at her, and she couldn't move.

"It sounded great, didn't it, Lora?" James wrapped his arm around Nick's shoulder as they walked toward her.

"Umm… yeah… great." Lora moved through the door before they got too close to her.

"How's Aunt Alice?" Nick asked him as they exited the pub.

Lora closed the door to keep her back to them, but she did want to know how her boss was feeling. Alice was kind to her and Lora prayed she wasn't hurt badly.

"When I talked to Jess, she said they think her leg's broken, but she was on her way to x-ray then." James walked back into the diner and checked all the windows.

"I locked them." Lora smiled.

She didn't feel as if he was double checking her work. It just seemed second nature to him. As if he needed to make sure they were all secured before he could leave.

"Sorry, I didn't even realize I was doing it. I do it at home too." James chuckled.

"You really should see a doctor about that." Nick teased as he flicked off the lights.

"What's going to happen if Alice has a broken leg? Will they close down *Jack's Place* until she can come back?" Lora was worried about how that would make Alice feel because the woman truly loved her business.

"That's where having a big family comes in handy." James grinned as he started down the stairs.

"Yeah, we'll get together to set up a schedule. Mom and Nan will take over the kitchen with Kit." Nick took the keys from her hand, and the light touch of his finger against her skin was like a spark.

When their eyes met, she couldn't turn away. Nick's hand still covered hers, and they both held the keys for what seemed an eternity. She swallowed as he slowly leaned toward her, and as if something drew her in, she leaned into him. Someone clearing their throat broke the spell, and she stepped back almost backing over the steps.

Nick caught her arm and glared at James at the bottom of the steps. When Lora glanced at Nick's brother, he suddenly seemed to find his boots very interesting.

"I need to go." Lora practically ran down the steps and across the parking lot to her car.

God, she almost kissed him. Lora had to get a better handle on her attraction to Nick. The last thing she wanted was to put him in the sights of the person stalking her. If the investigator on her case couldn't find the person, Nick wouldn't be safe even if he was a police officer.

He walked down the corridor of the high school as invisible as always. Sure, people said hi, and some smiled as he acknowledged them but none of them considered him important.

Not that he cared what any of them thought of him. There was only one reason he trudged down the hallway. He needed information, and he'd get it from her even if he had to beat it out of her.

He turned into her classroom and glanced around. A man with the short military haircut, beard and tattoos glanced at him. The man wasn't familiar and it pissed him off. He didn't have the time or patience to deal with anyone other than the woman he came to see.

"Where's Ms. Ross?" He snapped at the biker wannabe.

"She's out for a few days. I'm her substitute. Is there something I can help you with?" For a second, he felt intimidated when the man stood.

"No," He turned and stomped out of the room.

The fucking bitch had to be home with her kid. It's the only reason she would miss work. For as long as he'd known her, she'd never lost a day in front of the classroom.

"She won't be back until the end of next week. If you need help...." The muscle-bound ass shouted from the door of the classroom.

He ignored him because there was no possible way he had any information. Nobody in the fucking place knew anything. He slammed against the handle of the exit and stomped toward his vehicle.

"Well Ms. Ross, I guess I need to visit you at home." He grumbled to himself.

As he sped out of the parking lot barely missing the curb, a couple of students shouted at him for almost hitting them. It wouldn't be a huge loss, but that was a hassle he didn't need, and he especially didn't want to deal with any of the authorities inside the school. Not when they could ruin all his plans.

Chapter 6

"You're a fucking dick." Nick shoved James as he stomped by his brother on the way to his truck.

"Sorry, I didn't realize you were seeing each other." James strolled next to him.

"We're not." Nick yanked open his door.

"Could've fooled me." James snickered as he hopped into his vehicle.

Nick slammed his hands against the steering wheel as his brother pulled away. He'd almost kissed her right there on the step of *Jack's Place.* Considering why they'd been there together, it was a little inappropriate. Plus, she'd made it clear she wasn't interested in dating.

Not that she said as much, but Lora kept her distance. It was a whole new world for him because he'd never wanted a woman so badly that didn't want him back.

"Fucking idiot," Nick grumbled as he watched Lora drive out of the lot behind James.

The entire drive back to his place he continued to reprimand himself for getting lost in her beautiful eyes and forgetting where he was. The fact he'd just finished a song that reminded him of Lora didn't help the situation. He'd pictured himself singing it to her, which was probably why he hadn't heard anyone come into the pub.

He swung his truck in front of the bunkhouse when his phone vibrated in his pocket. Nick yanked it out as he slammed his truck door.

"Hello," He cringed for a moment because he sounded as if he was ready to kill someone.

"Who shit in your cornflakes?" Aaron grumbled on the other end.

This is just what I need.

"What do you want, A.J.?" Nick clomped up the steps and entered the house.

"I'm leaving the hospital and heading to the station. Cory found something, and I told him I'd call you. He said it's a connection." Nick heard a horn honk. "Do you not know what a fucking arrow means, fuckhead?" Aaron grumbled.

"Shouldn't you go after that guy?" Nick chuckled.

"If I was on duty, I would." Aaron snapped.

"How's Aunt Alice?" Nick grabbed his laptop and the briefcase with all his notes.

"Leg broke in two places and knee dislocated." Aaron's voice echoed presumably because he was on speaker phone.

"Ouch," Nick winced at the thought of how painful it sounded.

"Yeah, we'll be brushing up on our waiter skills." Aaron chuckled. "Anyway, I'll meet you at the station. Let's get this fucker."

Before Nick could reply, Aaron ended the call, but Nick was definitely on board with getting this evil prick.

The station was all abuzz over Alice's accident, and everyone offered to help out where needed. It was the great thing about living in a small town. Most people were there for each other without any ulterior motive behind it.

After a couple of waves to other officers and staff, Nick made his way to the conference room where Cory moved the evidence board. John wanted the room kept strictly for the task force investigating the case of the missing and murdered women.

Cory was hovered over something on the table when Nick walked into the room. His friend was a damn good police officer and Nick trusted him completely. However, there was something about this specific case that seemed personal to Cory, but Nick had no idea what.

"Hey. A.J.'s on his way." Nick rested his laptop on the table and dropped the briefcase on the chair.

"Yeah, Steve's with the second victim's sister. He's checking out a couple of things." Cory didn't even glance up as he shuffled the papers in front of him.

"You want to fill me in, or wait until the guys get here?" Nick walked around the table and glanced down at Cory's papers.

"A.J. and Steve already know." Cory stood up and turned to Nick.

"So, what is it?"

"Did you know all these women were single mothers?" Cory asked.

"I knew two of them were, but not all of them." Nick glanced at the five pictures on the board.

"Why didn't we figure that out before?" Cory seemed pissed.

"Why are you snapping at me?" Nick backed up but stared his friend in the eye. "I just came in on this case the first of May, remember?"

"I know, I'm more pissed at myself and Steve." Cory turned around and stared at the evidence board.

"Well okay," Nick nodded, but acid churned in his stomach. He knew another single mother similar to the victims.

"I sent Steve to talk to the sister because he remembered her mentioning a new boyfriend the girl had." Cory turned around.

"Why are you not using names?" Nick twisted around to the sound of his brother's voice.

John stood in the doorway his arms folded across his chest concern written all over his face. Nick remembered John and James always reminded him the one thing to remember was to use the victim's names because they are people.

"It's easier for us to number them." Cory didn't turn around.

"Cory, use their names. I know the first girl came to you about a stalker, but that's not your fault. These women were someone's daughters, sisters, mothers." John moved further into the room.

"Don't you think I know that." Cory snapped and slapped a file folder on the table.

John picked up a marker and began to write the five names of the victims under each of their pictures, *Amanda Tulk, victim one, Joy Lester, victim two, Aileen Pittman, victim three, Darlene Pike, victim four, and Gloria Everson, victim five.*

"Five women with no obvious connection except, they were working single mothers." John stepped back and scanned the board.

"And similar features." Cory sighed.

"Yeah, that's the part I don't like," John growled. "They have an eerie resemblance to Pam, Isabelle, Jess, Kristy, and Emily." John listed off his four cousins and Keith's wife.

"But they aren't single mothers." Cory reminded him.

"Lora is." Nick hadn't meant to say it out loud, but John and Cory turned to stare at him.

"God damn it. You're right." John sighed.

"Gloria could pass for Lora's sister." Cory tapped the last victim's picture.

"They all complained of being stalked." Steve stepped into the room and dropped files on the table.

"What about Joy's new boyfriend?" Cory asked.

"I doubt he's our guy. He was at Joy's sister's when I got there. He works on the rigs and only got back yesterday after three weeks out." Steve dropped down in one of the chairs.

"So, all five filed reports of stalkers." John skimmed through the folders Steve dropped on the table.

"Yeah, it was just a hunch. I called ahead and asked Blake Harris to search the victim's names. He handed me the reports when I got here." Steve nodded toward the folders.

Aaron walked into the room with a tray of coffee from the famous Canadian coffee franchise, *Tim Horton's*. He placed it in the center of the table and glanced at the board.

"We're using names now?" He glanced at Cory.

"Yeah." Cory walked out of the room without another word.

"Did he know that girl? Personally, I mean?" Nick seemed confused by his friend's visible distress over Amanda Tulk.

"Not that I know of. The only thing I know is, she filed the stalking report with Cory." Aaron took one of the large coffees from the tray and popped open the lid.

"Maybe I should take him off this." John sighed.

"Not a fucking chance, John." Cory stepped back into the room.

"Well, get your head in this." John pointed to the board. "And Nick?"

"Yeah?" Nick had been listening to the conversation going on around him, but his focus was on the pictures.

"I want you to keep an eye on Lora. Maybe check to see if she's ever reported having issues with someone bothering her." John stood in the doorway.

"I may spend my time at the diner and make sure she gets home safe." Aaron sipped his coffee.

"Fuck off," Nick growled.

"These women disappeared walking either too or from work." Aaron reminded him.

"She drives back and forth." Nick stuck his middle finger up at Aaron when the bastard tried to cover the knowing grin.

"Good." John nodded as he left the room

"She lives with her mom as well." Nick wasn't talking to anyone specific.

"Darlene and her son lived with her sister. Joy and her daughter lived with her parents." Cory put stickers under each photo with that information.

Nick couldn't pull his gaze away from the last victim. She had the strongest resemblance to Lora down to the way she wore her hair. Midway down the back with a slight curl on the ends. Although Gloria's eyes weren't the same sapphire-blue as Lora's beautiful eyes.

"We'll keep her safe." Aaron stepped next to him and lowered his voice

"Who?" Nick glanced at his brother.

"The pretty waitress both of us see in those pictures." Aaron grabbed Nick's shoulder and squeezed it gently. "Just so you know, the reason it took me so long to get here, wasn't because of traffic. I had a chat with Keith. He has Hulk keeping an eye on her house."

Bruce 'Hulk' Steel worked for Keith and Kristy's soon-to-be husband, Bull. Newfoundland Security Services was a high-end security company. Usually, companies hired them for bodyguards, security detail for dignitaries or politicians, or lately for protecting family and friends. Nick assumed the prior had to be lucrative, because if Keith and Bull were running the company from the latter, their business would be bankrupt long ago.

"You can't just have a guy watching her house without setting off alarm bells with her or her mom. Jesus, A.J., if someone is stalking her, the first thing she's gonna think is he's outside her house." Nick rolled his eyes.

Aaron meant well, and the truth was Nick was a little pissed for not thinking of it himself. Nick turned to study the pictures again. The pretty smiling women stared back at him as if they didn't have a care in the world.

Maybe she should be worried.

He pulled into the side of the road and stared at her house. He'd spent the last two days waiting for her to show, and it was pissing him off even more. He was growing impatient waiting to get the information he wanted.

"Where are you, bitch?" He growled as he slammed his hands against the steering wheel.

He grabbed the box on the passenger seat and pulled out the pictures of his love. She was smiling at the person he'd cut out of the photo. That fucker tried to take his place, but he'd put a stop to that and cut the brake lines. It was too bad he wasn't on a hill when the fluid ran out. It taught him a lesson though, because the coward ended things with her after that.

The sun started to disappear behind the trees on the back of the bitch's house. She still wasn't home, and he couldn't stay any longer. He had things to do.

"I'll be back tomorrow, and you better be here." His body shook with rage as he pulled away from the curb.

He'd come back every day, so he could finally be with his love again. There was no way that bitch didn't know something and he wouldn't give up until he had the information he wanted.

"We'll be together again, my heart. They can't keep us apart forever."

Chapter 7

Lora stood in her living room staring through the large picture window. The cup of tea in her hand almost spilled because her brain kept returning to Nick, and the fact she'd almost kissed him. The harder she tried, the more difficult it was to fight her attraction to Nick. He was sweet, handsome, and sexy as sin, but getting involved with her could be dangerous for him. Not to mention he had a playboy reputation.

Isabelle said Nick liked her, but did he, or did he want another notch on his bedpost? Lora's past wasn't virgin white, and for a short time in her life, she enjoyed the downtown scene. Not that she was proud of it, but she did have a one-night stand once or twice. Lora wished she didn't feel the overwhelming draw to him, because it would make resisting him a hell of a lot easier.

Movement at the end of the tree line drew her attention. Her mother asked Daphne if they could widen the driveway to clear some of the overgrown trees. It made it easier to see when someone drove in, and it saved the scratches on their vehicles. The only problem now, what she saw wasn't a car.

Lora slowly lowered her cup to the side table and moved behind the curtain. Had he found her again? She pushed the thick drape aside enough to see without being seen. Her heart thundered in her chest when a large figure walked deliberately by her driveway. She counted to twenty, and it moved again.

Her mother had taken Molly to the park, leaving Lora alone. The shadow was much too large to be her mom. She didn't want to have police swarming her place. What was she supposed to do?

Nick's face flashed in her thoughts. He'd been to her house before, and he wouldn't come with sirens blaring. The shadow moved again but slowed almost to a stop before walking again.

"Screw it," She pulled her phone from her pocket and scrolled to his number.

Nick's grandmother, Nanny Betty, added Lora to a group of friends and family. The sweet woman regularly sent texts about different events going on in the town, and with the O'Connor family. Lora would always politely decline.

When she found Nick's number, she hit call and waited while she focused on the end of her driveway. It rang several times before he answered out of breath.

"Hello," Nick panted.

"Hey, Nick. Umm… It's Lora Norris." Lora stammered over her words. "I hope I'm not… that you …. I hope I'm not interrupting."

"What? No, I was getting out of the shower and couldn't find my damn phone when it started ringing." He chuckled.

"Oh, sorry. I'll let you…" He stopped her before she ended the call.

"No, that's okay. What's up?" Nick's voice rumbled in her ear in a sexy deep tone.

"Well… I may be paranoid but…" Lora took a deep breath.

"I'm on the way." The call ended, and she stared at the screen.

Lora glanced through the window again in time to see the figure at the end of the driveway. Her heart hammered in her chest, and she took slow deep breaths to calm herself. She'd never been afraid of much, but this guy had her ready to jump out of her skin.

Lora was ready to burst into tears when she heard the footfalls on her front step. She covered her mouth as she glanced around for something to use as a weapon to protect herself. If he wanted to hurt her, she wasn't going to make it easy for him.

Her father's old baseball bat that he used when he coached ball, sat mounted on the wall. All the kids he coached signed it every year when they graduated. The school gave it to her mother when he died.

"Thanks, Dad." Lora ran to the fireplace and had her hand wrapped around it when she heard a familiar voice.

"Lora, it's Nick." Her two legs buckled to the point she went to her knees.

"I'm in the living room." She rested her arm on her mother's arm chair.

Nick walked in with another man behind him. She recognized the man from the pub but wasn't sure of his real name. Most everyone referred to him as Hulk.

"Are you okay?" Nick crouched in front of her while Hulk made his way through the house.

"Ah… I'm fine but what's he doing?" Lora asked as the large man opened doors, scanned inside the rooms and then moved to the next.

"He's making sure nobody's in the house. Are you okay?" Nick grasped her hands and helped her to her feet.

"I'm… someone kept walking back and forth at the end of the driveway…. I'm home alone and … I overreacted." Lora blew out a breath and dropped her head.

"First of all, if you didn't feel safe, you did the right thing. With everything going on these days you can never be too careful." He put his finger under her chin and forced her to look at him.

"House is clear. I'm going back to my post." Hulk disappeared out through the front door.

"His post?" Lora narrowed her eyes and stared at Nick.

"Yeah," His cheeks turned a cute shade of red as he met her eyes.

"It seems A.J. knew I was concerned about you being here with only you, your mom and Molly. He asked Keith to have one of the guys keep an eye on your place." Nick hadn't released her hand, and it was way too comfortable.

"Why would you.... Why are you worried about me?" Lora could barely breathe when his gaze met hers.

Nick's eyes traveled all over her face as he pushed a lock of her hair behind her ear. His touch soothed her rattled nerves but sent heat through her body right to her core.

"I thought it was obvious," Nick whispered.

"Not to me." Lora stared into his blue eyes, and it was as if they could see into her soul.

"Lora, how could you not know, I've been captivated by you? I've tried to ask you out so many times, and when I get the nerve, I chicken out." Nick cupped her cheek. "That's never happened to me. Until you."

"I don't think this is a good idea, Nick." Lora wanted to back up and put distance between them, but she couldn't.

"Why? Because of Molly?" Nick dropped his hand from her cheek but grasped both of her hands again.

"No… yes… no… maybe." Lora sighed as she slowly dropped into the chair behind her. "It's more than that."

"Lora, since the first day we met, you're walking around waiting for something to happen. If I ask you something, would you be honest with me?" Nick pulled her mother's footstool closer and sat on it, but didn't break eye contact with her.

"Yes," She knew she could trust him.

Before he had a chance to ask her anything his phone buzzed in his shirt pocket. He released her hand and held up his finger.

"Hello," Nick answered, but kept his focus on her.

His facial expression went from relaxed to tense in seconds. Whoever was on the other line told him something he didn't like.

"Thanks, get the reports, and I'll see what I can find out." Nick shoved his phone into his pocket and stood up.

"Nick," Lora didn't like the concern that tightened his handsome features.

"Do you know Wayne Drover?" Nick sat down in front of her and grasped her hands again.

"Yes," It figured he would know the Inspector working on her case.

"You reported a stalker?" Nick tilted his head

"Yes," Lora sighed.

"Why didn't you tell me?" Nick shook his head.

"It stopped when I moved here," Lora admitted, but she hadn't planned on telling anyone else in town, except Alice and even if it started again she was ready to leave the province.

"You moved here to get away from it?" Nick squeezed her hands.

"I moved several times when I lived in St. John's, but he kept finding me." She blinked back the tears that threatened to fall.

"You haven't had any issues since you moved to Hopedale?" Nick brushed his thumbs against the back of her hands.

"No... well yes... the figure at the end of my driveway but as I said..." Lora stopped when Nick chuckled.

"That was Hulk, and that figure will be coming further up the driveway starting today." Nick released her hand and pulled out his phone.

"Nick, that's not... I mean I don't need... I can't afford to..." He pressed his finger to her lips.

"You don't have to worry about any of that." Nick smiled then dropped his head to text something on his phone.

A few seconds later she heard thuds on her front steps. She didn't have to ask who it was because, from the size of Hulk, he would be the only one to sound that heavy on her steps.

"My mom will worry, and I don't want to scare Molly or worry Ethan." At the mention of her brother, Nick's expression tensed.

"Ethan?" His voice was hard.

"My older brother." Lora smiled because she recognized the green-eyed monster of jealousy when she saw it.

"He lives here?" Nick's expression relaxed.

"No, he's a pilot and lives in town, but he's coming here on his next rotation." Lora wished he would back up a little because the scent of his body wash was driving her crazy.

She'd noticed his freshly washed hair when he walked in, and the way his T-shirt clung to his body. Probably because he didn't completely dry himself and his body was still damp.

Damn, stop thinking about that.

"Lora, are you okay?" Nick cupped her cheeks in his warm hands.

"Yeah, I'm fine." Lora managed to tear her gaze from his, but it dropped to his full biteable lips.

"Your cheeks are flushed." Nick's voice lowered, but she couldn't rip her eyes away from his mouth. "Lora."

"Nick," she whispered his name and raised her eyes to meet his.

Nick held her face in his hand as his thumb grazed her bottom lip. Lora held her breath as he leaned closer, but as if he was a magnet, she moved toward him.

"Lora," Nick whispered.

His mouth brushed against her bottom lip. Then her top. Lora parted her lips when he covered her mouth with his, and her eyes fluttered closed. The kiss was slow, sweet and she got lost in it. Her hands rested on Nick's forearms, holding him as if he would disappear. It was the first time in a very long time she felt desired and as stupid as it sounded, safe.

When he pulled back slightly, he smiled and began to move in for another. If it weren't for the sound of her daughter's laughter outside, Lora knew she wouldn't have stopped him.

"That's my mom, and Molly." Lora didn't move, but Nick dropped his hands from her face.

"I kind of figured that." Nick gave her another quick kiss before he stood up.

"You want to know about the stalker, don't you?" Lora stood up as he moved toward the door.

"Yes, Lora, but I don't want you to discuss that in front of your daughter." Nick nodded toward the front door where Molly came scampering inside.

"Mommy, there's a superhero on our step." Molly jumped up and down and then stopped when she saw Nick.

"Hi, Nick." She ran to the man she'd only met once, and hugged his legs.

"Hey there, Lollipop." Nick picked her up in his arms and gave her a little toss in the air making her squeal.

"Did ya see the superhero?" Molly was wide-eyed as she stared at Nick.

"Who's the superhero?" Lora was completely confused.

"He's out in front of our house." Molly pointed. "Come on, Nick, and I'll show ya."

"She's talking about Hulk. All my nieces and nephews call him, Trunk, and Crunch that, because they always wear superhero shirts." Nick chuckled. "Hello, Mrs. Norris." Nick nodded to her mother.

"Oh dear, what's going on?" As usual, her mother was in panic mode.

"It's nothing, Mom. I'll explain later." Lora motioned toward Molly, and her mother understood it wasn't the time.

"Not again." Her mother turned away from Nick who still held Molly.

"Mrs. Norris, don't worry we've got the superhero out front." Nick winked at Molly. "Right, Lollipop?"

"Right, but I'm Molly, silly." Her little girl giggled when Nick tossed her up into the air again.

"Yeah, but Lollipop will be my special name for you if that's okay." Nick glanced at Lora.

"Okay, I like it." Molly wrapped her two little arms around Nick and hugged him.

"Molly, why don't you go with Nana in the kitchen and we'll get supper, okay?" Lora walked toward Nick and Molly.

"Okay, Mommy." Nick put her down, and she followed Lora's mother out of the living room.

Nick was about to say something to Lora, but Molly ran back into the living room as if something was chasing her. She stopped in front of Nick and tugged on his hand.

"You're stayin' fer supper too, right, Nick?" The hopeful glint in her little girl's eyes would make it impossible for most people to say no to her.

"I'm sure Nick has other plans, sweetie." Lora glanced at him.

"Nope. What are we having?" Nick winked and followed Molly into the kitchen.

"Nana, said were havin' sascedie," Molly said excitedly.

"Ah, okay... sounds great?" Nick glanced back at Lora with confusion.

"Spaghetti," Lora whispered.

"I love Spaghetti." Nick picked Molly up as he made his way into the kitchen.

Lora stood in the doorway and stared as Nick entertained her daughter. Molly was a friendly little girl with an infectious smile and inquisitive nature. It made Lora uneasy, especially when the letters and gifts began to arrive. It was why Lora frequently reminded Molly about stranger danger and how not everyone was a good person.

"What about Hulk's supper?" Molly jumped down from the chair and headed out of the kitchen.

"We'll bring him some outside." Nick caught her and lifted her back into the chair. "He likes to be outside."

"Why?" Molly tilted her head and stared up at Nick.

Lora did her best not to laugh because Molly was about to start a list of questions that would drive the most patient person to the brink of insanity.

"You see, when you're a superhero, you need to be outside to make sure you can keep people safe." Nick's explanation was ridiculous, but to Lora's shock and surprise it appeased her little girl.

"I played with Olivia and Gracie at the park, and they said they know lots a' superheroes." Molly turned to face Nick. "I like livin' here cause there's no superheroes at our old houses, and Mommy was scared."

Lora had been filling her plate when Molly's words had her almost drop it on the floor. Lora spun around and stared at her daughter. During the whole ordeal, Lora thought she'd managed to hide her fear and concern from her little girl.

"Since we came here, Mommy isn't scared no more." Molly turned back when her plate was placed on the table in front of her.

Lora glanced at Nick and then her mother. They both appeared as stunned as she did.

"That's why your mom moved here because she knew we had all the superheroes." Nick nodded at her mother when she placed a plate in front of him.

"I know, and now we got one on our step." Molly didn't speak anymore and started to dig into her supper.

Through the rest of the meal, they chatted about Alice and how the family would take over her duties. Her mother offered to help if they were able to take Molly to the diner or Lora was off.

Molly wanted to bring Hulk his supper, and her mother helped her out to the large man along with a bottle of water. Nick loaded the dishwasher while Lora cleared the table.

"You seemed shocked by what Molly said." Nick wiped off the stove.

"I was. I always made sure she was never around when I discussed it with Mom or Inspector Drover." Lora wiped off the table and flopped down in the chair.

94

"Kids are pretty perceptive. Trust me my nieces and nephews have seen a lot more than we wanted them to, but they're thriving. I think kids have a sixth sense. They know when parents are stressed." Nick took the cloth from her and held her hands in his. "If you want, we can go to the station, and you can tell me everything."

"I gave my statements to Inspector Drover. He has almost all of the things the weirdo sent me." Lora didn't know what else she could tell him.

"I know, but I'd like to hear it from you." He wasn't telling her something, but she didn't know what.

"Nick, you never really explained why Hulk's here." Lora could see the change in his expression. "Wait, this has something to do with those murdered women, doesn't it?"

"Yes," The whispered affirmation sent a cold chill through her entire body.

His patience was running out. She was out of town, and he had to wait for her to return. He'd hit a brick wall with getting any information on his love. He slowly spun around in the room taking in every single picture glued to his wall.

Pictures that he'd taken of her at work, at the park with her little girl, and of course his favorite was her beside him with a beautiful smile.

Of course, between her brother, father and the prick that knocked her up, he wasn't able to get close to her. The kid's father wasn't hard to get rid of, and nobody even knew he was at the bottom of the lake behind his parent's house. Even after six months, nobody reported the deadbeat missing.

The day her father died was the happiest of his life, because it meant there was nobody else around to keep him from the woman he loved.

She hadn't realized she was free once her dad died, and then she started dating the muscle-bound loser with the sports car. He'd taken care of him too but unfortunately not the way he'd wanted. The bastard had managed to pull his car into a grassy field when he ran out of brake fluid.

"My love, I know they have us separated but don't worry, I'll find you, and we can be together forever." He ran his finger down the picture of her in the shower. "Nobody will get in my way again."

Chapter 8

Nick despised the appearance of complete terror in her eyes. If someone punched him in the stomach, it wouldn't have gutted him as much. His first instinct was to pull her into his arms and protect her from everything.

"Don't worry, Lora. I won't let anyone hurt you, Molly, or your mom." Nick held her against him and covered the back of her head with his hand as he pressed his lips to the top of her head.

"You don't understand. I don't know who it is." Lora trembled against him.

"A.J. read the report, and Wayne told him you didn't know who it could be." What could he do to make all her fear go away?

"I made a list of every man and woman I knew or had any contact with during the day. It was hard to do because the truth is, you never think about how many people you interact with during a twenty-four-hour period." She pulled back but didn't meet his eyes.

They were silent for a few minutes with only the sound of Molly's sweet giggle floating in from outside. It calmed him and seemed to have the same effect on Lora. She took a deep breath and let it out again slowly. It was only then that she tipped her head up and met his eyes.

"If this starts again, I'm leaving Newfoundland," she said the words, but her eyes told him there was no way she wanted to leave her home.

"You know what that would do?" Nick ran his knuckle against her cheek.

"What?" Lora seemed to lean into his touch.

"Break my fucking heart." Nick smiled.

"I'm sure you'd survive." She rolled her eyes.

"I'm not sure I would. You've charmed me, Ms. Norris, and it makes me happy and terrified at the same time." Nick stared into her eyes. "I'm going to find this guy, so he'll never scare you again."

"You're going to do that all by yourself." Lora cupped his cheek and smiled.

"If I've got to, but I'm sure between my brothers and the superheroes, I'll have lots of help." Nick leaned toward her, and as their lips were about to touch, a small voice from the front door drew it to a halt.

"Mommy, come watch Hulk lift me with only one hand." Molly squealed excitedly.

"Big deal, she's what? Thirty pounds." Nick grumbled.

"Forty-one, actually." Lora laughed. "You should go show her that you can do it too."

"Nah, she thinks he's a superhero, and it makes her feel safe." Nick slipped his hand behind Lora's head and pulled her close. "I want both of you to feel that way." Nick pressed his lips to her forehead and reluctantly released her.

"I think, maybe you just stepped up to superhero level." Lora smiled as she backed out of the kitchen.

"I hope I can be yours." Nick followed her.

Nick stayed for most of the evening for a few reasons. He wanted to get all the information he could on Lora's stalker. As well as find out if Molly had knowledge her mother didn't realize the little girl had, but most of all he wanted to spend time with Lora.

"G'night, Nick." Molly jumped on the couch next to him and wrapped her little arms around his neck.

"Goodnight, Lollipop. Sweet dreams." Nick hugged her tightly.

He could hear Lora reading softly to Molly while he sat in the living room. He wasn't surprised when Sheila stepped up to the couch and sat next to him. For a moment she didn't speak. Then she turned to him.

"You care about my daughter, don't you?" Sheila didn't pull any punches.

"I do, but that's not the only reason I'm here." Nick kept his voice low.

"She's been hurt in the past, and last year she went through a very tough time." Sheila reminded him a lot of his own mother, especially with the mama bear scowl she gave him.

"I know about her stalker." Sheila's surprised expression told him not many people knew about her ordeal.

"She told you?" She seemed skeptical.

"That she had one, yes, but she's gonna tell me the rest after Molly goes to sleep. Is there anything you can tell me?" Nick figured Sheila might know something he didn't

"I'll leave that to Lora. I'm going to warn you, don't hurt my daughter, or you'll see a side of this soft-spoken woman not many people see." Sheila stood up and gave him a sweet smile.

"You know, I think you and my mother would be great friends." Nick chuckled.

"I've met her, and we've had lunch, but I might have to get some information on you, young man." Sheila winked and disappeared into one of the rooms Nick assumed was her bedroom.

While he waited, Nick checked email on his phone and scrolled through social media. Apparently, Molly's bedtime routine was an enormous production. There was water, a snack, several trips to the bathroom, and a story. An hour later Lora emerged from the room, closing the door softly behind her.

"I'm sorry that took so long." She entered the living room and sat on the opposite end of the couch.

"Are you kidding? You need to be at Ian and Sandy's place when they try to get four kids to bed." Nick smiled.

"I can't imagine, but after getting to know both of them, I'm pretty sure they're good at it." Lora tucked her legs under her and rested her arms on the back of the couch. "I know that's not why you stayed. What do you want to know?"

"If you'll have supper with me on Saturday evening." Nick rested his arm on the back of the couch, so he was able to reach across and touch her hand.

"Nick," Lora sighed.

"What?" He studied her features, but it wasn't like he'd ever forget any of it.

He'd memorized every inch of her beautiful face including the tiny scar she had just over her right eye. She had tiny freckles across her nose and he'd noticed she'd gotten more since the summer started. To him they were beautiful. Just like her.

"That's not why you're here." She glanced at his hand that now held hers.

"It's part of it." Nick winked.

"I don't know if that's such a good idea." Lora attempted to pull her hand away, but he gripped onto her fingers and pulled them to his lips.

"I think it's a great idea." He linked his fingers with hers.

"The last guy I dated was almost killed when someone cut his brake line." Lora's voice cracked.

"Is that when you moved here?" Nick tugged her closer.

"No, I moved once more before I came to Hopedale." Lora's eyes were fixed on the ring on Nick's finger.

"To get away from this guy?" Nick asked, but he knew the answer.

"It started just after my dad died." Lora ran her fingernail across the insignia on his ring. It was the graduation ring he received from law school. He didn't practice anymore, but the ring was part of him, so he still wore it.

"What happened?" He probably should take notes, but at that moment he didn't want to let go of her hand.

"My dad was a teacher, and he coached baseball in the summer and basketball during the school year. He was my superhero." Lora glanced at Nick with tears in her eyes.

"Aren't all dads superheroes to us as kids? I know mine was. Hell, my dad still is." Nick brushed his thumb against hers.

"I like your dad." She smiled.

"Me too. Go on." Nick managed to get her close enough, so he could tuck her under his arm.

"A week after the funeral, I got a card in the mail. Nothing really. We were getting tons of them from Dad's co-workers, students, old friends, and neighbors." Lora sighed.

"What was different about the card?"

"It wasn't a condolence card. It was like a card you'd give to a girlfriend." She shrugged.

"Do you remember what it said?" Nick absently played with her hair.

"You'll be my tomorrow; you own my heart. It was signed, for my one and only love." Lora shivered, and Nick kissed the top of her head.

"Were you dating anyone at the time?" The question was for one reason.

If Lora had a bad break up with some psycho, it was possible the guy wasn't ready to let go. Some men didn't take rejection well, and Nick saw more than his share of them. He couldn't count the number of times he'd been called to a domestic disturbance because a woman wanted to end things with some asshole who didn't take it well.

"Yes, I thought it was from him, and it was odd because we'd only been out on four dates. When he came by a couple of days later, I thanked him for the card. He told me he didn't send it, and I shrugged it off as someone being sweet." Lora snuggled closer and rested her head on his shoulder.

"But that wasn't the last one."

"No, that was only the tip of the iceberg. After that, they started coming at least two or three times a week. Cards, flowers, candy and stuffed animals." Her body relaxed against him.

"What made you move the first time?"

"About three weeks after it started, Roy, the guy I was dating mentioned he'd gotten some threatening texts. Basically, warning him to stay away from me."

"Then his brakes were cut." Nick nodded.

"Yeah, after he spent the night…. Sorry." Lora tipped her head and glanced up at him.

"Why are you sorry?" Nick was confused.

"I don't know, talking about Roy spending the night… seems weird." Lora rolled her eyes. "Stupid I know."

"It's not stupid." Nick put his finger under her chin. "Just so you know, I hate Roy."

"You don't know him." Lora giggled.

"He spent the night with you, and that makes me jealous." Nick ran his thumb across her lower lip.

"I'm pretty sure you had some overnight guests from time to time. Actually, if I'm to believe the rumors, you've had lots of slumber parties." Lora raised her eyebrow and smirked.

"I'm not proud of that." For the first time, Nick was embarrassed by his sexual exploits.

"Nick. I was kidding." Lora sat up and gazed into his eyes.

"Lora, I'm not going to pretend I was the good Catholic boy, but since I met you, the only woman I want, is you." Nick brushed his nose against hers.

"Nick, this is too fast." Lora sat up and sighed.

"I'll wait as long as I have to." He didn't reach for her because she'd probably bolt.

"Why would you wait? You don't know me at all." Lora stood up and turned to face him.

Nick stood and took both her hands in his. She trembled, and he squeezed her hands gently. Her head tipped back, and he could see the conflicted emotions all over her face. She'd spent almost a year avoiding any kind of relationship outside of her family. It was obvious she was terrified someone would get hurt, or worse.

"I want to get to know you. I want to be the one you feel safe with." Nick ran his finger down her cheek. "I know that's what's holding you back."

"What's holding me back is…" Lora dropped her head.

"What?"

"I'm terrified you'll get hurt," Lora confirmed what he thought.

"I'm a big boy. Don't worry about me." Nick held her face in his hands. "I'm going to find out who did this and I'm going to take that fear out of your beautiful eyes."

"You think my stalker killed those women, don't you?" Lora's voice cracked.

"I won't lie to you. It's possible, but I need to know more about the things he sent you." Nick pressed his forehead against hers. "Do you want to tell me tonight, or do you want to talk about it on our date Saturday night?"

Her laugh made Nick grin because it was exactly what he'd wanted. To distract her from the heavy subject of the murders and her stalker. She had to be told everything at some point, but Nick wanted her to be able to get a good night sleep before filling her head with the horrible facts.

"Pretty sure of yourself, aren't you? I don't remember agreeing to supper." Lora rested her hands on his hips.

"You didn't actually say no." He wrapped his arms around her waist and pulled her closer.

"I didn't say yes either." Lora smiled.

"Oh, just say yes before he starts begging." Nick glanced over her shoulder as Lora turned.

Sheila stood in the doorway a glass in her hand and a smile on her face.

"Mom, you shouldn't be listening to private conversations." Lora shook her head.

"Hmm…" Sheila turned around and disappeared into her room.

"Sorry about that." Lora faced him again.

"No need to be sorry. She wants you to say yes." Nick grinned.

"Fine, I'll go to supper with you." Lora took his hand and tugged him toward the front door.

"Am I getting the old heave-ho?" Nick pouted.

"Yes, you are." Lora stopped at the front door.

"Well, that can't mean anything good." Nick sighed.

"It means I'm finding it hard to resist your charms, Mr. O'Connor." Lora smiled, and it took his breath away.

"Good to know." Nick cupped her cheek and brushed his nose against hers.

"Tomorrow, I'll go to the station, and I'll tell you everything you need to know." Lora ran her finger across his lower lip.

"I'll pick you up." Nick kissed it.

"You don't…" Nick put his finger to her lips.

"I do, and I will. I got a text from Mom earlier, and we're meeting at the pub around two." Nick hated to go, but he did feel better because Hulk would be there all night.

"I have a question."

"Shoot."

"Does he need to come in here for the night?" Lora nodded toward the door.

"No, He'll stay in his truck," Nick replied.

"Will he be okay?"

"Trust me; he'll be fine." Nick brushed his lips across hers.

"Hey, we haven't been on a date yet." Lora pulled back from him.

"Yeah, I'm making tonight our first date, we had supper, we cuddled, we talked, and now I'm kissing you goodnight." Nick slid his hand behind her head and pressed his lips against hers before she could say another word.

He watched as she staggered up the length of her driveway linked into the man. It was more than clear they had too much to drink. The guy was the teacher from her classroom a few days earlier.

It figured she would go for that type of guy. Dulce looked like his love, but that was where their resemblance ended. His love would never go for a muscled, tattooed jock. No. His love enjoyed intelligent conversation, art, and would never sleep with just anyone.

There were a few errors in judgment she'd made, but she was only human, and he'd forgiven her for that. He blamed the men. They tricked her, and someone definitely deceived her again. He was sure of that, because his love would never go so long without seeing him.

All he had to do now was wait for the man to leave, and force Dulce to tell him where to find his love. He'd waited this long. What were a few more hours?

Chapter 9

Lora climbed into bed with an enormous smile on her face for the first time in almost a year. Except for Molly, Nick did something that nobody was able to do for a long time. Give her hope she could have a life without thought of some crazy man waiting to take her away, or possibly take her life.

"What time is Nick going to be here?" Her mother asked the next morning as Lora put breakfast in front of Molly.

"Nick's coming today?" Molly bounced excitedly in her seat.

"Yes, but he has to take Mommy to work. Maybe Mommy will invite him to supper again tonight. Right, Mommy?" Her mother grinned, and Lora didn't miss that glint in her eye.

It was hard for Lora to deny Molly anything that made her happy, and her mom knew it. Molly had fallen for Nick almost as hard as Lora. It also seemed like the feeling was mutual for Nick.

"I'll see. He may have to work." As she spoke, there was a rhythmic knock on the door that sent her heart racing, and Molly almost knocked her over to answer it.

"Nick. Nick. Nick," Molly shouted as she pulled open the door before Lora got out of the kitchen.

"Well, that's the kind of welcome a man could get used to." Nick scooped Molly up in one arm and tapped her nose with his finger. "Hey there, Lollipop."

"Nana said you could come for supper, but Mommy said you might be working." Molly paraphrased the conversation in one sentence.

"I'm not working tonight, so supper sounds great." Nick winked at Lora, and if it was even possible, she softened a little more.

Seeing the way he was with Molly; it was hard not to fall for the man. She didn't know how she couldn't fall for a man who treated her daughter as if she was a precious piece of gold. Not to mention he was sweet, kind, gorgeous and sexy. Who was she kidding? Nick was hot with a capital H.

"Yay," Molly wrapped her little arms around his neck.

"Come on, Molly. You need to finish breakfast if you want to go to the park and play with Olivia and Grace again today." Her mother shuffled Molly into the kitchen leaving Lora alone with Nick in the foyer.

""Molly adores you." Lora smiled.

"You think? I didn't realize." Nick arched an eyebrow. "The question is, how does her mother feel about that, and does her mom maybe like me too?"

"Well, her mom thinks its great that Molly likes you, and her mom may like you too. Just a little bit." Lora held her thumb and index finger about an inch apart.

Nick grabbed her arms and tugged her toward him. He wrapped her arms around his neck and rested his hands on her hips.

"How exactly could I get her to like me a lot?" Nick gazed into her eyes making it very hard to look away.

"Keep being you." Lora smiled and cupped the back of his head.

"I think I can do that," He whispered just before he grazed his lips against hers.

"Thanks for picking me up but it really wasn't…." Nick stopped her by cupping the back of her head and covering her mouth with his.

His kiss was slow, tender and made her knees weak. It turned her brain to mush, it was hard to think when her head was spinning. When he finally pulled away, Nick staggered a little.

"I could get addicted to kissing you," He whispered.

"I know the feeling." Lora rested her head against his chin and took a deep breath. He smelled incredible, and it didn't help her libido when his scent drove her crazy.

"Are you ready to go?" Nick asked as he took a step back.

Although he tried to be inconspicuous, Lora noticed him adjusting himself. She'd felt his arousal against her stomach during the kiss. It made her want to throw caution to the wind and ask him to take her somewhere private.

"Yeah, I need to grab my phone and purse." Lora scurried into the kitchen where her mother held both out to her.

"I'll see you later." Her mom had been eavesdropping again.

"I'm not sure what time I'll be back because I…" Her mother stopped her and smiled.

"Don't rush back. Do what you need to, and maybe after, let yourself have fun. Maybe with one of the handsome O'Connor brothers." Her mother kissed her cheek and sat down at the table with Molly.

"Bye, Mommy," Molly mumbled with a mouth full of pancakes.

"I'll see you later, baby." Lora kissed the top of her head and headed out of the kitchen.

She was about to tell Nick and the other officers everything about a person that maybe killing women. Lora didn't know a lot of details about the murders because she honestly didn't want to think about it. The nightmares were less frequent, but knowing the details of the case could have them return, or maybe even make them worse.

No, she didn't want to go there, and she certainly didn't want to scare her mother again with her screams. She'd only woken Molly once, because usually, the child slept like a rock, but she'd been sick and crawled into the bed with Lora. Luckily, Lora calmed her quickly and settled her back into a restful sleep.

It was hard to believe anyone would be so disturbed they'd send sick things to a woman. She didn't know if the police would ever find him, but for some reason, she had a new outlook. It almost seemed as if it could all be over, and she could go back to living a normal carefree life.

With Nick?

"I don't know...." His hand stung as he slapped her face again and she cried out in pain.

"I don't believe you. She wouldn't go anywhere without telling you." He pushed his covered face within inches of hers and gripped onto her chin. The last thing he wanted was for her to see his face. "You two joked all the time about being long lost sisters."

"I haven't talked to her in months. All she told me was she had to go away for a while. She probably left the province." Dulce sobbed, but it didn't bother him.

He stepped back and glared at her through the holes in the old hockey mask he'd found in the basement. It angered him when Sheila sold the house. It was supposed to be his home with his love. As luck should have it, the couple that bought it didn't protest at the request to turn the house over to him. Of course, they couldn't argue much with their throats slit.

"Please, let me go. I won't say a word. I have a little girl, and she's coming home…" He sighed as he slapped her into silence once again.

"Don't worry; you'll be going home really soon." He sneered as he left her locked inside the small soundproof room he'd built in the basement of the house. "You'll be going home to Jesus," He whispered as he secured the lock.

Chapter 10

Aaron, Cory, and Steve Parker were at the station when Nick arrived with Lora. They wanted all the information first hand, since the report Wayne gave them didn't appear to be very in depth.

It bothered Nick. Wayne was a highly decorated police officer and usually anytime Nick received information from him it was very detailed. John even mentioned Wayne's report seemed incomplete.

"The three other investigators are A.J., Cory, and Steve. I think you've met them all." Nick explained as he led her into a conference room.

"I know A.J. pretty well." Lora laughed nervously.

Aaron continually flirted with Lora. Nick knew Aaron only did it to piss him off and force him to finally ask Lora out. His younger brother probably got a thrill out of it too. Aaron seemed to enjoy fucking with his brothers by flirting with their women.

"Yeah, but he'll be more professional here. I hope." Nick smiled.

Nick sat next to Lora as Aaron, Steve, John, and Kurt entered the room. Kurt didn't usually get involved in interviews, and it struck Nick as odd to see his uncle. Not to mention, Alice was laid up with a broken leg.

"Nick, I need to talk to you." Kurt nodded toward the exit door.

"Can it wait? I wanted to be here for this." Nick wasn't comfortable with the idea of leaving Lora.

"It's important." Kurt's expression was unreadable, and Nick's stomach churned.

"I'll be right back." Nick touched Lora's shoulder.

Nick followed his uncle through the door feeling slightly annoyed with the man. When he turned back to the room, he got a glimpse of Lora's worried eyes as Cory closed the door. He was ready to give Kurt a piece of his mind as they turned into John's office.

"What's going on?" Something told him he wasn't going to be happy about what Kurt was going to say.

"Sit," Kurt demanded and motioned to the chair behind Nick.

"Okay," Nick eased into the seat.

"Are you seeing Lora?" Kurt didn't pull any punches.

"We haven't been out on a date or anything, but I did ask and she…" Nick stopped. "Wait, are you taking me off this because I'm involved with Lora?"

"I don't think it's a good…" Nick stopped him before he finished and jumped to his feet.

"Now wait one damn minute, Uncle Kurt. First of all, there's no way I'm sitting out on this with all the hours I've put in on this case. Second, I'm pretty damn sure John, James, Ian, Keith, and Mike were involved in the crap their women went through." Nick struggled to keep his tone calm.

"Nick, that's why I don't want you involved in this." Kurt sighed.

Nick linked his fingers and rested them on top of his head as he paced the office. There was no way he was staying out of the investigation. Primarily, since it was possible Lora was a potential target.

"No way, Uncle Kurt. I can't sit back and twiddle my thumbs while she's in danger." Nick swallowed the lump in his throat.

He never got emotional over most things, but the thought that Lora could get hurt, or worse, made him want to vomit. Nick shuddered at the memory of what that monster did to the murdered women. *No.* They weren't pulling him off this.

"See, that's why." Kurt pointed to his eyes.

"What? Because I've got feelings for her? That's not going to affect how I do my job. If anything, it'll make me do it better." Nick dropped his hands to his sides.

"And if Lora gets put in the line of fire, so to speak, will you risk your life?" Kurt asked.

"You're damn right I would," Nick shouted, and then dropped his head.

"When you do that, you get careless." Kurt finally got to the point.

"I'll be careful." Nick raised his eyes to meet his uncle's worried gaze.

"You boys have such big hearts, and like me, when that one woman comes along, takes your heart, grips onto it, you can't breathe when you think you might lose her, or she could be seriously hurt." Kurt's eyes filled with tears.

"Uncle Kurt, is Aunt Alice okay?" Nick didn't know if this was really about Lora at all.

"Yes, thank God." Kurt pushed his fists into his eyes, and a few seconds later dropped his hands to his sides. "I'm worried this fucker, maybe obsessed with one woman, and is hurting others until he can get to her."

There it was. Kurt spilled the beans and didn't even realize he did it. Nick had let the idea sit in the back of his head, but he didn't want to think it was true.

"You think this guy stalked Lora first, and when he couldn't find her, he started replacing her. When they don't match up, he kills them." Nick dropped into the chair next to the door. "Right?"

"I'm not the only one." Kurt leaned against the edge of the desk.

"The murders didn't start until after she moved to Hopedale." Nick tried to remember the first day he saw Lora, and it was just after Bull's niece died.

"Lora moved here in September. The first murder didn't happen until December. In between that time several notes and gifts sent to her old address after she moved. The last was two weeks before Amanda Tulk disappeared." Kurt pulled a piece of paper out of his pocket and handed it to Nick.

Nick unfolded the paper and read it. He jumped to his feet when he realized it was a statement from the person who lived at Lora's last known address.

"Why didn't I know Cory was doing this?" Nick snapped.

"John's in charge of this case, and he wanted all the information before he made the decision. He figured it would make it easier if I told you he's taking you off the task force." Kurt's expression went back to unreadable, but Nick was too furious to worry about it.

He ripped open the door and stomped down the hall to where he left Lora with the team. *Bastards.* They probably all knew about it. Nick yanked open the door to the conference room, and all eyes turned to him, but the tears in Lora's eyes almost broke him.

"What the fuck are you doing to her?" Nick stomped around the table and crouched in front of Lora.

"Keep your cool, bro," Aaron warned.

"We're asking about…" John started but Nick shot to his feet and glared at his oldest brother.

"I'm taking her out of here." Nick took her hand and tugged on it.

"Be reasonable, Nick," John growled.

"Fuck you. You didn't have the balls to tell me you're taking me off this case, and now you want me to be reasonable. Fuck you, John. Fuck all of you." Nick snapped then glanced down at Lora.

Lora hadn't moved from the chair as she stared at him with wide eyes. Her lips were pressed together but he didn't know if they frightened her, or if he did.

"You know the procedure." John reminded him.

"Was it procedure when you let Stephanie into the apartment of the person you thought was trying to kill her? Was it procedure to let James be involved in the team to find Marina?" Nick tried to keep his anger under control as he spoke, and Cory moved across the room to close the door he'd left open.

"Keep your voice down." Steve snapped.

"No, it wasn't procedure, and we broke it. Yes. Nick, I know how you feel, trust me, but if you'd listen to us." John took a step toward him, but Nick held up his hand.

"Why are you so angry?" Lora's quiet voice broke the tension.

Nick took a deep breath and let it out slowly. He crouched in front of her and captured her hands in his. She didn't appear to be scared, but her hands trembled.

"They're pulling me off the case," Nick kept his voice calm.

"Why?" Lora's gaze moved to John.

"Because we want him to be safe," John replied, and Nick rolled his eyes.

"You don't think he's good at his job?" Lora stared at his older brother, and Nick turned his head because he wanted to know the answer to that question as well.

"It's not that, Lora. Nick's a damn good cop, but sometimes when you care for someone, and they're in danger, it clouds your judgment." John sat in the chair next to her.

Lora turned to Nick and cupped his face. A tear slipped from the corner of her eye and ran down her cheek. It broke his heart to see one tear fall from her eyes. Especially because she seemed almost afraid to speak.

"That's why I tried to keep you at arm's length for so long." Lora sniffed. "I don't want you to get hurt."

A war raged inside him. What was more important to him? Being with Lora or working a case. He knew his feelings for her were more than he'd ever expected to feel, but he wanted to be her hero.

"There has to be a middle ground here." Aaron slapped his hands on the table startling everyone in the room.

"If you have an idea let's hear it." John shrugged his shoulders.

Aaron paced the floor for what seemed forever. Nick didn't release Lora's hand, and she'd dropped the one she'd touched his cheek with to cover his hands.

"Is he talking to himself?" Lora whispered as they watched Aaron mumble.

"I think so." Nick snorted.

"How about for this case, Nick takes over protection detail?" Aaron spun around to face everyone.

"Isn't that what Hulk and Crunch are doing?" Nick reminded his younger brother they'd already dealt with that problem.

"Not really. Hell, I don't know." Aaron threw his hands up in the air.

"How about we do it this way? Nick, you can stay on this, but if I see you putting yourself in danger, or jeopardizing your safety more than we already do, then I'll pull you." John raised an eyebrow.

For a moment Nick contemplated Aaron's idea. He'd be with Lora all the time. Then again, he didn't plan on leaving her side anyway.

"Deal," Nick held his hand out to John, and his brother tugged him into a hug.

"Am I forgiven now?" John smirked.

"For now." Nick laughed.

"Can we continue now that the drama queen is happy?" Cory grumbled.

"Fuck you, Asshat." Nick tossed a pen at his friend.

"Nice language to be using in front of your lady." Aaron sat next to Lora and gave her a wink.

"So, what we learned so far is all this started after your dad died." Aaron glanced down at the notebook in his hand.

"Yeah, but only cards like you'd send to a girlfriend. I thought it might be a mix-up." Lora met Nick's eyes.

"But your name was on them?" Nick wasn't sure if John was asking or confirming.

"Yeah, but I tried to brush it off." Lora glanced down at her hands.

Nick tried to stay at a distance to prove that he could keep things professional while they were there. He wasn't giving John any reason to pull him off the task force. If what Kurt suggested was right, Lora was in a lot of danger if that crazy fucker found her.

"How long was it before this guy started to get creepy?" Aaron motioned with a nod of his head to come closer, and Nick crouched next to Lora's chair as he captured her hand in his.

"The first thing was a doll." She shivered.

"A doll?" Aaron glanced back at John and Nick knew why.

"It wasn't a baby doll or anything. It was a Barbie doll with homemade …" Lora peeked at Nick under her lashes.

"Lingerie?" Nick ducked his head to see her face.

"It wasn't stuff I'd ever wear." Lora lifted her head, and as if she'd decided not to let this guy affect her anymore she looked Aaron right in the eye. "I would say it's probably something you would see on a prostitute."

"Why isn't the doll in with the other gifts you received?" Steve dug through the box Wayne had given them.

"It was the first weird thing. I tossed it out before Molly saw it." Lora sighed. "I didn't think…"

"It's okay, Lora." Nick squeezed her hand.

"Nick's right. Why would you keep that, but I do have a picture of something sent to another woman. Could you look at it and let me know if it's similar?" Cory held up a picture in his hand.

Lora nodded, and he placed the picture on the table in front of her. She released Nick's hand and picked up the photo. Nick had seen it. He'd seen all five of them. There was a doll sent to each of the dead women, and if Lora received the same one, it would prove what they suspected.

He'd give her one thing; Dulce Ross was one tough nut to crack. He'd beaten her every two hours for the last three days, and she still wouldn't tell him anything. He was beginning to think all his trouble was for nothing. Dulce was useless to him.

He poured a glass of whiskey and stared out through the kitchen window. The backyard needed mowing before he could move his love into the house. The little girl needed a place to play, and overgrown grass would not do.

As he scanned through the phone book for a company to do yard work, he noticed the neighbor poking around at the back of the yard. The broken fence needed repairing, but he'd buried the couple who owned the house close to where the bitch currently stood.

He opened the door that led to the backyard and shouted to the woman. She jumped, and her eyes grew large.

"Can I help you with something?" he forced a smile.

"Oh… I didn't… I was looking… I thought I saw my cat come through here." She stammered over her words as she backed into her own yard.

"I haven't seen a cat, but if I do I'll be sure to let you know, but if you don't mind, I'd rather you didn't trespass on my property." He started to head down the back steps.

"I apologize." She walked quickly to her back entrance.

"I'm a very private person." He nodded as he picked up the part of the fallen fence and leaned it against the opening.

He glanced toward the neighbor's house, but she'd already entered her residence and was peeking through the curtain. She must think he was a complete idiot if he couldn't see her big nosey snout between the thick drapes.

"Guess I better find someone to build a privacy fence as well." He mumbled to himself. "I think I'll try to break Dulce one more time, but if it doesn't work, I have to find another way."

With a heavy sigh, he picked up the knife from the counter and headed back to the basement. If she didn't give him what he wanted she'd have to pay the price.

Chapter 11

Lora's hand quivered as she picked up the photo. She didn't exactly want to see it, because if it was the same as the doll that was sent to her, it would give her the creeps. She examined the whole picture before she allowed herself to focus on the doll in the center.

A traditional Barbie with dark hair, cut in long layers and side bangs lay next to a yellow ruler. It was clear it had been cut, it wasn't a typical style seen with the famous toy. It was however the way Lora wore her hair.

When she finally allowed her eyes to move to the clothing, her stomach filled with acid, and she felt it bubble up into her throat. Black vinyl or leather wrapped around the doll's neck and chest, resembling a bra with the front open. He'd drawn nipples on the breasts as well as hair between the legs. It was visible through the black crotchless panties.

Not that all that wasn't creepy enough, but the doll's hands and feet were tied together. Similar to what she'd seen in Calgary when she went to the Stampede about ten years earlier. The guy next to her at the time called it hogtied. The last thing she noticed was the ball gag painted across the mouth.

Lora tossed the picture on the table and backed away with a shudder. Instantly, strong arms wrapped around her from behind and she turned into them. Lora knew instinctively it was Nick.

"It's the same. Exactly." Lora confirmed as she tucked her head into his chest.

"Is that the only one you threw away?" John's voice sounded apologetic.

"Yes. When the flowers came with the first drawing, I called the police." Lora turned her head in order to see John. "These women were murdered because he couldn't get to me, weren't they?"

"We don't know for sure, Lora." Aaron's hand squeezed her shoulder as Nick hugged her tighter.

"You suspect it though?" Lora knew the answer when John looked over her head at Nick.

"We don't know for sure." Aaron repeated, and it was sweet, but not knowing made it worse.

"I'm not going to fall apart if you tell me the truth. I just need to know." Lora turned around, but Nick didn't release his embrace.

"We think he's trying to recreate you, but when they didn't match his ideal idea of you, he got rid of them," John's matter of fact tone sounded cold, but she knew that wasn't his normal personality.

"Were they raped?" She needed to know what kind of torture the women endured.

"No, there were no signs of sexual assault." Nick cupped her cheek and turned her to look at him.

"There's something we need to know," Steve spoke for the first time since he told Nick to keep his voice down.

"What can do to help?" Lora leaned back against Nick, feeling safety in his embrace.

"We'd ask Nick, but I've …. Ow." Aaron received a smack on the back of the head from John.

"Shut up, Asshole." John snapped.

"We need to know if you have any tattoos or scars on your body. We also need to know where, and what they are." Steve ignored the brotherly situation between John and Aaron.

"I have two tattoos, and a scar from when I had Molly. I had a C-section." Lora tried to remember if she had any others.

"Do you have a tattoo with a cross on your shoulder?" Cory held up a picture.

"That's my tattoo. I got it the week after my dad died. It has his signature on it." Lora glanced at Nick.

"Is this your other one?" Cory held up another picture. A lock, in the shape of a heart, with a thin chain hanging from it. On the end of the string was a letter M, for Molly.

"Yes," She wasn't sure they even heard her say the word, but she was certain she might throw up.

"Is it on the front of your left shoulder?" Cory continued with his questions.

"Yes, right over my heart." Lora wiped a tear from her cheek, furious that she allowed it to escape.

The room was silent for a few minutes, except for the soft click of the air conditioner cutting in and out. Lora didn't want to know where they got the pictures of her tattoos. Mostly because she knew in her heart, they weren't hers. She had a good idea of where they got the pictures.

Lora glanced around at each of the men who seemed to be avoiding eye contact with her. She knew the answer to her question but needed to hear them say it.

"Were those tattoos on the murdered women?" Lora waited for an answer, but the only one to meet her eyes was Nick.

"Honey, he was trying to recreate you. They aren't real tattoos. He drew them on each of the victims. So, we know he's a very talented artist." Nick's hands were sliding up and down her arms as if he was trying to keep her calm.

"He couldn't use his talents for something else." Lora snorted as she tried to ease her anxiety with a joke, it didn't work.

"I'm sure he thinks what he's doing is art. Lora, we need to know who saw your tattoos, where you had them inked, and if you're comfortable with it, we need pictures of them as well as your scar." Nick released her as she lowered herself into a chair.

"Remember when I said I wasn't going to fall apart. I hope you don't mind if I do, just a little bit." Lora's heart pounded, and her body trembled.

There was no way to stop the sobs that escaped, as tears streamed down her cheeks. She gasped for air and wrapped her arms around herself. Lora wasn't scared anymore, she was pissed that this bastard hurt all those women because he couldn't get to her. The overwhelming wave of guilt felt like a brick wall on her back, and it was all his fault.

"You can feel whatever way you want, sweetheart." Nick knelt in front of her, and wrapped her in his strong arms as she tucked her face into the crook of his neck.

"Lora, we'll figure out who this is," John assured her.

"We got your back." Aaron placed a gentle hand on her shoulder.

Those four words from Aaron, and Nick's comforting arms seemed to give her the kick in the ass she needed to pull it together. This asshole had taken a year of her life. She'd uprooted her child, her mother, and herself, as well as pissed off her brother because she'd kept it from him.

Enough is enough.

The only good thing about the whole damn situation, was she met Nick and his amazing family. Lora took a deep breath, and Nick's incredible woodsy scent filled her senses. She wiped her hands across her cheeks and kept her gaze locked with the man who ultimately stole her heart.

"I'm a mess." Lora forced a smile.

"You're beautiful." Nick dragged his finger down the side of her face.

"Okay. I've got that out of my system. What do you want me to do?" Lora turned to John.

"We'll get someone to take a picture of your tattoos, and your scar. We'll bring in a female officer to do that." John picked up the phone.

"Unless you're okay with Nick… Jesus, stop hitting me." Aaron grumbled as John slapped the back of his younger brother's head.

"Stop being an ass," John growled.

"The tattoos aren't in private areas." Lora rolled her eyes.

"I'll get the camera." Aaron stood up and ducked immediately when John swung at him again.

"Over my dead body." Nick shot to his feet.

"I wasn't going to take them. Christ, you think I was a pervert or something." Aaron complained as he disappeared through the door.

"Are you okay with Nick, or do you want me to get a female?" John asked her.

"I'm okay with Nick." Lora didn't feel weird about having Nick take the photographs.

Nick closed the door to John's office, and her nerves suddenly got the better of her. Not because the tattoos and scar would reveal anything, but her body wasn't exactly perfect. Maybe she should have gotten a female, but she thought she'd be more comfortable with Nick.

"I can still get a female." Nick smiled as he picked up the camera.

"I'm okay. It's just… My body isn't exactly perfect." Lora dropped her head and sighed.

"Lora, look at me." She could see his feet appear next to hers and heard the slight thud of the camera he placed on the desk.

Lora peeked up and met his intense blue eyes. They reminded her of the cloudless summer sky, and she could stare into them forever. He tucked her hair behind her ear. Nick was the first man in a long time that she'd even thought about being intimate with and she dreamed about it. Constantly.

"You're beautiful, sexy, sweet, sexy, strong and did I mention sexy?" Nick smirked.

"Maybe once or twice." Lora smiled.

"But do you know the first thing I noticed about you?" he leaned against the desk and pulled her to stand between his legs.

"My great coffee making skills." Lora wrapped her arms around his neck.

"That's a great skill, but your smile made my heart do a flip-flop." Nick tapped her nose with his finger. "Yes, I noticed your curves and I'd be a liar if I said I didn't dream about you at night."

"Nick," Lora was breathless.

"But I want more than that with you. I want to spend time with you and Molly. Get to know both of you, and yes, when the time is right, I want to take you to bed and worship every inch of your incredible body." Nick pressed his forehead against hers. "To me, you are perfect no matter if you have one tiny scar, or a thousand."

"You're so incredibly sweet." Lora brushed her lips against his, as Nick cupped the back of her head, and his tongue glided along the seam of her lips.

When Lora opened her mouth and met his tongue with her own, she pressed her body against his. His kiss was demanding, but gentle. Lora moaned into his mouth when his hand cupped her ass and pulled her flush against his body. He was hard, and she pressed her aching center against his erection.

"Lora," Nick panted as he pulled his lips from hers.

"Nick," She breathed his name.

"Do you see what you do to me?" Nick kissed her cheek and brushed his lips across hers. "I can come just kissing you."

"I want you... but…" Lora sighed, and closed her eyes.

"You're scared," Nick whispered.

"Yeah, but not because I don't trust you. I do. More than I've ever trusted anyone." Lora opened her eyes and saw his smile.

"I'm glad." Nick's hands still rested on her ass.

"I'm scared because I've never felt this way about anyone before. Not even Molly's dad and I thought we were soul mates once." Lora rolled her eyes at the thought of that.

"I'm scared too, sweetheart. I've always been the guy that my brothers and cousins teased … nevermind." Nick's cheeks turned the cutest shade of red.

"Nick, I know you have a playboy reputation." Lora smiled because he seemed embarrassed.

"Aaron's a hell of a lot worse than I ever was," Nick grumbled.

"Can I tell you something?" Lora cupped his face in her hands.

"Anything,"

"I don't care about any of that. I'm no angel." She watched the flare in his eyes.

"Are you done with pictures in there?" John shouted through the door.

"Shit," Nick stood up straight. "We'll finish this conversation at supper," Nick whispered. "We were talking for a minute. I'm getting them now," Nick shouted through the door.

Lora pulled her arm out of her shirt sleeve to reveal both of her tattoos. Nick moved close with the camera and clicked a couple of photos of the one on the front of her shoulder, and then she turned around. She shivered as his finger grazed her skin when he brushed her hair out of the way. He clicked a couple more photos of the other tattoo, and then allowed her to fix her shirt.

"I can still get a female to take the photos of the scar if you want." Nick met her gaze as she unbuttoned her jeans.

"I'm comfortable with you, but just try not to get grossed out by the stretch marks." Lora pulled her thong down enough to show the scar.

When she heard his intake of breath, her head snapped up. The arousal in his eyes said he wasn't the least bit turned off by what he saw.

"I can't wait to see you in just those," Nick growled as he crouched in front of her.

After a couple of clicks of the camera, Nick stood up almost as quickly as he pulled her against him. He covered her mouth with his before she could refasten her jeans.

"Fuck." Nick pulled away from her lips and glanced down to where her jeans were still open. His finger ran along the edge of her thong, and she closed her eyes. "I've never seen a thong look so damn hot."

"Nick, what the fuck are you doing?" John grumbled through the door.

"I think you better do them up before my brother crashes in here." Nick gave her another quick kiss, adjusted himself and moved to open the door. "Here, I got a few of the two tattoos and the scar."

When Lora had her clothes presentable again, she followed Nick through the door. John's smile told her he knew they were not merely taking pictures in his office. Time for a distraction from the intense arousal she felt.

"What do I do now?" Lora asked.

"We've got all the information we were missing." John held up the camera. "Once we get a hard copy of these, we'll put them in our files. Aaron has the name of the guy who did both your tattoos, and he's going to go have a chat with him."

"Are you going to keep me in the loop?" Lora worried that once she left the station, they wouldn't give her any more information.

"Lora, you don't have to worry about that. We'll make sure Nick keeps you up to date on the investigation. This is not just a case to him or us. You're family, and we protect our own." John winked at her as he turned and dropped his hand on Nick's shoulder.

"Thanks, bro. I'm going to take Lora over to the pub and see if we can help with that situation." Nick reached behind him and grabbed her hand in his. "You ready?"

Lora nodded, and it was hard to hide the smile because the truth was, John's comment on her being part of the family, and Nick's unconscious act of taking her hand overjoyed her. Even with the stress of knowing it was a good possibility this guy was killing women because he couldn't find her. The fact he was drawing on them as well as scarring them was beyond terrifying.

"Is that okay with you?" Nick interrupted her thoughts as he opened the door to the truck.

"I'm sorry, what?" She was lost in her thoughts and hadn't heard a word he said.

"Are you okay?" Nick gently took her chin in his fingers.

"Yeah, I was just thinking about stuff." Lora smiled.

"I hope I'm included in that stuff." Nick pressed his lips to hers.

"You're always in my thoughts. You have been since the first time I saw you." Lora ran her hand down his cheek.

"I know the feeling." Nick gave her another quick kiss and opened the truck door for her.

For the first time in almost a year, she felt free. It was stupid, because her stalker was still out there. Nobody knew who he was or when he would hurt another woman. Still, Lora felt free to move on with her life.

"You still didn't answer my question?" Nick chuckled as he drove toward the pub.

"What question was that?" Lora lay her head back against the headrest and turned so she could see his profile.

"If we could have our date this evening instead of tomorrow." Nick glanced at her and then back to the road.

"Oh, so we're only going to have one date, huh?" Lora feigned a sigh.

Nick didn't say a word as he turned into the parking lot of the pub. He backed into a spot and turned off the truck. Lora reached for the door to get out, but before she could, Nick grabbed her hands and turned her toward him.

"Not if I can help it. If it's up to me, we'll spend every evening together. I don't care if it's just you and me, or you, me and Molly, or the three of us and your mom. I don't care if it's in the middle of a flash mob, but we'll definitely be having more than one date." Nick gave her a quick kiss on the lips and pulled back.

"I think if you're with me all the time you'd eventually get sick of me." Lora smiled at him.

"I'll never get sick of you, honey." Nick cupped her cheeks and stared into her eyes.

"We have an audience." Lora glimpsed over his shoulder.

Nick's grandmother, mother and Cora stood in front of his truck with enormous smiles. He turned as all three women held up their fists in the air with thumbs pointing to the sky.

"We got the thumbs up." Nick shook his head as he opened the truck door, stepped out.

"Why do I get the feeling I'm about to enter the lion's den?" Lora snickered as she met Nick in the front of the truck.

"You have no idea how right you are." He linked his fingers with hers and winked.

Inside the diner, trays of sandwiches and salads sat on the main counter and Nick's sister-in-law, Billie, was near the door to direct everyone as they came inside.

"Here are your orders, grab a plate, fill it with food, Jess or Isabelle will get you a drink, and then find a place to sit in the pub." Billie rested her hands on her baby bump, and gave them a sweet smile.

"Yes, ma-am." Nick gave her a salute as he picked up two plates from the pile at the end of the counter.

In his usual gentleman way, Nick held both plates while Lora filled them. It amazed her how much she piled onto his plate, because it would have fed Lora, her mom, and Molly. It obviously didn't negatively affect him. The man didn't have an ounce of fat on his body.

"Hey, got a couple of seats over here next to us." Another of Nick's sisters-in-law called from the other side of the pub.

"Hey, Steph," Nick placed both plates on the table and held Lora's chair for her to sit.

"John told me you guys left the station, so I saved you a seat. He's on the way with A.J." Stephanie placed her baby boy on her knee and proceeded to sway back and forth.

"Where are the rest of the kids?" Nick pulled his chair into the table.

"They're at the community center. Except for this guy, and Keith's little fella. They have some games and stuff there. A few of the local teenagers organized it." Stephanie cringed when little Brendan grabbed a handful of her blonde hair.

"Molly used to love pulling my hair too." Lora smiled at the baby when he giggled.

"Yeah, he likes to pull hair, noses, ears and he particularly likes to pull his sister's hair." Stephanie stood the little boy on her lap. "Don't you, my little prince."

A few minutes later Kurt's familiar voice echoed through the speakers of the pub. Everyone in the room turned toward the small stage as they continued to eat.

"Thank you, everyone, for coming today. I know most of you are on lunch break, or have shit to do, but I'm thankful you were able to come." Kurt pulled a sheet of paper from his pocket and placed a pair of glasses on the tip of his nose.

"He's finally wearing the reading glasses." Stephanie snickered as Jess sat down next to her.

"If he wants to be able to read, he has no choice." Jess laughed and gave Lora a little wave.

"The good news is Alice is home. The bad news, I'm in the dog house because I wouldn't bring her here today. You may receive a lot of calls or texts from her to make sure I followed her instructions." Kurt snorted. "First, all of you who told her you could fill in while she's off, she wanted me to thank you from the bottom of her heart. You have my deepest gratitude as well."

Lora scanned the crowd in the pub. She noticed not only were most of the adult O'Connors gathered there, but a number of the men from Keith's construction company and security firm were as well. She could also see plenty of Alice's customers, friends and a lot of the O'Connor in-laws.

"Okay, here we go." Kurt glanced at the paper again. "Kathleen, Cora, and Mudder are going to take over Alice's duties in the kitchen with Kit. Stephanie and Marina's mom, Janet, has volunteered to help in the kitchen as well. Emily's mom, Lynn Ann, and Billie's mom, Marg, will be helping in the pub and the diner. Thanks for that ladies. Kathleen has a schedule for the rest of this week. All you need to do is fill in your name where you can volunteer your time." Kurt glanced at the paper again. "Lora, you'll work your same hours. Alice doesn't want you to take time away from little Molly."

"I don't mind filling in when you need it, Kurt." Lora appreciated Alice's concern, but it wouldn't be permanent.

"Nope, she was firm on that, but she said to thank your mom as well for agreeing to work the coat check at the pub on Saturdays."

Lora hadn't realized her mother had volunteered, but since Lora didn't work on the weekends, it would be good for her mom to get out of the house for something besides her regular card club or committee meetings.

As Kurt listed off the duties for almost everyone in the pub, a lump formed in Lora's throat. It moved her to see a family so close that they would give up their free time to help. Not that her family wasn't the same.

Before her father died, he would stay after school to help kids with studies or volunteer as a coach for sports teams, drama clubs, art clubs, and even the chess club. He didn't play, but he said just because the school board cut back all extracurricular programs, didn't mean the kids had to suffer.

It made Lora want to volunteer her time at the school as well. Many of the teachers didn't have time because of family commitments. So, whenever her dad said they needed extra help, Lora and Dallas would be there with a few volunteers. Some university students, and students' parents would help too, but not nearly as many as was needed. According to Dallas, since Lora's father passed away, the school had lost most of the volunteers.

She wanted so much to go back to the school, but it was hard without her dad there. The kids would talk about how it wasn't the same without him, and the other volunteers would say how much they missed him.

"Lora, are you okay?" Nick touched her hand making her head snap in his direction.

She hadn't realized she'd gone off into a daze until he spoke to her. Lora was slightly embarrassed that she'd gone off in a daze again.

"Sorry, I was thinking about Dad." Lora sighed.

"Do you want to leave? I know what I'm supposed to do." Nick linked his fingers with hers.

"No, I'm good. All this just reminded me of him. If he were alive, he'd be the first one in line to help." Lora smiled.

"Sounds like a great guy." Nick lifted her hand and kissed the back of it.

"He was." Lora blinked back the tears.

An hour later, everyone had a copy of the first week's schedule. Kurt mentioned the Canada Day celebration may be cancelled, but he'd let everyone know once he talked to Alice. It was two weeks away, so there was still plenty of time to prepare if Alice was against it.

"How's your mom?" Lora asked Kristy as they made their way out of the pub.

"Surprisingly in good spirits, but I have a feeling that will change real fast if dad keeps hovering." Kristy laughed.

"Just don't give her a frying pan. She may beat him with it." Nick laughed.

"I'm keeping her out of the kitchen." Kristy chuckled.

"Where's Bull?" Nick glanced around.

Lora couldn't remember seeing Kristy's fiancé when she walked in, and it would be hard to miss the bald head. Plus, he rarely left Kristy's side when they were in the same room. He may be a big tough guy, but he was putty in Kristy's hands.

"He and Hannah went to make sure the old house is completely cleared out of their family's things. It's sold. They never want to go inside that place ever again after today." Kristy shuddered.

"Good," Nick gave Lora's hand a gentle squeeze.

She wasn't entirely sure what happened with Dean and his sister. All Lora knew was, Hannah's husband faked his own death, and tried to frame Hannah for the murder. It was a big news story, because Dean's family were one of the most well known in the province.

The only thing Lora was sure about was Dean was madly in love with Kristy. When they were in the same room, it was as if nobody else existed. Dean's sister was friendly and dropped by the restaurant often with a firefighter named Garrett. Although, she insisted he and her were just friends.

"Hey, I just saw Keith come in. I need to ask him something." Nick released her hand and left her standing next to Kristy.

"Well, it's about damn time." Kristy nudged her elbow.

"If you're referring to Nick, yes, it's about damn time." Jess appeared behind her sister.

"Don't go getting all excited. We haven't even had our first date yet." Lora rolled her eyes.

"Oh honey, you two are so beyond dates now." Jess wiggled her eyebrows.

"What are you… wait…you think… hold on… we haven't." It wasn't that she didn't want to, because the truth was she craved Nick.

"Oh, come on. A.J. said, you two were in John's office forever." Jess grinned.

"Oh, Lord. The only thing that happened in that office was Nick took pictures and… well, a kiss." Her cheeks felt as if they were on fire.

She was so embarrassed Nick's family thought they were fooling around in John's office. Well, they kind of were, but from the grin Jess gave her, Nick's cousin thought they did a lot more than just kiss.

"Seriously?" Jess sounded doubtful at first, but Lora turned to glare at Aaron as he strutted across the pub.

"A.J.'s in so much trouble." Kristy laughed.

"Why is A.J. in trouble now?" Nick appeared behind her and grasped her hand.

"I'll let Lora tell you, but you guys were in there a long time, from what I heard." Jess wiggled her fingers in a wave as she and Kristy walked away.

"Want to tell me why I've got to beat the shit out of A.J.?" Nick glanced over her shoulder in the direction where Kristy and Jess had left.

"Take me home, I'll tell you on the way." Lora wanted to get out of the restaurant before someone else said something.

Nick didn't say another word as they walked out of the pub and made their way to his truck. He waved to his family and from the grins on a lot of their faces, they'd heard Aaron's little story. Facing them again was going to be humiliating.

He was enraged. The bitch died before he had a chance to slit her throat, but he probably shouldn't have beaten her so severely. He was tired of being kept apart from his love and went too far.

He studied Dulce's beaten and bruised body. She was similar to his love, but her tattoos were different. He didn't know how to cover up tattoos, but something compelled him toward her.

"I'm tired of weak imitations of you, my love. I need you, and no cheap whore is going to take your place." He pushed Dulce's shoulder.

Her lifeless body tipped over in the chair and hit the concrete floor with a slap. He'd take care of the garbage later. It was Thursday night, and Sheila was a creature of habit. He would have to miss work, and if his boss gave him shit about it, he'd remind the bastard of the little video he currently possessed. The one that could ruin his employer's career and life.

His next step, surveillance outside that stuck up bitch's house. Daphne Hobbs was the key to finding his love, and she was probably the one who convinced Sheila to hide her daughter. Daphne never liked him, but that didn't anger him as much as it did when she snubbed him.

He pulled the black hat over his head and shoved his arms into the jacket. Between the dark clothes and his tinted windows, he could sit on the side of the road for days before anyone would notice. After all, his car resembled the high-end vehicles the snobs on that street owned.

As his garage door slowly went up, he got into his Black Mercedes Benz C-Class Coup. It was the one possession he owned that everyone admired. He'd used his family money to buy the one indulgence, even though he was mocked for wasting his money by his father.

He didn't care, because when he overheard his love say she'd love to get behind the wheel of one. He wanted to make all her dreams come true, and as soon as he found where they were hiding her, he'd let her drive his.

Chapter 12

Nick dropped Lora off at her home, but he was ready to explode. He hid his anger from Lora, even managing to make her laugh at the whole situation. Aaron didn't mean any harm, and Nick knew that. His brother had probably been joking with Jess, but it didn't calm his urge to pound the piss out of the ass.

If Aaron wasn't at the bunkhouse, Nick would beat him later. Nick's priority was to get ready for his date with Lora. He was a wreck, but he couldn't wait. He never got nervous before a date. Hell, most of the time he didn't even look forward to them.

His previous companions were not ones to introduce to mom, and the ones that did meet his family usually didn't last very long. Then there were the ones that wanted to say they'd bagged a cop. None had potential, but with Lora, he saw a future, and it had nothing to do with his Aunt Cora telling him she was the one for him.

By the time he pulled into the bunkhouse, Aaron sat slouched on the step with a beer to his lips. Nick's urge to punch Aaron subsided a little. At least until the fucker grinned at him.

"There's another in the fridge…." Aaron jumped to his feet when Nick pushed his head to the side. "What the fuck was that for?"

"You and your oversexed imagination." Nick stomped up to the door.

"It was a fucking joke. It's not my fault Jess took it seriously." Aaron followed him into the house.

"Watch what you say in the future." Nick pulled off his t-shirt as he headed into his bedroom.

He showered, shaved and dressed quickly. When he wandered back into the living room, Aaron was on the couch with his feet crossed over on top of the coffee table. He met Nick's eye when he walked into the living room.

"She means a lot to you, doesn't she?" Aaron wasn't his usual teasing self.

"Yes. She does." Nick flopped down in the armchair across from his brother.

"I'm happy for you, bro." Aaron rolled the beer bottle between his hands and dropped his gaze down.

"But…" Nick knew his younger brother probably better than he knew himself.

Aaron may be his brother, but he was also his best friend. Not that Nick wasn't close to the rest of his brothers, because he was. It was just that Nick and Aaron were only eleven months apart and growing up they were always together.

"It's just with this case; I worry you're gonna take too many chances if she's in jeopardy." Aaron glanced up.

"I won't. Yes, I'll do what ever it takes to keep her out of this guys clutches, but I'm not stupid, bro." It stung that Aaron would even consider Nick would do something careless.

"I know, but I can see Lora's it for you." Aaron smiled.

"Oh, so now you're the cupid of the family." Nick chuckled.

"Fuck no, but you're different with her, and it's good to see." Aaron sat back on the sofa.

"I'm sure you'll find someone too someday." Nick assured Aaron.

In high school, Aaron had fallen for a girl, hard. The year his brother graduated, she dumped him, left the province and never looked back. Very few people knew how much Aaron loved Bethany, and Nick had been sworn to secrecy. Nick believed it was the reason Aaron never dated a girl for more than a night or two. Aaron didn't want to go through that pain again.

"There isn't a woman out there who has the patience to deal with all this." Aaron wiggled his eyebrows.

"You may be right." Nick tossed a pillow at his brother.

With time to kill before his date, he called Isabelle to make sure everything was set. He'd booked one of the private booths at his cousin's restaurant because Isabelle insisted it was the most romantic.

Nick was watching a ball game with Aaron when his phone buzzed. He glanced at the screen, and his heart flipped in his chest at the sight of Lora's beautiful face.

"Must be the pretty waitress." Aaron chuckled.

"Hello," Nick slapped Aaron on the chest as he stood up.

"Nick, hey. Listen, I can't go out tonight." Lora sounded panicked.

"Is something wrong?" Nick spun and glared at Aaron.

He knew Hulk was at the house, so Nick was pretty sure that she wasn't in danger. This sudden change had to be because of Aaron's little joke.

"I… shit… I can't talk now. I've got to go." Lora ended the call before he could say another word.

"Fuck," Nick tossed his phone on the table and trudged to his room.

"What's wrong?" Aaron stood at Nick's bedroom door.

"She canceled." Nick snapped as he changed into his work out gear.

"Why?" Was Aaron that dumb?

"Why? Seriously?" Nick picked up his bag. "Why the fuck do you think?"

"She canceled because of what I said?" Aaron grabbed Nick's arm, and he dropped the bag.

"She didn't say, but why else. Now let go before I use you for a fucking punching bag." Nick snarled.

"Bro, I'm sorry." Aaron was sincere, but at that moment, Nick didn't give a fuck.

Aaron released him, and Nick snatched the bag from the floor. The gym would help work out some of his shitty mood. He wasn't angry with Lora. People thinking she fucked Nick in John's office had to be humiliating for her.

Nick never got sore over most things, but he had a feeling his chance with Lora was done. He cared about her more than any woman he'd ever met, and now it seemed as if she ended things before they even started.

His stomach clenched when he thought about how she would keep him at arm's length again. It would make it harder to keep an eye on her as well. Not that he didn't trust Hulk or Crash or any of the guys, but he wanted to be the one to keep her safe. Be her superhero. How pathetic was that?

Nick was falling in love with her, and it scared the shit out of him. Not because he was afraid of spending his life with someone, he was terrified of losing her. Could he admit that to her? Was he ready to acknowledge that to himself?

Sitting in the car was not only monotonous, but terribly uncomfortable. There hadn't been any movement in the house all day, and he wondered if the women had moved their club night to some other place.

If that was the case, then he needed to find out where the rest of the old bitches lived. The only one he knew besides Daphne was Sheila. It was going to take lots of patience to figure all this out. The first thing he had to do was get rid of the body at his house before it started to smell.

Since the sun set, it was probably the best time to drag the body out to one of the parks and let the idiot cops find her. He still laughed when he thought about how they hadn't figured out what happened to the couple that bought his house. Nobody even reported them missing. Hell, nobody even knew they'd bought the house. Sheila had done everything through an agent, so she never got to meet the couple, and she certainly didn't know he lived in the house.

The amount of stupidity he'd found in people was shocking. He'd fooled so many without a single one of them figuring it out. It was why it was so great that his love was the only one who knew how he felt, and the extremes he'd gone through to make sure they could be together. Yes, his love would be pleased.

How could she not? No other man in her life ever did so much for her. Nobody loved her like he did.

Chapter 13

Lora dropped her phone on the table at the sound of Molly crying from the other room. She'd hated to cancel her date, but when her mother brought Molly back from the park, the little girl had a fever and vomited all over herself.

"Mommy's coming, sweetie." Lora ran as she heard Molly gagging again.

"I just called Daphne and told her I'd be staying home from cards tonight." Her mother opened the front door. "I'm going to run to the pharmacy and grab some juice for Molly."

"Get the one they use for kids with all the electrolytes," Lora shouted as she made her way into the bedroom where Molly had the bucket in front of her again.

"My belly hurts, Mommy," Molly moaned.

Her daughter didn't get sick very often but when she did, it was usually bad. When Molly gagged again and stuck her head over the bucket, Lora rubbed her back until it settled.

A few minutes later Molly gave her the bucket and flopped back on the bed. Lora used a cool cloth to wipe down her little face and gave her a sip of water to rinse her mouth.

"Nana's gone to get you some special juice to make you feel better," Lora whispered and kissed Molly's forehead.

"Okay," Molly sniffed.

"Do you want to come lay on the couch?" Lora hated to leave Molly alone in the room.

"No, I'm gonna sleep." Molly turned onto her side, and her eyes fluttered closed.

"Okay, just call out if you need me. Mommy will hear you over the monitor." Lora pulled the covers over her daughter and tiptoed from the room.

When she walked back to the living room, she was startled by the man who stood at the open front door. She covered her mouth to stifle the scream until she realized who it was.

"A.J., you frightened the bloody crap out of me." Lora groaned.

"Sorry, I ran into your mom, and she said you'd be out in a minute." Aaron walked in and closed the door.

"What are you doing here?" Lora cringed, because her tone sounded rude.

"I wanted to apologize." Aaron shoved his hands into his pockets and gave her a sheepish grin. "I really didn't mean anything, it was a joke."

"You didn't have to come all the way over here to apologize." Lora smiled.

"Yeah, I felt terrible that you canceled your date with Nick over this." He looked so pitiful.

"I didn't cancel my date with Nick over that. Molly's sick." She realized why Aaron felt the need to come tell her he was sorry. "Oh my God, does he think that's why I canceled?"

"Yeah, he got pissed at me because he thought you were embarrassed and didn't want to go out in public." Aaron sighed.

"I need to call him. I swear that had nothing to do with me staying home tonight. I'm so sorry, A.J." Lora picked up her phone.

"Me too. It's just... I've never seen Nick this serious over anyone before." Aaron smiled. "He's a great guy, and I'm glad I didn't ruin things for you two."

"You didn't, and I know how great he is." Lora tapped Nick's number.

"I'll get out of your hair. I hope the little one gets better soon." Aaron waved as he opened the door. "If you need some medical advice give Dad or Ian a call." Then he was gone

Nick's phone rang several times and then went to voicemail. She tried again but still no answer. Maybe Aaron wasn't the only one to piss off Nick. She'd meant to tell him her daughter was sick, but Molly started to throw up again.

She tried Nick's phone a third time, and as she was about to end the call someone answered.

"Hello," It wasn't Nick, and she couldn't place the voice.

"Hi. I was looking for Nick." She glanced out through the living room window.

"Let me see if I can get him to stop pounding the shit out of the heavy bag." The man chuckled.

Now she really felt awful. He was at the gym taking out his frustration on a poor defenseless punching bag.

"Thanks," Lora replied.

She heard the guy tell Nick his woman was on the phone, but he didn't answer. Was he pissed at her too?

He rolled her onto the grass, then balled up the heavy plastic and stuck it down in a garbage bag. He'd burn it when he got home. He didn't like burning the plastic because it smelled terrible, but he couldn't take a chance.

He stuck it down under the spare tire in his trunk until he could make it out to the place where he disposed anything that could lead back to him. He wasn't stupid. The property his family owned was so far in the woods that he couldn't drive in there with his car. He'd bring his vehicle as far as he could and then pull out the ATV hidden in the trees.

He didn't have time for that right now. He had to get back to Daphne's house, in case Sheila showed up. Then he'd follow her until she led him to his love.

Chapter 14

Punching the leather bag wasn't helping with his mood. It just made him sweat. The music blared in his ears from his earbuds as if it was taunting him with *Love Hurts* by *Nazareth*.

"Hey, Nick," He heard the faint shout in the background and ignored it because he wasn't in the mood to talk to anyone.

He'd seen Bull, Trunk, and Keith when he stomped into the building, and knew they'd question why he was working out for the second time that day. Especially, when he'd mentioned his date with Lora earlier.

He was thankful Keith had a fully functional gym on his property, but he wished he was in one where nobody knew him. At least then nobody would harass him.

"Hey, Rocky," Bull tapped him on the shoulder.

"What?" Nick spun around as he yanked out his earbuds.

"Who the fuck pissed in your cornflakes?" Bull growled.

"What do you want, Bull?" Nick pulled the gloves off his hands.

"Your phone was dancing on the bench, so I answered it when I saw your lady's picture." Bull held up the phone. "You're welcome by the way, Dick smack."

"Fuck you, doorknob." Nick snatched the phone and mumbled thank you as Bull sauntered away.

"Hello," Nick tried to sound casual.

"A.J. just dropped by to apologize." Lora's voice was barely above a whisper.

"What are you talking about?" He appreciated Aaron had consideration enough to do that, but what good would it do?

"He seemed to believe I canceled our date because of what he said," Lora said with a scoff.

"Isn't that why?" Now he was confused.

"No, Nick. Molly's sick. She's running a fever and throwing up…." Nick stopped her before she said another word.

"I'll be there in an hour." Nick grabbed his bag and waved to the guys as he jogged out of the gym, but not before he heard Trunk shout after him.

"Another one bites the dust." Trunk laughed.

"Nick, she has a stomach bug that's probably contagious." Lora warned.

"Don't care. One hour. I'll see you then, sweetheart." Nick ended the call and ran from the gym back to his bunkhouse.

Forty-five minutes later he'd showered, changed, dropped by Isabelle's restaurant to pick up enough supper for four people, a separate order for Hulk, and stopped by the station to get a surprise for Molly. He had one more stop before he got to Lora's house.

He walked into Hopedale Pharmacy and went straight to the counter. The Pharmacist would know if there was something that could make Molly feel better.

"Nick, your father, and brother are doctors, and your cousin is a nurse. You couldn't ask any of them what to do?" Harold Lawton laughed.

"I didn't think of it, Mr. Lawton. My friend's little girl is sick, and I ran out to get whatever I could to help the little one." Nick knew he probably looked like a complete idiot.

Why hadn't he thought to call his father? Even his mother probably could have given him some advice, but Nick knew where that conversation would have led. His mother getting excited about another wedding.

Jesus.

Why did all thoughts of Lora make him think of the same thing? It was the first time in his life he ever thought of taking that long walk down the aisle. Maybe Cora wasn't wrong.

"That stuff should help, but it must be something going around. You're the second person to drop in for this today." Harold walked Nick to the exit.

Harold owned Hopedale Pharmacy and knew all Nick's family well. The Lawton kids went to school with Nick, his brothers and cousins. There was even a time Isabelle dated one of the Lawton boys for a short time.

"Thanks again, Mr. Lawton." Nick left the building with juice, and ice pops specifically for kids.

After Nick pulled into Lora's driveway, he grabbed the various bags and made his way up her steps. Hulk was on a bench with his feet propped up on the railing, but jumped to his feet to relieve Nick of a couple of the bags.

"Are you moving in already?" Hulk teased with a chuckle.

"Behave yourself, or you'll get none of Isabelle's Lasagna and garlic bread," Nick joked.

"Shit, sorry, bud." Hulk grinned.

Nick managed to knock on the door while he pulled out the separate bag for Hulk. Lora opened the door, and her mouth dropped open.

"What did you do?" Lora smiled as she stepped back.

"This bag has supper for me, you and your mom." Nick held up the cloth bag with the food from Isabelle's restaurant. "This bag has juice, ice pops, coloring book, and crayons for Molly."

"Nick," Lora stared at him as she choked out his name.

"That's me, but this is starting to cramp up my fingers so can I come in and put it on your table?" Nick adjusted the heavy bag of food.

"Of course," Lora motioned for Nick and Hulk to come in, and they made their way to the kitchen.

"What's all this?" Sheila sat at the kitchen table sipping on a cup of tea.

"Direct from *A Taste of Hopedale* to your table." Nick and Hulk carefully placed the bags down. "Also, some disposable plates so you won't have any dishes to wash."

"Nick, this is too much." Lora started to pull the containers out of the bags as Hulk made his way back out of the house with his own meal.

"You have to eat and so do I." Nick placed the other bag on the table next to the food.

"Mr. Lawton said this stuff would help keep Molly from getting dehydrated." Nick pulled the bottles of juice out of the bag. "These will have to stay in the freezer." He handed her the box of ice pops.

"Nick, this is great but…" Sheila stopped Lora before she finished.

"It's great you would think of Molly like this." Sheila smiled.

The two women grinned. Something with the looks they exchanged told him they were hiding something. Then he remembered what Mr. Lawton said earlier about someone else picking up the same items.

"You already have this stuff, don't you?" Nick sighed.

"Yeah," Lora touched his cheek. "But it was really thoughtful of you to think about Molly."

"I do have something you would never be able to get her." Nick held up the bag with his big surprise.

"Oh really," Lora tried to peek in the bag, but he held it over her head.

"Sorry, this is for Molly's eyes only." Nick winked.

"She's sleeping right…." Lora stopped when Molly's voice echoed through the house.

Lora walked around him and left the kitchen leaving Nick with Sheila. She'd spread the containers of food on the table and handed him a plate.

"You just earned major points with me, young man." Sheila winked.

"That's nice to hear, but it's not why I did this." Nick hoped Sheila didn't believe he only did everything to gain proverbial points.

"That's what makes it so great, Nick. Knowing what I do about your family, I'm sure you didn't even give it a second thought. You, young man, think with your heart, and that's a good thing." Sheila reached across the table and gently tapped his hand.

"Thanks," Nick smiled.

"Look, who wanted to get a drink." Lora walked into the kitchen with Molly perched on her hip.

"Hi, Nick." Molly smiled but her flushed cheeks and tired eyes made it obvious she was unwell.

"Hi there, Lollipop." Nick stood up and held up the bag.

"What's that?" She looked at him with a little sparkle coming back in her eyes.

"I got this from my work. We gave them away to boys and girls a few months ago at the hospital. We had some left over, and I was told this guy in here makes people feel better." Nick reached into the bag and pulled out his surprise.

Molly's smile was worth the pain of digging through the storage room at the station to find one of the stuffed Newfoundland dogs wearing a police cap.

"Wow," Lora smiled at Nick as she held the toy up for Molly.

"Now there's just one rule when you have this guy." Nick tapped his finger on the head of the dog.

"What?" Molly glanced up at him.

"You need to give him a name." Nick winked at the little girl.

Molly stared at the toy as if it required a lot of thought to name a stuffed dog. After a few minutes, she stared up at Nick and smiled.

"I'm gonna call him Gus." Molly hugged the dog to her.

"Gus is a great name." Nick tapped her nose with his finger.

"Gus is really a mouse, but I like it." Molly smiled.

Nick glanced at Lora, but she didn't give him any indication as to what Molly was talking about. She just smiled at him as if he'd given her the greatest thing in the world.

"Do you want to watch Cinderella and show Gus where he got his name?" Lora glanced at Nick, and it all came back to him.

He remembered the character from the old Disney movie. His nieces loved it, and he'd watched that one, as well as most of the princess movies when he babysat. Nick didn't mind, but it was a lot more fun for him to watch his nephews.

"Okay," Molly nodded.

"How about we let Mommy and Nana get some supper while you and I watch that movie? Do you know it's one of my favorites?" Nick took Molly from Lora and walked out of the living room.

"You like Cinderella?" Molly's eyes went wide with surprise.

"Are you kidding me? It's my very favorite." Nick sat on the couch with Molly on his lap.

Lora entered the room and handed Molly a small glass about half full of juice. Nick met her gaze, and his heart did that flip-flop it seemed to do every time he was near her.

"Drink it slow, sweetie." Lora crouched in front of Nick.

"We're good here, Mommy. You get something to eat." Nick winked and took the glass from Lora.

Lora stayed for a few minutes staring at him. At first, he thought he might be overstepping his boundaries, but when she smiled and mouthed the words thank you, Nick knew he'd done the right thing.

Everyone knew being a single parent was difficult, even when a person did have help, but considering Lora's situation, she needed all the extra support she could get.

Nick cared about Lora, and it felt right to help with Molly. If he and Lora were going to start a relationship, her daughter would be a part of that. Plus, he was already in love with the cute little girl now snuggled into him.

Yep, he wasn't only falling for Lora, but Molly had also wrapped her little arms around his heart. He'd never pictured himself as a father, but Molly was making him wish he was hers.

He grinned as several cars pulled into Daphne's driveway and women walked toward the large house. None of them were Sheila, but in all the years these women had been getting together, his love's mother never missed a night. All he had to do now was wait.

"These women are creatures of habit." He counted them as they entered the house.

They were all there except the one he waited for. Anger grew inside him, and he slammed the palms of his hands against the steering wheel, but it didn't help with the rage.

"I'll find you, my love." He growled through gritted teeth. "They can't keep us apart for much longer."

Another car pulled into the driveway, and he stared as the driver's door opened. Since the car parked in a dark part of the driveway, it was hard for him to see the occupant. Excitement swelled inside him as the figure moved into the light, but then disappointment.

"Your boss is here. What could that bitch possibly be doing at Daphne's house?" He leaned back in the car when Dallas stopped and turned.

He practically stopped breathing until she shrugged and continued to the entrance of the house. When she disappeared inside, an idea hit him.

"I think I might have made a mistake. Dulce was the wrong one to get information out of. If anyone knows where you are, it's Dallas Ball."

He settled back in the seat and waited for his chance to get answers from the only other person that they would trust outside of her family. Yes, they would definitely let her know where they'd imprisoned his love.

Chapter 15

Lora stood in the entrance to the living room for a few minutes and watched Nick and Molly. She was in such awe of this man. Except for kissing, and a really hot moment in John's office, they hadn't even been on a date. Yet he showed up as soon as he found out Molly was sick. Not only did he bring food for Lora and her mother, but things for Molly to make her feel better. Was he real?

"That has to be the cutest thing I've ever seen," Her mother whispered in her ear.

"Yeah," Lora smiled and turned away from the scene that was making her ready to tear up.

"Hey, this is a good thing, Lora." Sheila took Lora by the shoulders.

"Is it? Mom, if the guy that's killing those women is out to get me, then I can't expect Nick to be in the middle of this," Lora whispered.

"He's already involved. Isn't he one of the investigating officers?" Her mother was right, but the conversation with John earlier in the day about Nick taking chances still stuck in her mind.

"Honey, don't overthink this. Enjoy it. That man out there obviously cares about you and Molly." Her mother cupped her face.

"I'm falling for him, Mom, and it terrifies me." Lora sighed when her mother pulled her into a hug.

"That's an amazing thing." Her mother kissed her cheek as she hugged her tightly.

"He's so great. The whole family's incredible." Lora pulled back and walked into the kitchen with her mom.

"You don't have to tell me. This food's incredible too." Her mom grinned.

After she'd eaten and put a plate together for Nick, Lora put the mass amounts of leftovers into the fridge. Her mother planned to stay home from her club night because Molly was sick, but since Nick was there, Lora talked her into going.

"I think I might just spend the night at Daphne's place." Sheila winked. "Just so I don't have to drive back in the dark."

"You drive back in the dark every Thursday night. Why is tonight so different?" Lora knew her mother wanted to give her and Nick some privacy. Not that they would get much with a sick child.

"I'm changing it up a bit." Her mother kissed her cheek and disappeared down the hall to her room.

Lora grabbed the plate of food, and a bottle of beer for Nick. After what he did for her and Molly, she would make sure he ate.

She entered the living room and stopped. Nick sang along with the song, *So This is Love* from the movie. The man's voice gave her goosebumps, and she was entranced.

"I'm gone."

Lora jumped at the sound of her mother's voice behind her. Luckily, she was able to keep from dropping the plate and the beer.

"Okay, Mom. Drive safe." Lora glanced at her.

Her mother walked into the living room and kissed Molly on the cheek. When she leaned over to kiss Nick on the forehead, Lora shook her head. The expression on Nick's face was priceless as her mother walked away from him.

"Bye, Nick. I'm going to be gone all night so feel free to stay if you want." Her mother smiled as she walked out of the living room.

"I... ah.. okay... bye, Mrs. Norris." Nick stared at her mom as she walked out through the door.

Lora placed the plate and beer on the coffee table in front of him. Molly was sleeping, but before Lora could move her, her daughter sat up. Lora knew by the wide eyes and grey color what was about to come next.

"Mommy," Molly squawked, and before Lora could do anything, Molly threw up all over Nick.

"Oh, God." Lora cringed. "Nick, I'm so sorry."

"Don't be." Nick didn't even flinch as he jumped to his feet and carried Molly into the bathroom with Lora hurrying behind them.

"That's okay, Lollipop. Get it up." Nick smooth calm voice filled the tiny bathroom. He held Molly while she bent over the toilet. "Get that ol' germ out, girlie."

Lora hurried to Molly's room to grab clean pajamas for her daughter. She remembered her brother asked her to store some of his old clothes until he had time to go through them. In the back of Molly's closet, she tore open a box and yanked out a pair of track pants and a t-shirt.

Ethan was not quite as muscular as Nick, but he was close in height. Hopefully, Nick wouldn't mind the clothes being a little snug. At least they'd do until she washed the clothes he was currently wearing.

Lora felt awful that Molly threw up all over him, but when she re-entered the bathroom, Nick had a cloth held to Molly's forehead as he reassured her sobbing daughter Gus hadn't gotten covered in vomit.

"Molly, why don't you let Mommy get you into some clean pajamas while Nick goes to the other bathroom to clean up." Lora knelt on the floor next to Molly.

"Nick, I'm sorry." Molly's lip stuck out.

"You don't have to be sorry, Lollipop. You couldn't help it, and it's nothing I can't wash off." Nick cupped her cheek and kissed the top of her head. "She feels really hot."

Lora grabbed the thermometer from the medicine cabinet and placed it in Molly's ear. Nick didn't move as she waited for it to beep.

"It's a little high, one hundred and one." Lora sighed.

"Do you have something for fever?" Nick didn't even seem to care that he was still covered in vomit.

"Yeah, I'll give her something when I get her changed." Lora started to strip off Molly's pajamas.

"Maybe I should call Ian or Dad." Nick's concern was heartwarming.

"Maybe you should change." Lora smiled and nodded toward the clothes she left on the sink. "They're my brother's, but they should be okay until I get your clothes washed."

"I don't care about that. Isn't that a really high fever?" Nick touched Molly's head again.

"Nick, trust me. Once I give her some Advil the fever will come down." Lora smiled at him.

"Okay, if you're sure, but I know they'd be here in minutes if you need them." Nick finally grabbed the clothes.

"I know. You can wash up in the master bathroom off my room. Leave your soiled clothes on the bedroom floor, and when I get Molly settled, I'll toss them in the washer." Lora nodded toward her room.

"I probably should shower, if that's okay." Nick finally seemed to notice the mess.

"Towels are in the linen closet." Lora chuckled as she washed her daughter and helped her into clean pajamas.

Molly wanted to go to her bedroom, and although Lora would rather she be next to her, she knew her little girl was just a kid that wanted to be in her own bed when she was sick.

"Mommy, tell Nick thank you for Gus." Molly yawned as Lora covered her little girl with a thin sheet.

"I will, sweetie. Try and get some sleep, okay. If you need Mommy just call out. I have the monitor next to me." Lora kissed Molly's head.

Lora heard the water running as she left Molly's room. The thought of Nick naked in her shower made her body warm with desire. It was so long since she'd been intimate with anyone or even wanted to.

She pushed open her bedroom door and saw the pile of clothes next to the bathroom. He hadn't closed it all the way, and she could hear him humming softly inside the shower. As she picked up the clothes, she finally realized what he was singing. It was one of the songs from Cinderella. It made her smile.

She made her way to the laundry room off the kitchen and tossed his clothes in the washer. When she heard her phone beep she hurried to grab it off the kitchen table. The text was from an unknown number, and immediately Lora's guard went up. She opened the text, and her whole body went cold.

Unknown: I finally got your number again. Did you know they were trying to keep us apart, my love?

Lora dropped the phone on the table as another text popped up from the same sender. She reached for it with a trembling hand.

Unknown: Those others couldn't measure up to you, my beloved. None of them are as beautiful as you. None of them looked at me the way you always do. We'll be together soon.

"Oh, God." Lora gasped.

"Hey, what is…" Lora turned the phone toward Nick before he could finish.

"He knows where I am." Lora's knees buckled, and Nick grabbed her before she hit the floor.

"Hulk, get in here." Nick knocked on the window.

Lora couldn't hear anything after that. The room started to spin, and it was as if she could hear whooshing in her ears. He knew where she was, and admitted he killed all those women. Now, he was coming for her.

Daddy, please watch over us.

He was slightly disappointed he didn't have to hurt or even bother to talk to Dallas. After she'd entered the house, he made his way to the side of her car, so he could grab her when she left.

He noticed something shiny on the grass where she'd driven her car over part of the lawn. He grinned from ear to ear when he realized it was Dallas's smartphone. Not only had she dropped it but it was still unlocked.

"Someone is certainly watching over me," He whispered as he quickly moved to his car, jumped inside and closed the door quietly.

The last thing he needed was someone to hear his door slam. Especially since another car pulled into Daphne's driveway. He didn't even care that it was Sheila, because he'd found the contact for his love. It had her full address and phone number.

"Oh, my love. I've found you." He kissed the picture on his phone and entered the information into his contact list.

When Sheila entered the house, he quickly returned the phone to where he'd found it and made his way back to his car. He couldn't wait to tell her that he would be with her soon. He pulled his laptop over and brought up the website he'd created for sending texts that couldn't be traced. He sent her a text and smiled. Once he'd sent the second, he pulled his car onto the road and made his way back to the house to prepare for her arrival.

Chapter 16

The panic on Lora's beautiful face practically gutted him. She'd managed to hide her fear of this guy from most everyone. Probably because the fucker didn't know where to find her. How the fuck *did* he find her?

"What's after happenin' now?" Hulk stormed into the kitchen gun in hand ready practically shouting the Newfie phrase which basically meant, what happened.

"She got a couple of texts. They're from that fucker." Nick carried her into the living room and carefully sat her on the sofa. "It's okay, sweetheart. He isn't going to get close to you."

"You can fucking say that again." Hulk had his phone to his ear.

"I need to phone John." Nick hated to call his brother when he was at home with his family, but since they were all on this case, John needed to know.

"I'm on it." Hulk pointed to the phone he held to his ear. "You stay with your pretty lady."

Hulk disappeared through the door, and Nick blew out a breath. Lora's eyes were glazed as if she was lost in some memory. Hopefully, not one that would make her run again. He couldn't let her leave him.

"He wants to kill me. Like the others," She whispered when her eyes finally focused on his.

"I don't care what he wants. He's not going to hurt you, Molly or anyone else." Nick kissed her forehead.

"My mom. She's in town…." Lora tried to stand up, but Nick kept her on the couch.

"I'll call her. What's her number?" Nick pulled his phone out of his pocket.

Lora managed to calm a little when Nick was able to get in touch with Sheila. Of course, her mother wanted to come right back to Hopedale, but Nick assured her that Lora and Molly were perfectly safe, and he'd send someone to stay with her.

"John and Cory are on the way, as well as Keith." Hulk appeared in the doorway.

"I hate to have them come here. It's after nine, and they should be home with their families." Lora glanced toward Molly's bedroom.

"I can go check on her if you want." Nick offered.

"No, I need to see her." Lora stood up and hurried back to Molly's bedroom.

Nick stared after her as she practically ran to her daughter's room. For the first time in his life, Nick understood how it felt to love someone so much that it physically hurt to think of losing them. If it took moving heaven and earth, he'd make sure Lora and Molly were safe.

Nick paced the floor while he waited for his brothers and Cory. Hulk messaged Sandy and started her working on tracking the texts. If anyone could trace them, it was Sandy. His sister-in-law was one of the best computer analysts in the country, and she knew her way around the not so legal ways of getting information as well.

"I'm here." Aaron's voice echoed from the front entrance.

"Who called you?" Hulk asked.

"John. He said to meet him here. Steve can't make it he's at the hospital with his mom." Aaron sat in the chair next to Hulk.

"Is she okay?" Nick asked.

"She had some chest pain." Aaron tapped his fingers on the table.

As everyone arrived, Nick felt guilty they practically took over Lora's kitchen. Especially with Molly sick. He made his way to the bedroom to check on Lora and Molly. Hoping the noise didn't wake the little girl.

Nick's heart felt as if it dropped in his stomach when neither of them were in Molly's room. He hurried to the master and blew out a breath. Molly was curled up next to Lora in the middle of the large bed. Lora met his gaze when he walked toward her.

"I just needed to hold her, and her bed is too small." Lora gave him a weak smile.

"That's fine. The guys are here as you can probably hear. If they get too loud let me know." Nick leaned down and kissed her forehead and Molly's as well. "Try and get some sleep."

Lora nodded, and he closed the bedroom door behind him. John had Lora's phone in his hand when Nick got back to the kitchen. He was on his own phone and reading something to whoever was on the other end.

"That's all I've got." John sighed.

"It's Sandy," Keith answered Nick's unasked question.

"Did she find anything?" Nick knew it was probably a long shot, but maybe she could find the address of this guy.

Nick wanted to pound the shit out of him. Chances were, finding the man wouldn't be easy. He'd managed to elude the police at every turn.

"She said it wasn't sent from another phone. It's one of those sites that you can send texts from your pc." Keith was reading something on his own smartphone.

"If you can find anything let me know. Get Smash on this too." John ended the call and shoved the phone into his pocket.

"How's Lora doing?" Cory leaned against the counter.

"She's in her bed with Molly." Nick didn't have to say anything more as all the men in the room nodded.

"What's next?" Aaron asked.

"We add this to the case file and hope to hell Sandy or Smash can find something from those texts. In the meantime, make sure Lora keeps track of anything else that comes in on this phone." John placed the cell in the middle of the table. "I'd say to change her number, but if we want to get this asshole, we need him to fuck up somehow."

"How about you take that phone, and I'll get her a new one with a new number?" Nick didn't want Lora to have to deal with getting messages again.

"Are you sure she's going to be okay with that?" John asked.

"I'll ask, but take it with you, and if she doesn't want to do it, I'll pick it up tomorrow." Nick walked the guys to the door.

"Hulk's staying, of course, and Crash will be here to relieve him in the morning. I think it's better if you stay here as well." John said, then turned around and headed down the steps.

"Thanks, I'm not going anywhere." From the moment he saw Lora's face after reading the text, he'd made that decision.

Nick locked up the house and messaged Lora's mom to let her know to call his number if she needed anything. Nick crept into Lora's bedroom to make sure he didn't wake them. Molly was on her back, and Lora curled up asleep next to the little girl.

Lora's bed was obviously a California King, which left lots of room for him to lay next to them. He eased onto the bed and pulled the covers over Lora and Molly. Nick placed his lips on Molly's head to check her temperature, a trick he'd learned from his mother. She always said it was easier to test it with your lips.

Thankfully she was cooler than earlier and seemed to be sleeping soundly. When he glanced at Lora, she was staring at him with a smile.

"She's cooler," Nick whispered.

"I know." Lora pushed Molly's hair back from her face.

"You don't mind if I stay here with both of you?" Nick reached over Molly and ran his finger down the side of Lora's face.

"I don't mind." Lora closed her eyes as he touched her.

"Good, because I'm going to be under your feet for a while." Nick cupped her cheek.

"I'm not going to argue." Lora covered his hand with hers and kissed his palm.

The full moon filled the room with a dim light that allowed him to see her beautiful face. He rolled onto his side so that he could watch her and Molly. There was no way he'd be able to sleep, because the truth, Lora was the love of his life. She and Molly had filled a place in his heart that he didn't know was empty.

"Go to sleep, sweetheart." Nick pulled Lora's hand over where Molly was softly snoring and pressed his lips against her fingers. "I'll be right here."

Forever.

Several times he'd sent a message, but she didn't respond. Were they allowing her to see his texts? Of course they weren't. That bastard father of hers must have made sure they knew to keep her under lock and key.

"It's okay, my love. Your Romeo will be with you soon." He ran his finger down the picture next to his bed. Her smiling face looking at him. It was the same day she told him she loved him.

She hadn't used the words exactly, but he knew, and that was the day he'd swore they'd be together. It was also the day his father laughed at him and told him to move on. His own father thought he didn't deserve someone like her.

"You might as well look elsewhere for a woman." the bastard laughed.

He was calm and told his father he'd let Lora make the decision. That same day Lora cried to her father about the little girl's father and how the fucker stopped paying child support. That day he tracked down the bastard and made him pay.

He bided his time for what seemed decades, but when he finally had her, it would be worth the wait. Having her in his bed would be worth everything he did to get to this point.

"Soon, my love." He closed his eyes and drifted off into a deep content sleep.

Chapter 17

Lora woke to the sound of Molly's giggles floating in from the kitchen. The sound always made her happy, but usually meant her daughter was being mischievous. She tossed the blankets off and practically tripped over her own feet to see what her little girl was up to.

The aroma of fresh coffee and the sight of Molly standing on a chair next to Nick took her by surprise. He stood by the stove quietly chatting with Molly and flipping something sizzling on the pan.

"Mommy puts blueberries in the pancakes." Molly tipped her head all the way back to look up at Nick.

"Why don't you get them, and we'll toss them in." Nick held Molly's hand while she climbed down from the chair.

Lora stepped back so they wouldn't see her and continued to listen. The sound of Nick and Molly in the kitchen brought tears to her eyes. Her little girl didn't know what it was like to have a dad, but Lora did. For as long as she could remember every Sunday morning, Lora, her dad and Ethan would cook breakfast for the family while her mother got a couple of extra hours sleep.

Sure, it wasn't Sunday, and Nick wasn't Molly's father, but the scene made her miss her father and fall a little more for Nick O'Connor. If that was even possible.

"Are you sure you're feeling well enough to eat these, Lollipop?" Nick asked.

"My belly feels all better, Nick." Molly sounded confident, and Lora heard the scrape of the chair being dragged across the floor.

"Okay, but why don't you start with half a pancake and see how that goes." Lora moved into the doorway as Nick placed the plate in front of Molly.

"Hi, Mommy." Molly grinned from her seat.

"Good Morning," Lora walked over and kissed the top of Molly's head.

"Already, checked that. Her temp is normal." Nick kissed Lora's cheek and handed her a cup of coffee.

"You didn't have to do all this, Nick." Lora sat next to Molly who was already halfway through her half pancake.

"Yeah, I did, I was hungry." Nick grinned. "I didn't get to eat supper, remember?"

"Oh right," Lora smiled, but then the memory of what happened after Molly got sick made her stiffen.

Lora scanned the table and the counter but didn't see it anywhere. Nick placed a plate in front of her and sat down with one himself.

"What's wrong?" Nick asked.

"Where's my phone?"

"John has it. We're going to go get you a new phone and number today," Nick said casually without even looking at her.

"Nick, I've got important things on that phone. I need it back." Lora didn't mean to snap at him, but if she lost some of the pictures on that phone, it would devastate her.

"I'm sorry, I just…." Nick glanced at Molly and stopped.

Lora never raised her voice around Molly, and if the expression on her little girl's face was what happened when she did, then it would never happen again.

"Sorry, I just have important pictures on the phone I can't replace." Lora smiled at Molly. "Pictures of Molly with my mom, my dad, and my brother."

"Papa's in heaven with the angels." Molly glanced at Nick.

"My Pop is too." Nick took Molly's little hand in his.

"Heaven has lots of people," Molly informed him as she dug back into her breakfast.

"Molly, why don't I bring you another pancake into the living room, and you can watch tv while Nick and I clean up the kitchen." Lora placed the other half pancake on Molly's plate, relieved her daughter was obviously feeling much better.

"Okay," Molly jumped down from the chair and ran out of the room. A few seconds later she came back and ran to Nick. "Thank you for breakfast, Nick." She hugged him

"You're very welcome, Lollipop." Nick grinned as Molly scampered out of the kitchen.

Lora returned once Molly was settled with her favorite tv show and her breakfast. Nick had placed the last of the dishes in the dishwasher when she entered the kitchen again.

"You could have let me at least help." Lora walked up behind him and wrapped her arms around his waist.

"Cause it was so difficult for me to put a few plates and a frying pan in the dishwasher." Nick wrapped his arm around her and pulled her in front of him.

"I'm sorry for snapping at you." Lora rested her cheek against his chest.

"It's okay; I shouldn't have let John take it without asking." Nick hugged her against him and kissed the top of her head.

She could stay in his arms forever. The warmth of his embrace calmed her. His heart thudded steadily in his chest, and Lora listened as if it were some sort of metronome.

She still had a couple of hours before she needed to go to work, and if she could spend it wrapped in Nick's arms that would be fine with her. Of course, the world conspired against her, because their peace was interrupted by shouting outside.

"What the…" Nick released her and peered through the window.

"What's going on?" Lora froze when Nick held up his finger for her to stay put.

"Who the fuck are you, and why won't you let me go into the house?" Lora recognized the voice instantly and ran after Nick as he yanked open the door.

"Ms. Norris never said she was expecting visitors." Hulk stood in front of her brother, but Ethan didn't seem the least bit worried.

"I'm her God damn brother. She knew I'd be coming I just got… I'm not explaining this to you. Get the hell out of my way." Ethan stepped to the left, but Hulk blocked him.

"Hulk, it's okay. He's my brother, Ethan." Lora stepped around Nick and out onto the front step.

"Okay," Hulk stepped back and held out his hand as if he didn't just try to keep her brother from entering the house. "Nice to meet you."

For a moment, Ethan stared at the man as if he was insane. Lora stifled a giggle when her brother glanced down at Hulk's large hand, and then back up to his face. Hulk not seeming the least bit offended, shrugged his shoulders, and proceeded down the front steps to stand there like he'd done all week.

"Lora, what the fuck is going on?" Ethan kept his eyes on Hulk as he pulled her into a hug.

"Come inside, and I'll explain." Lora waited for him to pick up the luggage that he probably dropped when Hulk stopped him.

Nick disappeared into the living room with Molly, but before Lora could turn Ethan into the kitchen to explain, Molly heard him and ran to him.

"Uncle Ethan," Molly practically leaped into his arms.

"How's my Molly Dolly." Ethan kissed her cheek.

"I throwed up yesterday, and I had temture." Molly tried to say temperature, but it was probably one of the few words she couldn't say correctly.

"You seem much better now." Ethan chuckled.

"Yep, she bounced back quick." Nick braced his shoulder against the doorjamb with his arms folded across his chest.

"And you are?" Leave it to her brother to be rude to a man inside her house.

"Ethan, this is Nick O'Connor my..." Lora didn't know what to call him.

"Boyfriend," Nick grinned as he finished her sentence.

"I see. I'm guessing by Lora's confusion of your status, this is relatively new." Ethan chuckled.

"Yes," Lora rolled her eyes.

"Nick's a policeman, and he calls me Lollipop." Molly reached for Nick and maneuvered herself so she could move to Nick's arms.

"It's nice to meet you," Nick reached out his free hand to her brother.

"You too, but who's the mountain out front?" Ethan hitched his thumb over his shoulder.

"Hulk," Molly answered.

"Appropriate name," Ethan chuckled.

"Come have a cup of coffee, and I'll explain." Lora linked into Ethan's arm.

"Lollipop and I are going to watch Cinderella." Nick sounded way too excited about watching the princess movie again.

"You watch the Little Mermaid too?" Ethan called over his shoulder.

When Nick began to sing one of the songs from the movie, Ethan threw his head back and laughed. Lora chuckled, but she was nervous to tell her brother the stalker had reappeared in her life. Especially when she'd hidden it from him for so long beforehand.

"Molly seems smitten with that guy." Ethan sat on one of the kitchen chairs.

"She is," Lora placed a cup in front of her brother and sat across from him.

"That smile says you are too." Ethan sipped the coffee and met her eyes.

"He's an amazing man, and he has a great family. His aunt's my boss." Lora folded her hands in front of her and glanced down at them.

"Dallas is his aunt?" Ethan confusion reminded her that he'd probably forgotten she left her job at Ball's Interior Design.

"I don't work for Dallas now, remember?" Lora sighed.

"Oh yeah, you're a waitress now." Ethan chuckled.

"Nothing wrong with being a waitress." Lora chastised.

"I didn't say it was, sis. Do you want to tell me what's going on here?" Ethan tapped his finger on the edge of the cup.

Lora couldn't keep it from him this time. He'd been so angry she hadn't told him when it first happened, and she didn't want to deal with that again. Plus, things were a little more intense this time.

"You may need a refill on that coffee for this." Lora retrieved the coffee pot and filled both their cups.

An hour later Nick sauntered into the kitchen as Lora finished explaining her situation to Ethan. Nick glanced back and forth between them as if he was afraid he was interrupting.

"It's okay, Nick. Come in." Ethan smiled.

"I don't know if I should have stopped this or not, but Molly's asleep on the couch." The guilt on Nick's face was amusing.

"It's fine. She's probably still dragged out from being sick yesterday." Lora motioned to the chair next to her.

"Okay, because Sandy gets really pissed if any of us let Gracie have a nap. That kid can go a week on two hours sleep." Nick smiled.

"She's very… umm… active." Lora saw how energetic Nick's niece could be, and she thanked her lucky stars Molly was on the calmer side.

"Yeah, out of all of my nieces and nephews she's the most hyper." Nick laughed.

"How many do you have?" Ethan asked.

"Ten and three on the way," Nick replied.

"Jesus, how many brothers and sisters do you have?" Ethan's eyes were wide with surprise.

"Six brothers, no sisters but I have four cousins who are like the sisters we never wanted," Nick joked.

"Big family." Ethan smiled at Lora.

199

Her brother knew Lora always wished she had more siblings. She also dreamed of having a lot of children herself, but at almost thirty, her chances of having more than Molly were slipping away.

Lora checked on Molly while Nick talked with Ethan. There was something odd about her brother showing up without calling first. Sure, he was supposed to be coming to visit on his turn around, but that was over a week away. Not that she wasn't thrilled to see him, because she truly missed him. They drifted apart over the last year because she'd kept things from him. That would never happen again because the last thing she wanted to do was lose her brother.

He stood in the trees that separated her house from the only other home on the small road. It was secluded, and it would be easy to save her, if it wasn't for the brainless muscle head at the bottom of the steps.

It didn't look good now that her brother was back. He hated her brother. There was also that pretty boy who slept in her bed the night before. They didn't do anything, but she let the asshole touch her. Even if it was just on the cheek. He knew what the fucker was up to. Men like that did everything to charm their way into a woman's pants.

It was even more critical now that he save her. That player wanted to soil her, and that would not do. It was enough that he had to clean the other losers from her soul, but she was his love. She wanted him to save her. It wasn't her plan to hide in the tiny God forsaken town. They brought her there and he would be the one to save her from them. She was waiting for him.

"I'm here, my love," He whispered behind the thick tree.

Chapter 18

Nick liked Ethan, and he was relieved the guy didn't seem too put off about the whole situation. Nick didn't know how he'd feel if he walked into one of his cousins' houses and found strange men he hadn't met.

"Considering the situation, Lora does seem happy." Ethan poured another cup of coffee, and Nick was sure it was Ethan's forth cup.

"I'm happy she's here." Nick smiled.

"I'm not going to bore you with the whole, I'll kick your arse if you hurt her shit. One, you're a cop, and I don't want to go to jail for threatening a police officer. Two, I haven't seen her smile like that in a long time." Ethan sat across from Nick.

"Trust me if I ever hurt Lora, my aunt, my grandmother, my mother and probably most of the women in my family would kick my ass." Nick chuckled but stopped when he saw Ethan's face turn serious. "Something else is on your mind."

"This bastard that's killing those women, Lora says you think he's trying to replace her with them." Ethan wrapped his hands around the mug. "Or something like that."

"It seems that way. It's why we're cautious." Nick wanted to be more careful, but he knew if he told Lora she couldn't go to work she'd probably kick him in the balls.

"Well, you've got me here to help too." Ethan emptied his cup again.

"I'm sure Lora and your mom appreciate that." Nick watched Lora's brother fill his cup again. "You must love coffee."

"Yeah, too much sometimes." Ethan sat down. "The last two days, it's probably been eighty percent of my diet."

"That's not good." Nick could see something was on his mind.

"I quit my job." Ethan raised his head to look at Nick.

"Why?" Lora's shocked voice from behind him startled Nick.

"I miss home, and as much as I love to fly, I hated the job." Ethan slouched in the seat.

"Does Mom know?" Lora sat next to her brother and placed her hand on his.

"No," Ethan sighed.

"I'm glad we'll get to see you more often." Lora smiled.

"Yeah. Now I have to figure out what I'm gonna do with my life." Ethan chuckled. "I'm thinking there isn't a gym in this town either."

"As a matter of fact, you would be wrong there." Nick laughed. "My brother has a full gym on his property."

"Keith wanted to make sure his employees were able to keep in shape and not have to make trips to town to do it. Since one of his businesses is security, it's necessary the men and women are physically fit." Nick explained.

"Your brothers are either cops or bodyguards." Ethan shook his head.

"No there's a doctor, and a lawyer. I was a lawyer for a while, but it wasn't for me, and I joined the police force." Nick felt his phone vibrate in his pocket.

"That's cool." Ethan nodded.

"Excuse me." Nick stepped into the hallway to answer the call from John.

"Hey, what's up?" Nick glanced into the living room where Molly was curled up on the couch, snuggled into the stuffed dog Nick gave her.

"We have another one," John growled.

"Fuck," Nick gritted his teeth.

"It's a lot worse this time, bro." John's voice was quivering.

"Tell me." Nick braced himself.

"He beat this woman to death, and her child is missing." Nick could hear the horror in John's voice.

"Boy or girl?" Nick pressed his fist against the wall.

"Girl, six years old." John stopped. "We got to find this little one before he does God knows what."

"I'm on the way." Nick was about to end the call, but John stopped him.

"No, you need to stay with Lora." Nick knew better than to argue with John from his tone.

"Okay, I'll tell her, and we'll have to get someone to cover her shift at …." Nick stopped when Lora stepped in front of him.

"I'm going to work." Lora crossed her arms over her chest.

"Keep me in the loop." Nick ended the call and shoved the phone into his pocket.

"Don't give me that look, Nick." Lora met his gaze, and he cupped her face in his hands.

"Sweetheart, it's better…" She held up her hand to stop him.

"What's happened?" Lora sighed.

"There's another woman." Nick didn't know if it was a good idea to tell her about the child, but then again, she would find out if she watched the news.

"Oh, God." Lora covered her mouth and tucked her head under his chin.

"Lora, there's more." Nick swallowed.

"What?" She wrapped her arms around him, and he did the same.

"He wasn't gentle with this one, and her six-year-old little girl is missing." Nick knew the minute the shock hit her, because her body stiffened, and she pulled back from his embrace.

"He took her…" Her voice came out in barely a whisper as she turned around toward where Molly still slept.

"Lora, nobody's going to get near her." Ethan stood in the doorway of the kitchen.

"I need to do something." Lora turned and paced from the kitchen doorway into the living room and out again.

"Let Nick and the rest of the police deal with this." Ethan glanced at Nick as if he knew what was coming next.

"No, this guy is killing women, beating them, and now taking children. I need to find a way to get him to come for me." Lora's eyes were filled with anguish.

"That's not going to happen. You need to think about Molly. If things go wrong, and trust me, they can go wrong, he could hurt you. Plus, John would never agree to that, and if he did, I'd beat his ass." He didn't like the look in her eyes, but she wasn't putting herself in a situation where she could get hurt or worse.

"Nick, those women. That little girl." Lora slowly lowered herself to the floor and covered her face with her hands.

Nick lifted her into his arms and carried her into the bedroom. Inside the room, Nick sat on the bed with Lora curled up on his lap. Since the day he met this beautiful woman, he'd never seen her so broken. She trembled as she sobbed in his arms. He swallowed the lump forming in his throat as he let her get it out of her system.

"Why is he doing this? I hate feeling helpless and crying all the time," She whispered when she'd calmed a little.

"Honey, there's no sane reason, you'd drive yourself crazy trying to figure out why people do these things, and there's not a thing wrong with you crying. Most people would in your situation." Nick grabbed the box of tissues next to the bed.

"There has to be something I can do." Lora wiped her nose and sighed.

"Making yourself a target isn't one of them." Nick pressed his lips to her temple.

The thought of Lora even thinking about putting herself in a situation where this guy could get his hands on her made him ill. He wasn't strong enough to sit back and allow the woman he loved to put herself in danger. He did love her, and it was at that moment he realized it was time to tell her

Nick leaned back so he could see her face. Her eyes glistened with tears as she stared at him. He cupped her cheek with his hand and swiped his thumb over her lower lip.

"I couldn't deal with it if I lost you," Nick whispered. "I'm in love with you, Lora."

"Nick," Lora stared into his eyes as a tear slipped out of the corner of her eye and slowly ran down her cheek. "I'm head over heels in love with you, but the thought of you being in danger because you're with me, scares the shit out of me."

"I've never said that to anyone before, and I'm scared too, but not because I could be in danger, but because some sick fuck is out there and wants to take you away from me." Nick pressed his forehead against hers.

"This feels… Real, with you." Lora ran her hand down the side of his face.

"I know. I don't think I could breathe if anything happened to you or Molly." Nick wrapped his arms around her tightly.

"Nick, who's the woman?" Lora wrapped her arms around him, and her voice was soft against his cheek.

"John didn't tell me her name." Nick didn't ask either.

"Do you have to go to the station?" Lora's arms squeezed tighter when she asked the question.

"No, I'm your personal shadow until this is over." Nick pressed his lips against the side of her neck and closed his eyes as he inhaled her scent.

"I'm not going to complain," Lora whispered.

Even with another victim, Lora still refused to stay home from work. Kurt gave Nick an earful when they walked into the diner.

"What did you want me to do, lock her in the closet?" Nick sat on the stool closest to the entrance.

"You could have been firm with her, and tell her she was …." The laughter behind the counter drew Kurt's attention, and Nick glanced around his uncle.

"Been firm…" Kristy held onto her stomach.

"Now young lady you're staying home, because I'm the man." Jess put her hands on her hips and made her voice deep. Nick assumed it was supposed to be her father's voice.

Lora stood next to them laughing hysterically. Nick couldn't help but laugh himself at Kurt's expression. His uncle seemed like he was ready to explode.

"Is that how you handled Mom today, Dad?" Kristy asked through her laughter.

"Yes, he told me under no condition was I going to be here today." Alice snorted from where she sat behind the cash register on a stool with her leg propped up on another chair.

"And your response was?" Lora chuckled.

"I said, yes dear, and pushed my wheelchair out to the car." Alice smiled as she rang in the takeout order for the woman currently laughing along with the rest of them.

"Yeah, Uncle Kurt. I've got about as much control over Lora as you have over Aunt Alice." Nick laughed and pulled back when his uncle made a playful swing at him.

"Damn women," Kurt muttered as he plopped back down on the stool next to Nick.

"What was that, honey?" Alice raised her eyebrows and glared at her husband.

"I love you, baby." Kurt grinned.

"That's what I thought." Nick chuckled as Alice turned back to the rest of the women. "They do learn eventually."

Alice resigned herself that she couldn't run the restaurant and pub by herself while she was injured, but she'd refused to stay home and do nothing while she healed.

"Kurt, you know better than to even try to control a woman. Especially in this family." Nick's father sat at the booth next to the window with Nick's mother and grandmother.

"I don't know what's wrong wit dat lad." Nanny Betty grumbled as she sipped her tea.

"There's nothing wrong with me. It's the God damn women in this family." Kurt muttered under his breath.

"Watch yer language, young man." Nanny Betty whipped her head around and glared at Kurt. "I'll bust yer arse if I hear dat again."

"Mudder, shouldn't you be losing your hearing at your age?" Nick's father laughed, but quickly stopped when Nanny Betty hit his knuckle with her spoon.

"I'm not too old to clout ya on da head." Nanny Betty pointed her finger at Nick's dad.

Nick glanced at Lora and smiled. It was good to see her laughing, but who wouldn't where his barely five-foot grandmother was concerned. It didn't matter how old any of them got, Nanny Betty kept them in line.

Between the lunch and supper rush, Nick helped Lora clear all the tables and washed them down. Nick wasn't supposed to be on the schedule to help, but Kurt made a quick change to the calendar, so Nick would be there with Lora at all times.

"I can still stay if you want." Jess pulled Nick aside. "At least it will give you a second set of eyes."

"I'd appreciate that, Jess." Nick hugged his cousin and made his way to the kitchen.

"Nicky, dat lass out dere is gonna be fine. My heart goes out ta da poor family of dat woman and da little one." Nanny Betty stood at the sink washing a large pot that probably weighed as much as she did.

"Nan, let me do that." Nick tried to push her aside, but she slapped him away.

"Ya get out dere and keep an eye on our girl." Nanny Betty pointed toward the diner.

"Jess is there with her too, Nan." Nick reached for the pot again only to get slapped harder.

"Get." Nanny Betty didn't say another word as she ordered him away from the sink.

Nick pushed through the swinging door and immediately spotted Lora next to one of the booths with her back to him. A man and two women stared at her with strange expressions. Nick glanced toward Jess on the other side of the room. She was watching Lora intently and seemed to be uneasy with the situation.

For a few seconds, he held himself back in case there was nothing to it, but with the rigid way Lora stood next to the table, he knew something wasn't right.

Lora stepped back from the table and turned. Nick was by her side in seconds. Her face was pale, and the tears in her eyes didn't sit well with him.

"What's going on?" Nick pulled her into the kitchen before she had a chance to respond.

"That woman who was murdered…" Lora took a deep breath.

"What about her?" Nick grasped her shoulders.

"She… I volunteered with her…. At the school where… my dad worked… She was a teacher." Lora inhaled again and wiped her hands across her cheeks.

"How do you know that?" Nick glanced through the small window in the door toward the table where Lora had been standing. "Who are those people?"

"One of the women is my old boss, Dallas." Lora sighed. "The other woman is Mom's friend Daphne, and the man is the principal of the school."

"He knew you were here as well?" Nick asked.

"No, he told Daphne to tell Mom about Dulce." Lora glanced down at the floor.

"Dulce?" Nick was confused.

"It's her name." Lora looked into his eyes. "Her little girl's name is Alexa."

"You knew them both?" Nick didn't like this at all.

"Yeah, a lot of people used to think we were sisters. We were close, but I couldn't tell her where I was going because we wanted as few people to know as possible." Lora shook her head. "I've got to get back out there."

"Lassie, ya take a rest." Nanny Betty appeared next to them with a glass of water. "Ya lost a friend. Ya need time ta deal wit dat."

"Thank you, Nan." Lora smiled at his grandmother.

"Nicky, give her a minute and take over fer her." Nanny Betty took the notepad from Lora and shoved it toward him.

"Nan, I want to …" Nick should have known better than to argue with his grandmother.

Before he could finish the sentence, Nanny Betty had him shoved out through the swinging doors. The worse thing was, Lora didn't seem to argue about him leaving her. It bothered him, but then he realized she probably needed time to pull herself together.

"Is she okay?" Jess whispered.

"I'll tell you later. Right now, I want to talk to them." Nick headed back toward the table where the man and women were sipping coffee, but Lora's mom had joined them as well.

"Mrs. Norris," Nick nodded toward her when he stood next to the table.

"Oh Nick," Sheila glanced around the table and then back to him. "This is Lora's boyfriend."

"It's so nice to meet you," one of the women held out her hand. "I'm Dallas."

Nick shook her hand as Lora's mom introduced to the other woman. Daphne was friendly and gave him a genuine smile as she nodded at him.

"Clyde Spencer," The man shook his hand, but it was as if he couldn't look Nick in the eye.

"Nice to meet all of you." Nick nodded. "I'm sorry, Lora needed a moment. Can I take your order?"

He kept his eye on Clyde for any kind of reaction, but all he did was continuously glance anywhere but at Nick. The man was definitely nervous about something.

"It's okay, Nick. Jess took our order." Sheila smiled.

"Is Lora okay?" Dallas didn't look at all the way Nick expected.

Lora mentioned her old boss a few times. She appeared to be around his age, and dressed in an old t-shirt and jeans she' didn't resemble a businesswoman at all.

"She's taking a moment to herself. It was a bit of a shock." Nick nodded.

"I understand you're one of the men working on this serial killer." Clyde glanced at him but quickly looked away when Nick met his eyes.

"Yes," Nick nodded.

"Why haven't you put out any warnings to women in the province?" Clyde's accusatory tone stung.

"We need to keep the information close to the vest, Mr. Spencer. If we put it all out there, then this guy could disappear before we get a chance to catch him, and we *will* catch him." Nick tried to sound calm.

"Six women are dead, Mr. O'Connor. Including a very dear friend and colleague." Clyde scolded.

"Clyde, that's enough. Nick isn't to blame for all this." Daphne snapped.

"That's right. Don't you dare blame Nick for any of this. The one to blame is the man who killed Dulce and took her daughter." Lora stood next to him, and she was pissed.

"I wasn't blaming him." Clyde narrowed his eyes and glared at Nick.

"It sounded like it to me." Lora bent over the table. "Clyde, when my dad died you were there to help us through everything, and I appreciate it very much, but don't you ever speak to Nick with such disrespect again."

Lora spun on her heels and stomped toward the kitchen. It was the sexiest damn thing he'd ever seen in his life. As he turned back to the table the expression on Clyde's face was laughable. He seemed furious that Lora spoke to him with such anger, and that made the hair stand up on the back of his neck. He looked like a typical pencil pushing nerd sporting a Dr. Phil haircut.

"I apologize, Mr. O'Connor." Clyde almost seemed to choke on the words.

"It's okay Mr. Spencer, but just so you know, we're going to find this guy, and when we do he'll pay for every one of those women's deaths." Nick meant what he said, but he also wanted to see if his statement got any reaction out of Clyde.

"I hope you do." His voice was almost a whisper.

Nick stepped back as Jess appeared with the order for the table. He nodded to Sheila and made his way to the kitchen. As he stepped through the door, his mother nodded toward Alice's office.

"I can't believe he was such an ass to you." Lora stopped pacing when Nick entered the office.

"Sweetheart, he lost a friend, and he's probably hurting as much as you are." She rested her head on his shoulder as soon as he pulled her into his arms.

"Clyde doesn't have feelings." Lora snorted.

"Why do you say that?" Nick rubbed his hand up and down her back feeling her relax as he did.

"He treated all his staff as if they were idiots. My dad almost came to blows with him the first year Clyde became principal." Lora pulled back and looked up at Nick.

"Over what?" Nick was curious as to why a teacher would be so angry it would almost get physical.

"Mom said it was something about the way he treated the female teachers, but Dad just said it was because Clyde had a stick up his ass." Lora smiled.

"Did he ever say anything to you?" Nick tucked a stray piece of hair behind her ear.

"He knew better." Lora scoffed.

"Because of your dad?" Nick smiled.

"You've never seen a picture of my father, have you?" Lora smirked.

"No, but I'm guessing since he coached sports, and from the size of your brother, he wasn't a very small man." Nick laughed.

"Dad was about your height. Not as muscular, but next to Clyde, my dad looked like Arnold Schwarzenegger." Lora sighed.

"Did Clyde ever say anything after your dad died?" Nick saw the light come on in her eyes.

"You think Clyde could be the guy?" Lora stepped back and stared up at him.

"He's a little odd, and I get a strange vibe from him." Nick shoved his hands into his front pockets.

"He is odd, but I seriously doubt he would hurt anyone." Lora seemed as if she was trying more to convince herself then him.

"Was he on the list that you gave us?" Nick was going to have Cory check into the school principal.

"I think so." Lora leaned against the desk and gripped the edge with her hands. "You have to find Dulce's little girl, Nick."

The tears in her eyes appeared again, and it broke his heart. It was obvious she felt guilt over the missing child, and if he thought about it, so did he. How could he not? They hadn't found whoever was killing these women and leaving their children motherless.

"We have every available officer searching for her as well as a lot of Keith's guys." Nick grasped her shoulders.

"But will they find her in time." Lora choked out the words and then threw herself into his arms. "I held that little girl in my arms when Dulce brought her to the school for a visit, Nick. I have pictures of her with me. Dulce was my friend, and she's gone, and it's all my …. fault." Lora's body tensed.

"This isn't your fault, baby." Nick held her against him. "The only one at fault is the sick bastard doing this."

They needed to find out who was doing this, because until they did, Lora would keep blaming herself. Especially if anyone else was killed.

What was he going to do?

He knocked on the door to the small house and waited for the owner to answer. He grew more impatient as he rapped again. Someone was home since the television was loud enough he could hear it through the door.

"Jesus H Christ, I'm coming, God damn it," A raspy voice shouted from inside the house.

He stepped back with the door opened and a man that looked to be in his seventies stood with a cane in one hand. The man was hunched over and tiny, and if the wind blew too hard, the old bastard would probably fall over.

"What the hell do you want?" The man snapped.

"Good afternoon, sir. I've been sent from the senior center to talk to you about…" He got cut off by the man.

"I'm not interested in anything from that damn center. It's nothing but a bunch of suck-ups trying to get a good reputation." The man started to close the door.

He couldn't let this man stop him from his plan. He needed to stay in the house to keep on eye on his love until he could figure out how to rescue her.

"But, sir…" The man cut him off again.

"Are you deaf? I said I'm not interested." The man started to close the door.

He knew he could take the old man but didn't want anyone to hear the man if he shouted for help. There was a fair bit of distance between where they kept her and this old bastard's house, but he couldn't take a chance.

Before the man could close the door, he kicked the door, and the man fell to the floor. As luck should have it, he was able to get inside and close the door before the man got his wits about him. He stood over the man and pointed a knife at the man's face.

"If you keep your mouth shut, I won't hurt you." He growled at the elderly man.

"Okay... Okay. Take what you want. I don't got much." The man stammered over his words.

"I don't want your crap. I need to stay here for a few days until I can get what I need." He grabbed the man's hand and pulled him to his feet.

Thirty minutes later he had the man secured to an old recliner. He told the old fart that he'd gag him if he made a sound, and from what he saw the man wasn't going to make a peep. The old man pissed himself when he saw the knife.

The house was small, but it was perfect for him to be able to sneak back and forth to keep an eye on her. He thought about telling her he was close by, but that would only send her captors into a frenzy, and they'd spoil his rescue.

No, he'd been patient for the most part. He couldn't screw this up now that he was so close to saving her and spending his life making her happy.

"Soon my love," He whispered as he peeped through the window.

Chapter 19

Lora sank into the hot bath water and let the lilac scent invade her senses. The bubble bath always helped her relax after a long day, but the only thing she saw when she closed her eyes was Dulce and poor little Alexa.

Their pictures had been plastered all over the papers and news programs all day long. She was pretty sure if she still had social media that it would be all over that as well. Nick told her the police tried to get in touch with Alexa's dad, but he was currently out of town. He and Dulce had joint custody of the little girl.

Her eyes were closed when there was a soft knock on the bathroom door. She opened her eyes as her mother stuck her head in through the door.

"I don't want to disturb your bath, but Nick's sister-in-law is here, and wants to know if Molly could spend the night with Gracie."

Before Lora could respond, Molly burst into the bathroom. She jumped around and squealed about packing a bag and princess movies.

"Oh, Mommy. My very first sleepover. I need pajamas, and I got to take Gus. Mommy, I'm so happy." Molly clapped her hands excitedly.

"Honey, I don't know if…" Lora started, but her mother interrupted.

"Sandy said to tell you Molly will have a great time." Her mother then mouthed the words 'she'll be safe' when Molly turned away from her.

"Please, Mommy. Please." Molly knelt next to the bathtub with her hands folded as if she was praying.

Lora sat up in the bathtub and cupped her daughter's little face. She didn't want to be away from Molly, but the little girl was so excited about sleeping over to her friend's house.

"Okay, sweetie. Let me get out of the bath and pack your bag." Lora started to stand, but her mother held up a bag.

"Already done." Her mom grinned. "I'm going to Daphne's again tonight, and Ethan is coming with me."

Molly kissed Lora and ran out of the room shouting to someone in the living room. She assumed it was Sandy. It was strange for her mother to go to Daphne's house when it wasn't Thursday.

"Mom, why do I get the feeling you're up to something?" Lora pulled her knees up to her chest.

"I'm just giving you some time to yourself. Do me a favor and forget everything for a while." Her mother bent down to kiss her forehead.

When her mother closed the bathroom door as she left, Lora sat back in the bath and stared at the door. This was the first time she'd be alone with Nick for more than a few minutes. Could she do what her mother asked and forget about everything, and just enjoy being with him?

She certainly wanted to, because her body craved him. Ached for him. Lora wanted his touch, his kiss, his warm naked body against hers. She'd never wanted anyone as much as she did Nick.

She lifted her leg out of the water and rested against the side of the tub. The sudden realization she needed to do some significant body maintenance hit her like a ton of bricks. She sat straight up in the tub and hoped Nick didn't get tired of waiting for her to finish.

In less than an hour, she was smooth, dry and dressed in a tank top and jean shorts. Before she walked out of her room, Lora took several deep breaths and glanced around to make sure it wasn't a mess. Not that he hadn't seen her room already.

Lora found Nick in the kitchen singing along to a Luke Bryan song playing on the local country station. He turned around, and his eyes traveled down her body and back up again.

"I'm not a country girl. I'm a Newfie girl, and I'm not shaking anything." Lora grinned as she walked toward him.

"That's fine with me." Nick wrapped his arms around her waist and pulled her against him.

"You look pleased with yourself." Lora glanced around him to the stove.

"I've got some good news, and I've made supper. Why wouldn't I be pleased with myself?" Nick winked.

"Supper smells amazing, but I could use some good news." Lora slid her hands up over his chest and around his neck.

"Alexa was found. She's safe and sound. She was on vacation with her dad in Ontario." Nick's thumbs gently glided up and down her spine.

"That's great news. Although now the poor little thing has to deal with losing her mom." Lora tried to keep her emotions under control.

"At least she has her dad." Nick kissed her forehead. "But for tonight, can we have a nice supper, and enjoy a night alone."

"I've wanted to be alone with you for a long time." Lora stood up on her toes and pressed her lips against his.

"If you keep kissing me, I think supper may have to wait." Nick moaned when her tongue glided across his lower lip.

"Nick, I want you." Lora didn't care about supper because the only thing she wanted was him.

"I want you too, but you haven't eaten all day." Nick's voice sounded strangled as she moved her mouth across his jaw to his earlobe.

"I can eat later," Lora whispered into his ear.

"Fuck," Nick shivered when she sucked his earlobe into her mouth.

"That sounds good to me." Lora purred against his neck.

"Lora, you're killing me." Nick's hands cupped her ass, and he squeezed as he pulled her against his hard body.

She could feel his arousal against her stomach, and it only urged her on more. Lora nibbled her way down his neck and across his shoulder through his t-shirt. Nick's face nuzzled the crook of her neck, and his mouth did amazing things to the skin on her shoulder.

"Lock the door." Lora groaned as she forced herself to pull away from him. "I'll meet you in my room."

Before she turned and practically ran out of the kitchen, she glanced at his groin. If the bulge there was any indication of how big he was, she was about to become a very lucky woman.

Lora sat at the foot of the bed and leaned back with her hands behind her. Her heart pounded in her chest, and her body felt as if it vibrated with anticipation. She wanted Nick so badly.

Nick's muffled voice floated in from the front door and disappointment poured over her. They were going to be interrupted, and if that was the case, it wasn't going to be good news.

Lora flopped back, laying flat on the bed. She was sure Nick was about to come in and say they had company. Her eyes closed when he entered the room, but when she heard the click of the door, Lora opened one eye and peeked at him.

"Who were you talking to?" Lora turned onto her side and rested her chin on her hand when she saw he was alone.

"I told Hulk we're calling it a night." Nick reached behind his head and yanked his t-shirt over his head in that sexy way that men do.

Lora barely contained the gasp as she took in his hard chest and defined abdominal muscles. His body could be used on the cover of a romance novel or fitness magazine. Nick was hard muscle and tanned skin perfection. Her gaze went to the tattoo on the left side of his chest. It wasn't English, and for a moment she wondered what it said. At least until he unbuckled his belt.

"Are you just going to watch me undress?" Nick opened the button of his jeans.

"It's become my favorite thing." Lora grinned.

"Do you know what my favorite thing is?" Nick unzipped his jeans but stopped there as he stalked toward the bed.

"From the look of your body, working out comes to mind." Lora pushed up to her knees and kept her eyes locked with his.

"Kissing you." Nick cupped the back of her head and covered her mouth with his.

His tongue plunged into her mouth, muffling the groan that escaped. Nick's arms wrapped around her waist and pulled her body flush against his. Lora could feel the heat of his skin through her tank top, and she snaked her arms around him, trying to press her body even closer. All the months of wanting him, craving him, had her frantic to feel his skin against hers.

"Fuck, Lora, baby." Nick gasped when he pulled his mouth away from hers. "I can't get close enough to you."

Nick lowered them both to the bed as one of his hands slipped under the waistband of her shorts and cupped her bare ass. She could feel the coldness of his zipper against her belly, but it didn't do anything to tame the fire she felt inside.

Lora tipped her head back so she could see his face. He met her gaze for a moment, but when she ran her tongue across her top lip and bit her lower lip his eyes flared with arousal.

"As much as I don't want to move away from you right now, I want your clothes gone. I need to feel your skin against mine." Nick pulled away from her.

Lora was out of her shorts and tank in ten seconds. Nick chuckled as she tossed them over her shoulder. When she removed her bra and knelt in front of him in just a lacey thong, he growled.

"You're so fucking beautiful." Nick reached for her, but she straddled his legs and grabbed the waist of his jeans.

"You're pretty beautiful yourself, but if I'm down to my skivvies, I won't be alone." Lora scooted down his legs as she struggled to remove his jeans.

The only thing between them once she'd tossed his jeans aside, was the very sheer thong she wore, and his boxer briefs. Lora kept her gaze locked with his as her hands gently massaged the hard muscle of his thighs. Nick cursed as her hands glided up the length of his legs until her fingers reached the leg opening.

"You're killing me, baby." Nick propped himself on his elbows making the muscles in his stomach flex.

"I'm only getting started." Lora smiled.

She'd always been very open sexually, and was never shy about what she wanted, or what she was willing to do. She was self-conscious of her body since Molly was born, but with Nick, all that self-doubt disappeared.

The way he looked at her made her feel beautiful and sexy. A way she hadn't felt in a long time. The last couple of partners she had didn't do much to make her feel very beautiful. Especially when they pointed out her imperfections.

"You do know it's illegal to torture a police officer." Nick grinned.

"I haven't even started the torture yet, Officer O'Connor." Lora grabbed the waist of his boxers and slid them slowly down his muscular legs.

She wasn't wrong about Nick's package, because he was gifted in that department. Hell, who was she kidding the man was gifted everywhere. His underwear flew over her head, and she forced his legs apart with her knee.

Nick's grin disappeared when her tongue glided up one inner thigh and then back down the other. She did it several times inching closer and closer to his sack.

"You know what payback is right?" Nick gasped as her tongue flicked lightly against the side of his balls.

"I guess I better make this good then." Lora licked from the bottom of his sack to the tip of his throbbing erection.

"Fuck," Nick's head dropped back, and the word came out strangled.

"Not yet, but definitely later." Lora licked around the head a couple of times and then sucked it into her mouth.

"Lora, fuck…. baby. I … God…. I love this, but I need to be inside you." Nick stammered over the words in between her licks and sucks.

Before she knew what happened, he flipped her over on her back and ripped her thong down her legs. He pushed them open, but he didn't push inside her. Instead, Nick buried his face between her thighs and slipped his tongue deep inside her.

Lora arched off the bed with a shuddering moan. It was as if he knew every one of her secret spots. His rapid tongue movement, and pressure of his thumb pressed against her clit made it hard to catch her breath. She'd never had an orgasm hit her so fast. Even when she masturbated, it usually took a while, but Nick had her on the brink in less than a minute.

"Nick, yes… there. Oh, God… right… there." Lora moaned.

"Your so fucking responsive, baby. I've never tasted anything so fucking delicious," Nick spoke in a low growl as he continued to stimulate her with his hand.

Lora's body quaked as the tingle started in the tips of her toes and slammed through her body like an electric shock. He didn't stop as she fisted the sheets and spots formed in front of her eyes as she roared his name. Her back arched off the bed again, and for a moment she thought she'd tossed him on the floor, but he'd only moved to his knees.

"I could watch that all night," Nick grinned.

"If all you want to do is watch, I have some toys I could use instead," Lora responded teasingly.

"Not a fucking chance. At least not right now." Nick grabbed his jeans and pulled a strip of condoms from his pocket.

"Well, someone is confident in himself." Lora giggled as he tore one off the strip and tossed the rest on the nightstand.

"I've been waiting for this for nine fucking months, so don't think it will be one and done." Nick rolled the condom onto his thick cock and braced his hands on either side of her head. "Just so you know, the only sex I've had in those months was with my hand, and I was thinking about you."

With that statement, he slowly slipped inside her filling her completely. It had been a while for her and Nick was larger than most. He must have sensed it because he stilled and allowed her to adjust to him as he kissed her senseless.

He shook with rage as he watched the small monitor in front of him. How could she be smiling when he was doing that to her? She was his, and that oversexed cop would pay for soiling her.

With all the chances he took in the past couple of nights, he couldn't believe he hadn't been able to prevent her from being touched by another man. He'd make it up to her once he freed her from the prison where they kept her.

He was thankful that the tree line next to the house made it easy to maneuver himself to the back of the house and not be seen by the brainless thug parked in the front of the house. He couldn't believe that these men who were supposed to be professional security only checked around the house once every hour. In the hour he was able to place a small camera just inside her bedroom window. It would be hard for someone to see it unless they knew exactly what it was.

Now he sat watching as the ape rutted and pounded into his love. As much as it angered him, he couldn't help the arousal when he saw the perfect body of his love. He glanced back at the recliner where the old man had fallen asleep and grinned.

At least he could relieve himself while he pictured himself as the one taking her body. He unzipped his pants, pulled out his erect dick, and began to stroke himself. He could hear her words and closed his eyes as he pictured her saying those very words to him.

Chapter 20

Nick wasn't going to be able to hold back for long. Being with Lora was something he'd wanted since the first time he saw her at the grocery store. Little did he know at that time he would end up falling head over heels in love with her.

He'd always loved sex, but with Lora, it was better than he'd ever thought it could be. He knew the minute he pushed inside her that she was it for him. Nick never felt such a connection with a woman in his life, and feeling her inner walls squeeze his dick was the best thing he'd ever felt.

"Baby, don't stop." Lora panted as he pumped in and out of her.

"I don't think I could if I tried." Nick sucked her hardened nipples into his mouth.

"Oh... yes. Nick, that feels so good. You feel so good." Lora's body trembled as her muscles inside tightened around his cock.

"Fucking beautiful." Nick murmured as he slammed into her once more and quaked with his own release.

For a few minutes, the only sound in the room was their heavy breathing. Nick's body convulsed a couple of times as he ejaculated inside her, and he dropped his head into the crook of her neck.

"That. was…" Lora breathed.

"Yeah," Nick managed to push himself up, so he could look into her eyes and he didn't put all his weight on her.

"I love you," Lora whispered.

"I don't know if love is the right word for how I feel about you. Love doesn't seem strong enough. I adore you, crave you, and nobody in the world has ever made me feel the way you do. I do love you. More than I could ever tell you." Nick never thought of himself as an emotional man, but the feelings he had for this woman were so intense it made a lump form in his throat.

"Nick, you're so incredible." Lora cupped his cheeks, and her eyes searched his.

"You're the amazing one." Nick kissed her tenderly.

He didn't want to let her go, but he needed to dispose of the condom. He pulled out of her with a groan because surprisingly he'd started to harden again. He never had issues with recovery time, but it was never this immediate. He practically sprinted to the bathroom to get rid of the latex.

When he returned, Lora was in the middle of the bed, a tear running down her cheek. She smiled at him, but the tears confused him.

"Why are you crying?" Nick was next to her in seconds.

"These are happy tears." Lora pulled one of his hands to her lips. "Do you know how long I've dreamed of a man like you? My whole life I always wanted a man who loved me the way Dad loved Mom. It wasn't long ago I'd given up on ever finding it. Then I met you, and it was everything I could do to keep my distance, because it scared me the way my heart pounded when you were close." Another tear rolled down her cheek.

"Honey, you weren't the only one scared." Nick flirted with her, but mostly because he thought it would never happen.

"Now I'm terrified." Lora sighed.

"Why?" Nick held her face between his hands.

"The man killing those women is crazy, and if I'm the one he wants, what's to stop him from hurting people to get to me. Hurting my daughter, my mom, my brother." Lora sighed. "Hurting you."

"I don't want you to worry about me. That sick son of a bitch won't hurt you or your family. As for me, I'll kill the bastard if he even tries." Nick pulled her into his arms and lowered them both to the bed.

He held her against him pressing his lips to the top of her head. As scared as she probably was about this guy, Nick was equally as terrified. The thought of anyone taking her away from him made it difficult to breathe.

"Why are you the only one of your brothers with the cleft in your chin?" Her head tipped back as she ran her finger over the indent on his chin.

"Now how would I know that?" Nick chuckled.

"Isn't it genetic?" She kissed it.

"Yes, and just so you know, my grandfather on my dad's side had one. So does my dad." Nick took her hand and linked his fingers with hers.

"I noticed your dad has it too." Lora kissed his cheek. "Just so you know, it drives your sexy factor up. If that's even possible, because Nick O'Connor, you're sexy as hell."

"Ms. Norris, you could be the poster girl for sexy." Nick kissed her lips softly.

"Nick, you're the best thing that ever happened to my daughter and me." She cupped his cheek.

"I love you, Lora." Nick stared deep into her eyes.

"Nick, I love you so much." She ran her hand across his cheek, and he covered it with his.

Nick wished he could freeze time and stay with her like this forever. He finally understood what his brothers meant when they said, nothing compared to holding the woman you love. It felt peaceful.

Nick knew the minute she drifted off to sleep. Her body relaxed in his arms, and her breathing was deep and even. He even smiled when she let out a little snore for a few short seconds.

Nick managed to pull the bedsheet over them and turned his head to look through the window at the sky. The crescent moon was high, and except for a couple of clouds, it was clear. The breeze moved the thin white curtains as it blew in through the slightly open window.

With the warm air blowing across his face and constant movement of the curtains, his eyes fluttered closed. It was the most relaxed he'd been in a long time. Holding the woman he adored in his arms helped him drift into a deep content sleep.

Nick woke with a start. Something was wrong. He turned to the other side of the bed, but Lora was still curled up next to him. He dropped his head back into the pillow and blew out a slow breath.

"Do you always wake up this early?" She groaned.

"It's after nine, sweetheart." Nick chuckled.

"Holy crap." Lora sat up and reached over him for her phone.

Nick grabbed it from her hand and flipped her over onto her back. She wiggled under him until he took one of her nipples into his mouth.

"That's not fair." Lora sighed. "I need… ah… to get up."

"You. Don't. Need. To. Do. Anything." With each word, he placed a soft kiss up the side of her neck and across her jaw.

"I have … Nick… God… Molly." Lora moaned as he slowly slid his hand under her to squeeze her sweet ass.

"Molly's safe with Sandy and Ian." Nick kissed his way down her chest to the dip of her belly button.

"Don't you… Oh… my…" The minute his tongue slid between her folds she gasped.

"That's it, baby. You like that, don't you," Nick whispered against her wetness.

"Oh … Nick." Lora squirmed as he flicked his tongue against her swollen clit.

His finger slid into her opening as he sucked her swollen nub into his mouth. Lora's moans edged him on more, and he slipped a second finger inside her.

"God, yes." Lora's hips thrust up against his hand and mouth.

"Let go, baby. Come for me." Nick sucked her clit and thrust his fingers in and out of her.

Lora arched off the bed and screamed his name as she came undone. Nick watched the pleasure on her face, and it was the most beautiful thing he'd ever seen in his life.

They made love twice before she finally convinced him they had to get out of bed. It also helped that his stomach growled loud enough she giggled at the sound.

"I'm sure your stomach thinks your mouth went on strike." Lora laughed as she turned the bacon on the frying pan.

"Maybe, but I was pretty satisfied with the appetizer this morning." Nick wrapped his arms around her waist and nuzzled her neck.

"You're insatiable." Lora laughed.

"When it comes to you, yeah." Nick kissed her cheek.

"Is it safe to come inside?" Nick growled at the sound of Aaron's voice from the front door.

"Yes, A.J." Lora called over Nick's shoulder.

"Hey you two." Aaron sauntered into the kitchen holding a large yellow envelope. "Something smells great."

"I've got lots, do you want some?" Lora asked.

"No, he doesn't." Nick poured two cups of coffee and held one out to Aaron.

"Nick," Lora chastised him.

"He's right. I just finished lunch. Most people are up before noon." Aaron winked at Lora and Nick glared at his brother.

"What are you doing here?" Nick pulled one of the kitchen chairs out from the table and sat down.

"I just wanted to bring this over to Lora. John had Sandy copy all the files and pictures from her phone and put them on a flash drive. She also printed all the pictures." Aaron handed the envelope to Lora.

"They didn't have to do that." Lora pulled the pan from the burner and took the thick envelope from his brother.

"He said it was the least we could do for stealing your phone." Aaron chuckled.

"It's okay. I actually have a better one now." Lora grinned.

"Don't know how it could be better. That cracked screen is a rare treasure." Aaron teased.

Lora rolled her eyes as she pulled the pictures from the envelope and shuffled through them. He knew the minute she found the photo with her father. She smiled but he didn't miss her swallowing hard.

"So… I should probably go." Aaron must have noticed as well because he tossed back the rest of his coffee and put the empty cup in the sink.

"I'll give you a buzz later." Nick walked Aaron to the door.

"Don't forget we're playing at the pub tonight." Aaron reminded him.

"I thought that was Saturday." Nick completely forgot about it.

"Umm… today is Saturday, bro." Aaron shook his head and laughed.

"Fuck," Nick growled.

"If you need to be here we can work around the playlist." Aaron glanced behind Nick.

"No, he's going to be there because I've never heard you guys play." Lora wrapped her arms around Nick from behind and pressed her lips against his shoulders.

"What about Molly?" Nick glanced at her.

"I can watch her tonight if you guys want to go out." Nick turned at the deep voice.

"Hulk, you're gonna babysit?" Aaron laughed.

"Kids love me, and little Molly is no exception. I'm just not watching none of those princess movies that pretty boy watches." Hulk pointed his finger at Nick.

"I can't ask you to do that, Bruce." Lora had started calling the big burly man by his real name when she'd finally figured out what it was.

"You didn't ask. I offered, and I know you won't enjoy yourself if you're worried about the youngster." Hulk winked and jogged down the front steps.

"Those guys that work for Keith are a big bunch of softies." Lora snickered.

"With kids, yeah. Just don't get on their bad side." Aaron laughed.

"I guess I'll see ya tonight." Nick waved as Aaron sauntered to his truck.

"Be there by nine. I'll take care of the soundcheck," Aaron shouted as he drove off.

The rest of the day they spent with Molly. Nick was technically supposed to be on duty, but John got his shift covered, and Nick was considered on special assignment. Nick had no issue with that.

Molly was extremely excited that Hulk was babysitting her while her mom and Nick went out. He'd lost a bet with her and was required to watch at least one princess movie. Nick knew the little girl had Hulk wrapped around her finger when he sat on the sofa, and she climbed onto his lap.

"Molly, be a good girl for Bruce, and I'll see you in the morning." Lora kissed her daughter's head.

"I thought Hulk was staying with me." Molly pouted and glanced up at Nick.

"He is, Lollipop." Nick smiled as he crouched down to her level. "Bruce is Hulk's real name."

"Is it like a secret name?" Molly tried to whisper to Nick, but it was nowhere near a whisper.

"All superheroes have a secret name that only all their friends know." Nick winked at the little girl.

"Ohhhh… I won't tell a single soul." Molly grabbed Hulk's face in her little hands and made him look at her. "I promise."

"Good girl." Hulk smiled.

Nick and Lora managed to get to the pub just before nine. He made sure she was surrounded by his family before he made his way to the stage in time to grab his fiddle for the first song.

"About time." John chuckled.

Nick gave him the middle finger just before the lights flicked on the stage. Aaron started with his signature first song by *Alabama* except, they tweaked it a little. Instead of singing about Texas they used Hopedale. People loved it.

Although, the pub was considered by most an Irish bar, most of the music and bands that played there were country groups. *Rockin' The Law* was a combination of country, Irish and a few Newfoundland jigs for the locals. They also did some old-time rock and roll from time to time.

"Hope everyone is here to have a great time tonight," Aaron spoke into the microphone after the song ended.

A loud cheer was the response, and Nick laughed as Sandy shouted for Aaron to shut up and get the music going. His sister-in-law didn't get out to enjoy herself very often, but when she did, she could be a handful. Still, Nick felt better she was at the same table with Lora and his other sisters-in-law.

The fact that most of Hopedale was in attendance helped as well. There was no way anyone would get close to Lora without someone from his family or a friend seeing it. Nick caught her eye and gave her a wink before he relaxed and enjoyed the rest of the evening.

He sat in the corner of the overcrowded hole in the wall. Nobody seemed to notice him, and he managed to stay far enough away that she wouldn't recognize him.

He'd managed to slip by Sheila at the coat check when a crowd of people surrounded the small window she stood behind. If she saw him, she'd wonder why he was in the town. Nobody could know he was there until it was time, and if they saw him, they'd probably take his love away again.

He could see her through the horde of people drinking and dancing to the loud music. He wasn't a fan of this type of entertainment. He enjoyed more quiet forms. Reading, or the soft sound of classical music.

He could see her stuck between two of the women he'd learned were part of the family keeping her away from him. He rolled his eyes as one of the women stood up and told the band to play more music.

His love had to be miserable with these people. She didn't like any of this, but he had to admit she was great at acting as if she wanted to be there. He knew it was just to keep them fooled until he could get to her.

"Soon, my love. Soon."

Chapter 21

Lora's stomach hurt from laughing. Sandy was always entertaining, but alcohol infused Sandy was hilarious. Especially with Billie's friend Abbie next to her. Abbie Martin's personality was as big as Sandy's, and all Lora could think was if Dallas was there with them the pub would never be the same.

According to Marina, they all didn't get to have a night out together very often. All of them had kids, and if anyone understood that it was Lora. Apparently, all the kids were abducted by the various grandparents giving all the brothers and their significant others a kid-free night.

"I'm so freaking happy." Sandy wrapped her arm around Lora and Abbie.

"I can see that." Lora laughed.

"No, seriously. You and Nick." Sandy hiccupped. "Awesome."

"Thanks." Lora smiled.

"Now, if we could just get this one here to get her head out of her ass and make a move on Trunk, we'd be all set." Sandy motioned her head in Abbie's direction.

"If you start that again, I'm going to get Ian to cut you off." Abbie pointed a finger in Sandy's face. "Trunk is an ass with a capital A."

"But you want to ride him like a bucking bronco." Sandy laughed.

"Ian," Abbie shouted, but Sandy covered her mouth before she could get his attention.

"I swear those two get together and they're worse than sailors that were out to sea too long." Billie laughed and ran her hand over her swollen belly.

"That's a good description of them." Lora glanced toward the stage.

"Looks like A.J. won't be going home alone tonight." Billie nodded toward the blonde at the end of the stage dancing as if she should be spinning around a stripper pole.

"Isn't that the blonde that comes into the restaurant?" Jess leaned toward Lora.

Lora nodded, because it was the same one that had been eyeing Nick like he was on the menu a few weeks before. Aaron was giving her all the attention she seemed to want, but Lora didn't miss the bitch's glances toward Nick.

"Who is she anyway?" Billie asked.

"She works at the dance club up the road. I think her name is Jocelyn." Kristy squeezed herself between Billie and Lora.

"So why is she here?" Jess sipped her drink.

"Isn't that obvious." Billie shuddered, and Kristy gagged as Aaron crouched down to whisper into the giggling woman's ear.

"He's such a whore." Sandy rolled her eyes.

"He's single and hot." Abbie pointed out the obvious. "Why shouldn't he get it when he can?"

"From what I've heard about her, he better double bag it." Kristy snickered.

"You guys are terrible." Lora laughed.

"And now you're one of us." Sandy hugged Lora and kissed her cheek.

"Run. Now. While you still can." Abbie laughed.

Lora did feel like one of them. Especially, when Nick managed to come down from the stage. He'd pull her out to the dance floor for a slow dance and a sweet kiss. Of course, he made sure she was okay and having a good time.

On her third trip to the lady's room with Marina and Billie, Lora felt a chill run down her spine. It was so intense it made her turn around. She didn't see anything, but almost bumped into a woman walking behind her.

"Something wrong?" Marina asked as Lora walked into the bathroom.

"No, I just got a weird chill." Lora shook it off.

While she waited for the two pregnant women to relieve themselves, Lora fixed her hair and reapplied her lipstick. It was impossible not to smile as the two women complained about how often they had to pee.

"I swear this child is using my bladder as a squeeze toy." Marina sighed as she waddled to the sink.

"How much longer do you have?" Lora asked.

"Seven weeks." Marina beamed.

"I've got five weeks left." Billie came out of the stall.

"I'm finally getting my little girl." Marina's happiness was evident on her face.

Lora assumed after three boys, having a little girl would be a gift for the family. Molly was a joy, and Lora couldn't imagine her life without her daughter.

The door to the bathroom swung open, and another very pregnant O'Connor wife hurried through the door. Emily scurried to the nearest stall and let out a huge groan of relief

"Oh yeah, leave the other preggo to fend for herself." Emily narrowed her eyes at them when she came out of the stall.

"You know, I'm starting to think being around you women could be dangerous." Lora laughed, but having another baby wouldn't be the worst thing in the world.

"Yeah, it's contagious." Billie rubbed her shoulder against Lora. "There, now you've been infected."

"I've been vaccinated." Lora retorted.

"Oh, those O'Connor men can find there way around those vaccines." Emily laughed.

"How long do you have left?" Lora asked Emily.

"She is due the day before me," Billie responded before Emily could answer.

"Maybe I could go early; then we could get a group rate." Marina laughed as they left the bathroom.

Lora had just made it back to the table when someone grabbed her arm and tugged her from the chair. Lora clenched her fist ready to fight whoever was trying to pull her away. She snapped her gaze up to see Nick smiling at her.

"Did I scare you?" Nick pulled her into his arms and kissed her cheek.

"Enough that you almost got a fist in the face." Lora held up her fist.

"Nice to know you can defend yourself." Nick ran a finger down her cheek. "I'm sorry for startling you."

"You can make it up to me with a dance." Lora tugged him toward the dance floor.

As she wrapped her arms around his neck, she got lost in the music and Nick's embrace. She never felt safer than when she was in his arms.

It was difficult to keep his control as he watched her in that cop's arms. He'd been so close to her, but then that stupid woman stepped in his way, and he lost his chance. He could have saved her right then and there.

He needed to get back to the house before the old man woke up. He slipped a couple of sleeping pills into the man's food and waited for him to fall asleep before he made his way to the pub. The last thing he needed was that old man spoiling his plan by calling for help.

The old man lived alone and had no family, or at least none that the old man cared to talk about. That was a good thing, because he didn't have to worry about anyone spoiling his plan. The only thing that could, was if the old bastard woke up before he got back to the house.

"Soon, my love," He whispered as he disappeared through the exit.

Chapter 22

It was the first time the band had two gigs so close together. Nick wanted to make sure he was ready to sing the song he'd been working on for the Canada Day celebrations. The one just for Lora.

There hadn't been any more missing women, but it made Nick nervous. Cory and Steve questioned the people on Lora's list again, but there wasn't anything new. It was as if they hit a wall in the investigation.

John kept a close eye on Lora's old phone, but except for several texts sent the same day she'd received the first ones, the phone was quiet. The one thing that terrified Nick, was Lora stopped hiding in Hopedale.

"What's the point of trying to keep out of town? He knows where I am anyway." Lora argued when she wanted to have lunch with her old boss, Dallas.

"You can't make it easy for him, baby." Nick tried to reason with her, but as if something in the universe wanted to make his life even more complicated, Nanny Betty scurried into the diner.

"Are ya ready ta go ta town?" Nanny Betty smiled at Tom as he entered the diner, he'd offered to help out during rush hour.

"I'm just waiting for Jess, Nan." Lora raised her eyebrow.

He knew what she was doing. It was dare to argue the point with his grandmother. Lora knew that none of them would ever challenge Nanny Betty.

"Dats grand. Jess never told me she was comin' too." Nanny Betty fixed her collar and glanced up at him. "Nicky, if ya go out wit dat face ya'll scare da sun away."

"Gee, thanks, Nan." He bent to kiss his grandmother's cheek.

"He's a little upset that I'm going to town." Lora smiled at him.

"Why?" Nanny Betty stared up at him.

"We still don't know who this guy is, Nan...." Nick wanted to groan when his grandmother held up her hand.

"Isn't da big fella Hulk comin' wit us?" Nanny Betty glanced at Lora.

"Yes," Lora's amusement with the situation was obvious.

"And Jess?" Nanny Betty tipped her head as if she was questioning his sanity.

"And don't tink I'm gonna let her outta me sight." She pointed a finger at him.

Nick dropped his head back and stared up at the ceiling to keep from rolling his eyes. Nanny Betty probably would hit him with her purse. His grandmother was barely five-feet tall and maybe a hundred pounds, but whatever she carried in the bag was hard.

"See, Nick. I'll be perfectly safe. Plus, Dallas will be there too." Lora rested her hands on his hips, and he gazed into her eyes.

"I'm calling the station and getting off early." Nick was on duty and only dropped in for lunch because he knew Jess was working with Lora at the diner.

"No, you're not," Lora warned.

"But…" Lora pressed her finger to his lips.

"I'll be safe." Lora ran her thumb over his lower lip, and he kissed the tip of it.

"I'm ready, let's go." Jess's voice sounded from behind him.

"Okay, now Nicky get back ta work." Nanny Betty fixed her ever-present black purse on her arm and linked the other into Jess.

"I'll be fine." Lora cupped his cheek and placed a soft kiss on his lips. "I promise, I'll stay close to Bruce and Jess."

"I don't like this." Nick sighed.

"I got this." Nick felt the big hand on his shoulder.

"Thanks, Hulk." Nick didn't look at him he just kept his gaze on Lora.

"I love you," Lora whispered against his lips.

"I love you too." Nick cupped the back of her head and pressed his lips to her temple and inhaled her scent.

Lora smiled as she walked around him to join Nanny Betty and Jess at the exit. Hulk was behind them as they walked through the door. His heart thudded in his chest when she disappeared from his sight.

"If you want, I can tag along with them." Bull appeared next to him. "Kristy's working today, but I'm off."

"Are you sure you don't mind?" Nick couldn't shake the bad feeling.

"Not at all. I got you, bro." Bull quickly exited the restaurant with Nick behind him.

Nick stood on the step as Hulk drove out of the lot with Jess, Nanny Betty and Lora in his SUV. Bull pulled out behind them in his truck and gave Nick the thumbs up as he followed behind the love of Nick's life.

At least knowing Bull and Hulk were with them made him feel a little less tense. Jess was with her too, and his cousin was a damn good cop who would protect Lora no matter what. Plus, he was pretty sure nobody would get close to Lora with Nanny Betty around.

Before he could think about anything else a call came over the radio and he made his way to the cruiser to help the officer in need of assistance.

The soft knock on the door startled him. He'd been at the old man's house for almost two weeks, and it was the first time anyone came to visit.

"Who's at the door?" he whispered to the old man.

"It's the Lawton girl. She comes here to clean the place." The old man shifted in the chair. "If ya don't answer she'll go on her way. It's what I do when I don't want her here."

Footsteps sounded back and forth on the front deck, and he held his breath. He pressed his body against the wall as he saw the shadow against the large window. He'd closed all the blinds and drapes, but he couldn't take any chances. Not when he was so close.

"Mr. Batten, it's Sunshine Lawton," The girl shouted through the door.

"Keep your mouth shut." He growled at the old man.

"Mr. Batten, I'm here to do your cleaning," The girl yelled, and he pressed his lips together as the doorknob rattled.

If this girl didn't go soon, she'd ruin all his plans. He crept to the front door to see when she left. After she'd knocked once more, he heard her footsteps click down the steps.

"About fucking time." He peeped through the opening in the curtain.

The girl walked down the driveway and hopped on a bicycle. When she turned left at the end of the path, he stepped back and walked back to Albert.

"Why didn't you tell me about her?" He grabbed the old man by the front of his shirt.

"I forgot about her. I'm old for Christ's sake." Albert snapped.

He had to give Albert credit. Only once did he show he was afraid of what would happen. The old bastard was snarky and sarcastic which he respected. It was probably why he hadn't killed him yet.

"Well, you better think real hard and remember if there will be any more visitors." He warned Albert.

"Look, I got no family that comes here. I was never married and no kids. I live here by myself, and the only one comes by is that girl. She cleans the dump, and I pay her. I don't like people and you being here is getting on my last arthritic nerve." Albert grumbled as he lit a cigarette.

"You're a cranky old bastard, aren't you?" He shook his head.

He didn't like when Albert smoked because it smelled. It was also the reason he drugged the man every time he left the house. He couldn't take the chance of him not only calling for help but catching the dwelling on fire.

"I'm not cranky. I like to be alone." Albert blew out the smoke and started to cough.

He sat at the computer and kept glancing at Albert. He'd drugged his coffee, and he was waiting for the old bastard to fall asleep. He needed to be ready when she went to town. He heard the argument she'd had with the cop before she left the house that morning. He needed to follow her and see if it was his chance to finally save her.

Chapter 23

Lora sat across from Dallas and Jess. Nanny Betty was next to her, and both Hulk and Bull took a table across from them in the downtown coffee shop.

She'd argued with Nick all morning about going to town, but the truth was, now that she was at the old coffee shop where she went every day, she felt uneasy. Lora glanced around the place she hadn't been inside in almost a year, but nothing looked out of place.

Most of the staff were the same except for a young woman wiping down the table across the room. Lora felt a chill on the back of her neck, and she spun around in her seat.

"Lora, is something wrong?" Jess grabbed her hand, and Lora turned back to face her.

"Yes… no… I'm just paranoid. I'm sorry." Lora forced a smile.

"Doncha be sorry fer bein' worried. Dis is a nice shop." Nanny Betty sipped her tea. "Bruce, ya look like ya lost yer best friend. Smile," Nanny Betty shouted across to the table where the two men sat.

"Nan, don't bring attention to them." Jess sighed.

"It's not like every woman in da place is not staring at dem." Nanny Betty huffed. "Maybe if he smiled he'd find a lass fer himself."

Dallas had a huge smile on her face and was definitely enjoying Nanny Betty's company. Lora adored the woman. Nanny Betty said what was on her mind and didn't care who heard her.

"Mrs. O'Connor, could you adopt me." Dallas reached across the table and placed her hand over Nanny Betty's.

"Not if ya keep callin' me dat. Mrs. O'Connor was me mother-in-law and let me tell ya; she was a witch." Nanny Betty popped a piece of her muffin into her mouth. "Ya call me Nan, and we'll talk."

Dallas threw her head back and laughed so loud that everyone in the entire shop turned to look at them. Lora covered her face, but Jess laughed right along with Dallas. She loved her friend, but Dallas was loud, and a lot like Nanny Betty. Her friend said what was on her mind and didn't care what people thought.

"I still can't believe how lucky I was with my damn phone," Dallas said a little while later.

"No kidding. I've lost two in the last year, and the damn things are a pain in the ass to replace." Jess nodded to the waiter who appeared at the table to refill their cups.

"I've never lost mine, but changing my number so often was a pain in the ass," Lora remembered talking to the provider and them questioning why she was changing her number so often.

"Did you ladies want anything else besides coffee and tea?" The attractive waiter asked and smiled at them.

"Your number." Dallas propped her elbows on the table and rested her chin in the palms of her hands.

"Umm… I… Yeah." The waiter blushed and stammered over his response.

"He's a little young fer ya, Dallas. We'll take ya to see my Cora. She can help ya." Nanny Betty patted the waiter's arm, and he scurried away.

"I'm drawing up the adoption papers for you to sign, Nan." Dallas chuckled.

Lora still couldn't shake the feeling of being watched. She glanced at Hulk, and he raised an eyebrow. Maybe she wasn't as brave as she tried to make Nick believe. Lora had secluded herself in Hopedale for so long, that it was unnerving to be in a place where she wasn't surrounded by the safety of the small town.

Her phone buzzed, and she pulled it out of her pocket. It was from Hulk.

Hulk: What's up? You look spooked.

She was about to send him a return text, but a loud crash drew her attention. Lora glanced up at the table directly behind Hulk and Bull.

The pregnant waitress dropped the coffee pot and was in the process of slapping away the hand of the customer she served. Not that he tried to help her pick up the mess. His hand was on the back of the girl's leg under the hem of her uniform.

"Looks like you got lottsa spark, ducky." The man laughed as he slapped the woman's ass.

"Don't touch me." She snapped, but anyone with ears could tell she was frightened.

"Why don't ya sit here on my lap and we'll talk about the first thing that pops up." He grabbed the girl's arm and pulled her towards him but she managed to pull away.

"I told you not to touch me." The girl was practically in tears, and Lora wanted to punch the man.

"I'll touch you if…." The man reached for her again.

"I believe the lady said she didn't want to be touched." Hulk growled as he turned in his seat.

"That's my lad," Nanny Betty whispered and continued to sip her tea as if nothing was happening.

"Mind your own business, Asshole." The man didn't turn to look at Hulk.

"Oh, this is gonna be good." Jess chuckled as she spun around in her seat to watch the scene.

"I am an asshole, but you're about to be in traction," Hulk said in a calm voice as the guy jumped to his feet.

"I'd like to see you try, prick." The man stood next to Hulk's seat.

Hulk sat with his coffee cupped between his hands, and Lora could see the slight grin on his lips. If she was being honest, she couldn't wait to see the guy's reaction if Hulk stood up.

"Sit down before you hurt yourself." Bull laughed at the man.

"Stay out of this, Kojak." He didn't take his eyes off Hulk as he snapped at Bull.

"Someone get a body bag." Dallas laughed.

"Come on, Asshole. Let's see if you're man enough to put me in traction." The guy pushed Hulk's shoulder.

Was this guy blind or just stupid? Sure, the guy was big, but as soon as Hulk stood up, he was going to realize he wasn't as big as he thought.

"Stop this now." The girl stepped between the man and where Hulk still sat.

"Back off, bitch." He pushed the girl to the side almost sending her sprawling on the floor.

The man that was with the idiot caught her before she hit the floor. He also seemed ready to bolt at any second.

"Give it up, Howard." The guy seemed a little more reasonable than Howard.

"Fuck off, Gilbert. This guy don't got the guts to stand up." Howard chuckled and pushed Hulk's arm again.

The coffee shop had become absolutely silent as Hulk calmly pushed his cup back, and turned in his seat. Howard laughed and took a step back from the chair.

"Ooooo…. Look, Gilbert. He's gonna stand up." The guy shook his hands in front of Hulk's face. "I'm real scared."

Hulk slowly stood and the expression on Howard's face went from, *I'm a tough guy*, to, dear *God what have I done*. Even the waitress had taken three steps back when Hulk stood to his full height of about six feet, four.

"Oh, my. That man is just a mountain of sexy, tattooed muscle, isn't he?" Dallas fanned herself with a napkin.

"I know." Jess sighed.

"He's a good lad, and he won't hurt dat fool." Nanny Betty didn't show the slightest interest in what was happening right next to their table.

"I'm standing. Was there something you wanted to say to me?" Hulk spoke with the same calm tone Lora had come to know, and crossed his arms over his chest.

The look on Howard's face was priceless as he tipped his head back to look up at the enormous man he'd challenged. Gilbert's eyes looked like they were about to pop out on his cheeks and his jaw dropped.

"I... I was... just a joke... I." Howard stumbled over his words.

"Apologize to the lady," Hulk ordered.

"She... I was just shagging around." Howard glanced back at the pretty waitress.

Her eyes hadn't moved from Hulk. She stood with her hand on her swollen stomach, and her other hand gripped the back of a chair.

"Apologize," Hulk growled through his teeth.

"Okay, okay." Howard stepped back further from Hulk and turned to the woman.

"Caroline, I'm sorry. I was just fucking around." Howard didn't meet her eyes as he kept looking over his shoulder at Hulk.

"It's fine," The woman whispered.

"Now, I think it's time you gentlemen leave." Hulk's gaze moved to Caroline. "After you tip the lady of course. I think a twenty-dollar tip would make up for your disrespect."

Howard pulled a couple of bills out of his pocket and tossed them on the table. He and Gilbert practically tripped over each other as they hurried out of the coffee shop. Lora could see the two men jump into a truck across the street and speed away.

"Yar a good boy, lad." Nanny Betty stood up and walked over to the waitress. "Are ya alright, Lassie?"

"I'm... yes, ma'am... thank you." She stammered as Nanny Betty took her hands.

"Good," Nanny Betty cupped the woman's cheek and walked back to the table. "I'm ready ta go now."

Nanny Betty grabbed her purse and hung it over her arm. The coffee shop slowly went back to normal as the young waiter Dallas had hit on ran over to clean up the broken coffee pot, and another waitress guided Caroline to the back of the shop.

"Never a dull moment when you go out with the O'Connor family." Bull chuckled.

"I'm starting to figure that out." Hulk puffed but he was still glancing in the direction of the waitress.

As Lora stood up, she felt the hair on the back of her neck prickle. She whirled around, but people in the shop were deep into conversations or their smartphones.

"That's the second time I've seen you spin around like that. What's wrong?" Jess stood next to her and spoke softly.

"I just got a weird feeling." Lora glanced around once more but shrugged as Jess did the same.

"I have to thank you for the entertainment and of course the eye candy." Dallas hugged her. "Keep in touch."

"I will." Lora hugged her friend back. "Don't forget to come out for the Canada Day party."

"I'll be there, if I can get away." Dallas hugged her once more and headed out of the coffee shop.

With Hulk behind her, Bull in front of her, and the other two women next to her, they headed out of the coffee shop. Hulk made sure she, Nanny Betty and Jess were in the SUV before he got in himself. He waited for Bull to give him the go-ahead, then pulled out and headed back to Hopedale.

She looked right at him because she sensed him there. He could see the smile she tried to hide from the women she was with.

He had to give them credit; they made sure she was never alone, and that would make it hard to save her. He'd heard her mention Canada Day. The posters around that stupid town about the huge party were everywhere. That cop and his untalented band were supposed to be the entertainment.

It was probably going to be his only chance to save her and bring her home. Once she realized he was her hero, then he'd bring the little girl. He knew her mother and brother would try to convince her to stay away from him, but his love knew the difference. She loved him, and that was all he needed.

He glanced at his watch and tossed a twenty-dollar bill on the table. It was time to get back to that dinky town and put his plan in motion. He had three days, and he'd finally have her. He couldn't wait.

Chapter 24

Canada Day was an enormous celebration in Hopedale. Not only was it the country's birthday, but it was also the same day the town got its name. Nick hated to leave Lora that morning, but he needed to help Aaron, John, Mike and another member of the band Jason Brenton to set up the equipment on the beach.

The firefighters were installing the tents for the barbeque to have them ready for when the festivities started. The police and firefighters would be preparing the burgers and hot dogs as soon as everything started at noon. All money raised from the sales went back into the community.

"Cory's still at the station," John grabbed a guitar from Aaron in the back of the cube van and handed it up to Nick on the stage.

"What's he doing?" Aaron continued to bring the equipment to the opening of the truck.

"The tattoo guy finally called him back." John grabbed some of the cords and tossed them onto the platform they'd set up as a stage.

"Hopefully he can give us something to get this bastard." Aaron jumped down from the van and slammed it shut.

Nick wanted nothing more than to catch this guy. Lora seemed to get edgier over the last couple of days and started waking up during the night gasping or crying. He failed her because he couldn't keep the damn nightmares away.

An hour later the band equipment was set up as well as the computer for the recorded music when the band took breaks. Newfoundland Security Service was hired to do most of the security for the event because they were highly recommended to the committee by the Chief of Police. Having people in high places was convenient sometimes. Nick wasn't sure if he'd enjoy the celebration because he wouldn't be with Lora if she needed him.

Something in his gut told him he needed to stay close. He'd managed to make sure Lora wouldn't be in any vulnerable situations. Not only did Hulk promise to stick to Lora like glue, but the rest of his family agreed to keep her close to them.

"Steph just got to the pub." John interrupted Nick's thoughts.

"Yeah?" Nick wasn't sure why John was telling him this.

"Lora's there with Molly, and her mother. Her brother is headed down here to help with set up." John shoved his phone into his back pocket.

"Is Hulk with her?" A wave of panic hit him in the gut.

"Yes, but did you really need to ask that question?" John put his hand on Nick's shoulder.

"I guess not." Nick still wasn't comfortable with her being in a large crowd.

Lora gave an outward appearance that she wasn't scared anymore, but Nick knew that wasn't the case. After Dulce's funeral, she'd made a vow that she needed to take back her life. She told Dallas she'd be returning to her old job as soon as Alice was back on her feet and found a replacement for Lora in the diner. Of course, there was no way Lora would be going anywhere without Hulk, Crash or Nick.

John wasn't able to give him as much time off as he'd wanted, and Nick understood. In a small town, there were only so many officers employed by the department. John tried to have shifts covered in Hopedale with officers from other communities, but it wasn't an easy task.

Technically everyone was on duty for the day, but because John, Nick, Cory, and Aaron were performing during the celebrations, they would only be required in the event something got out of control. So in between the sets, Nick could spend time enjoying the festivities with Lora and Molly, and he couldn't be more excited.

"We're starting the first set at two, and if Cory's not here by noon, A.J.'s going to Deejay until he gets here. Hopefully, he'll come here with the name of the asshole and we can end Canada Day on a high note." John walked with Nick up Beach Road toward the pub.

"Yeah," Nick muttered, but he hadn't really heard all of what his brother had said.

"You love her?" John asked as they turned onto Harbour Street.

"With every beat of my heart." Nick turned his head to meet John's smile.

"Isn't that the lyrics to a song?" John chuckled.

"Yeah, Taylor Dayne comes to mind." Nick laughed.

"That line is in a lot of songs, Gladys Knight back in the fifties, and Rod Stewart had one in the eighties. I know there are more." John continued.

"How fucking old are you?" Nick pushed John's shoulder as they ran up the steps to Jack's Place.

"Not too old to kick your fucking ass." John shoulder checked him and headed into the diner.

Lora, Kristy, and Pam were sat at the counter talking to Alice. They turned when Nick and John walked in, and Lora gave him a bright smile that made his heart skip a beat, and he was pretty sure he fell more in love with her.

"Daddy," Olivia shouted as she ran right into John's arms.

"Hey, how's my best girl?" John kissed her cheek as the little girl wrapped her arms around her father's neck.

Before Olivia said another word, Molly ran toward them shouting as she practically flew into Nick's arms.

"Nick, Nick." Molly squealed.

"That's the kind of welcome a man likes to get. Hey there, Lollipop." Nick tossed her into the air.

"Olivia, Gracie and me are going to the beach, and we're gonna play on the bouncy castle." Molly's animated expression made him smile.

"That sounds like lots of fun." Nick glanced at Lora.

"That's only if you eat all your lunch." Lora reminded Molly.

"She's almost eated it all." Grace skipped toward Ian. "Daddy, Lily said she's too big for the bouncy house."

"Yeah, Lily's a big girl now." Ian crouched to wipe the food from Grace's face.

"Lily and Evie said bouncy castles are for babies." Grace turned to where her two older sisters sat in a booth with James' two oldest boys.

It seemed since Danny, Mason, Evie, and Lily entered the dreaded pre-teens, they'd made a point of letting the younger siblings know just how big they were getting.

"Daddy likes bouncy castles. Does that make him a baby?" Sandy knelt on the floor next to Ian and Grace.

"Nooooo," Grace giggled.

"Mommy likes them. Am I a baby?" Sandy tickled Grace.

"Noooooo," Grace giggled again.

"Maybe your sisters don't enjoy it anymore, but that's ok because you have Molly, Olivia, and Colin to play in the castles with you, and all your friends from playgroup will be there too." Sandy might get overwhelmed with the number of children that both she and Ian had, but she was a great mother and the best person in the world for his brother.

The walk back to the beach was a combination of telling kids to stay close and the pleasure of spending time with Lora. Nick could see himself in the future with Lora and Molly enjoying family outings. Possibly even with one or two more to add to the growing brood of O'Connor children.

Nick held Lora's hand as they watched Molly in one of the three bouncy castles set up on the beach. Lora glanced at him and smiled when Nick pulled her against him and kissed the top of her head.

"Isabelle told me that you play four different instruments." Lora wrapped her arms around his waist.

"Yeah, I play guitar, drums, piano, and fiddle." He shrugged his shoulders.

"I only saw you play the guitar and fiddle the other night but that's incredible." Lora's eyes widened in awe.

"Not really. A.J. plays the piano, guitar, accordion, saxophone, drums and fiddle." Nick smiled.

"Are all your brothers musical like you two?" Lora asked.

"Pretty much. Dad and Uncle Kurt can play most instruments as well. My grandmother has never been able to read music, but once she hears a song and you give her a day or so, she can play it on the piano." Nick laughed as Molly flopped down on her butt in the bouncy castle.

"You need to relax." She must have sensed the tension in his body even with the casual conversation.

"I'm trying, sweetheart." Nick wrapped his arms around her and squeezed her tightly.

"Well you better relax because in thirty minutes you have to go up on stage. You'll disappoint all the women if you look all surly." She cupped his face in her hands.

"You're the only woman I'm worried about, so make sure you're at the front of the stage. I've got a song I'm singing just for you." Nick brushed his lips against hers and she sighed against them.

"I'll be front and center," Lora whispered. "Or so Hulk told me."

Forty minutes later Nick jumped up on the stage and received a glare from the rest of the bandmates. Lora sat on the ground in front with the rest of the family and smiled at him as he pulled the fiddle from the stand.

"It's about damn time." Aaron grumbled through gritted teeth.

"Sorry, it's hard getting through the crowd." Nick wasn't lying, because once he'd realized the time, he practically dragged Lora through the crowds of people surrounding the stage.

"Yeah, couldn't tell time while his tongue was down Lora's throat." Mike chuckled.

Nick turned his back to the crowd and gave his brother the one finger salute as he ran the bow across the fiddle. It was time to get the crowd on their feet.

He despised large crowds but needed to keep near her. He couldn't miss his chance again. His love was close enough he could practically smell her scent from where he hid under the stage. The heavy black curtain that ran around the stage, gave him the perfect spot to observe everyone and move when the time was right.

The only issue was the stomping and loud music above his head. He'd probably end up with a tremendous headache by the time he got out of there, but it would be worth every bit of discomfort to finally save her from her abductors.

"You're so lovely," He whispered.

He froze when it appeared as if she looked right at him. He'd poked the hose camera through a small tear in the curtain so that he could watch her. When she laughed at something the blonde sat next to her whispered in her ear, he knew it was just a coincidence. All he had to do is be patient.

His father called him a pathetic loser that no one loved, but it was his dad that was the loser. The man did nothing but watch sex videos and share them with his perverted friends. No, what he had with his love was pure, and one day everyone would know.

Chapter 25

"I swear, John sings that song because he knows it makes me hot and want to rip his clothes off," Stephanie shouted into Lora's ear.

"Guess he's getting lucky tonight." Lora wiggled her eyebrows at the pretty blonde.

"You have no idea. I don't know what it is but when he sings that song… Let's just say, I'm glad the kids are going to Sean and Kathleen's house tonight." Stephanie snickered.

Lora completely understood why Stephanie would feel that way, because when Nick walked up to the microphone, he smiled down at her and her heart kicked up a notch. Then he started to play the same song he'd sang in the pub the day Alice got hurt. His eyes never moved from her through the entire song. If it was possible, Lora fell even more in love with him.

"Oh, you two got it so bad." Kristy squeezed in between Lora and Stephanie.

Lora laughed as Nick's cousin knelt between them. Her fiancée stood next to Hulk and kept his eyes focused on Kristy. Nick's family were funny and teased each other mercilessly but they were there for each other, and from what she'd seen, they'd bend over backward to protect each other.

It was the reason she felt safe in such a large crowd. Then again, she felt safer in Hopedale than she ever did in St. John's. At least until her stalker found her again and killed all those women. Lora constantly felt the hair on the back of her neck prickling, and the nightmares were back.

She didn't tell Nick about the uneasy feeling. Nick would think she didn't trust him to keep her safe. Lora wished the police could find the stalker, so she could get back to her life. It figured when she finally found the man of her dreams something would threaten to destroy her happiness.

"Hey, are you okay? Marina took Lora's hand and spoke in her ear.

"Yeah, sorry I was watching the kids playing." Lora forced a smile.

James' wife didn't seem to believe Lora's explanation of why she'd drifted off for a few minutes. Marina didn't say anything, just squeezed Lora's hand and laughed as her youngest son started to dance to Mike's version of *Hippy, Hippy Shake*.

"I swear Colin is getting as foolish as A.J." Marina laughed.

They were right next to the stage and had to shout when they spoke to be heard over the music. Lora glanced behind her when she felt someone brush against her back. Nick's mother smiled down at her and smoothed her hand over Lora's head.

"I thought I might find all my daughters-in-law down here." Kathleen chuckled as she unfolded a blanket and spread it out on the ground behind Lora, Marina, Stephanie, Kristy, and Emily.

"Where else would we be?" Emily shouted.

"How did you and Marina manage to get down on the ground in your condition?" Sandy appeared and plopped down next to her mother-in-law.

"Getting down is easy. Getting up might take some help," Marina shouted.

"I keep telling you to come to the house and try yoga with me," Sandy replied.

Lora laughed when Emily held up a fist and then slowly wound her hand as if she was turning a crank. Her middle finger gradually raised to give Sandy the one figure salute.

"Kathleen, do you see what she's doing to your favorite daughter-in-law." Sandy linked into Kathleen's arm.

"Billie's not even here." Kathleen glanced around with a grin.

"Thanks a lot." All of the women married to Kathleen's sons shouted together.

"Stop it. You know she loves all of you the same." Kristy rolled her eyes.

That was what it was like to be in the middle of the O'Connor family. It was fun, and Lora wished one day that she could be included with the banter as one of the O'Connor wives.

Wait? What?

Lora never thought about marriage before, even with Molly's father. She always believed it wasn't necessary if you were with the right person, but with Nick, she wanted to be married to him. She desired to take his name and if it was possible to have his baby.

"Mommy, I need to pee." Molly leaned over and whispered in Lora's ear.

"Okay, let's go." Lora stood up and clasped Molly's hand.

"Where are you going?" Kristy was on her feet in seconds.

"Molly needs to go to the bathroom," Lora told Nick's cousin.

Before Lora knew it, Emily, Marina, Sandy, and Kristy were behind her with a line of children who also needed to relieve themselves.

As the line of them made their way to the portable toilets, she couldn't help but giggle. It was comical. Each child lined up to go inside, and when they came out stood in another line to wait for everyone to finish. Hulk and Bull stood behind Lora, and it was honestly starting to get on her last nerve.

It wasn't that she didn't appreciate what they were doing, she was just tired of having a shadow anywhere she went. Lora knew it was necessary, but she couldn't wait for the day when she could take a walk on the beach by herself.

After the parade to the bathroom had returned to the stage for the third time, the sun had set, and the firefighters set off the fireworks. Molly managed to get through without falling asleep, and Lora couldn't help but smile at the amazed look on her daughter's face. With each explosion Molly would squeal excitedly at the multitude of colors in the clear night sky.

Molly enjoyed it, but didn't hesitate when Lora's mother and Kathleen asked if they wanted to go home. Lora waved to Molly as she watched Kathleen, Cora, her mother, Nanny Betty, along with Stephanie and Marina's mom herd the tribe of young children to Nick's parent's house.

"I love all those women." Sandy pressed her hands against her chest.

"I can't believe they're going to keep all the kids for the night." Lora shook her head in awe.

"That's what it's like to be in this family." Billie showed up just before the fireworks.

"It's a breeze for those women. There were times all of us stayed at Aunt Kathleen and Uncle Sean's place all weekend." Kristy laughed. "Think about it. Seven boys and four girls camped out in their living room."

"And we weren't always the angels that we are today." Jess smiled sweetly.

"Angels?" Sandy almost choked on her water.

"Sounds fun." Lora laughed, but the truth was, it did sound incredible.

The band still had another hour in their final set, and the crowds were starting to thin out. The firefighters broke down all the booths that were set up for the games and food. Some people still hung around to enjoy the music, but not as many as earlier.

"I have to pee so bad, and I'm not using that stinky box they call a toilet." Kristy wrinkled her nose.

"Me too." Emily struggled to get to her feet.

"Let's go to *Jack's Place*. That way we won't get the kids all upset if we all show up at Aunt Kathleen's to pee, and then leave again." Kristy suggested.

The three women squeezed through the smaller crowd, but they were stopped by Bull and Hulk. The two men stood in front of them with arms folded across their chest.

"Where are you going, Kitten?" Bull gazed down at Kristy.

"I'm going to relieve my bladder." Kristy tried to step around him, but he took her hand.

"The potty is right there." He nodded toward the large blue boxes.

"I'm not using that. It's gross, and God knows who else was in there all day." Kristy kissed his cheek.

"You let all the kids go there earlier." Hulk chuckled.

"Yeah before all the drunks got in there. There's probably piss all over the floor and the seat." Kristy gagged. "We're just going to the pub, relieve ourselves, and we'll be back."

"I'm coming with you." Bull cupped her face in his hands as he brushed his lips lovingly against her forehead.

"Are you going to do this the whole time?" Kristy groaned in annoyance.

"While you're carrying precious cargo, yes." Bull smiled at his fiancé.

"You're pregnant?" Emily gasped.

"Shhh… We aren't telling anyone yet." Kristy covered Emily's mouth with her hand.

"Why?" Emily asked when she managed to push Kristy's hand away.

"Because I don't want Kurt kicking the shit out of me for knocking up his daughter before the ring is on her finger." Bull chuckled.

"That's not true." Kristy rolled her eyes.

"Sure it is." Hulk grinned.

"Shut up, Hulk." Bull slapped his friend on the chest.

"Look, I would really like to finish this little chat, but I'm going to pee in my pants if we don't go now," Emily complained.

Bull and Hulk filed in behind the women as they made their way toward *Jack's Place*. Kristy complained several times that Bull was smothering her, but he managed to quiet her when he whispered something in her ear that made her eyes flutter and her breath hitch.

"That's mean," Kristy whined.

They'd just arrived at the pub when they heard a voice from behind them. Keith sauntered up to them with a huge smile on his face. He went straight to Emily and wrapped his arm around her shoulder.

"Princess, why didn't you tell me you were coming here?" He kissed the top of her head.

"I didn't realize I needed to tell you when I had to pee." Emily did the, *I have to pee* dance, as Kristy opened the door to the diner.

Emily practically pushed Kristy and Lora to the side once the door was unlocked. Lora followed her into the bathroom with Kristy close behind.

A few minutes later they left the ladies room with Kristy laughing at Emily's impersonation of Keith when he was hovering over her. Apparently, the middle O'Connor brother was a little too overprotective of his pregnant wife. According to Emily, he was even worse with the second pregnancy.

"Your voice is not quite deep enough to be me, Princess." Keith narrowed his eyes.

Before she could respond, she let out a squeaked and glanced down at her feet. Lora followed her eyes and realized what had the woman standing stock still.

"Did your water just break?" Kristy gasped.

"Yes." Emily held onto her stomach.

"It's too early." Keith took her hand and helped her walk toward the chair that Bull held.

"It's only four weeks, and I went early on Noah too." Emily eased down in the chair.

"But I can't drive you to the hospital. I've had a few beers." Keith crouched in front of her.

"I can drive you both." Bull ran for the door. "My truck's in the parking lot. Kristy come on."

"I'm not going. I'm going to let everyone know what happened."

Bull clenched his teeth and was about to say something when Emily grabbed her stomach and groaned. He glared at Kristy for a second and then ran out through the door.

"Come on, Princess." Keith lifted Emily into his arms.

"Keith, put me down. I can walk for Christ's sake." Emily grumbled.

"Not a chance." Keith stomped toward the exit.

"Keep us up to date," Kristy shouted, then turned and glanced down at the puddle still in the middle of the diner floor.

Without another word, Kristy hurried toward the kitchen. Lora grabbed the disinfectant behind the counter and proceeded to clean the seat of the chair where Emily had sat.

Fifteen minutes later the mess was cleaned up, and they headed out with Hulk a few steps in front of them. As Kristy locked the door to the diner, Hulk pushed open the main entry.

A loud roar from Hulk had both Lora and Kristy spinning around to see what happened. He staggered back from the entrance gasping, with his hand over his eyes.

Before Lora knew what happened, a figure entered through the door. He was dressed in black from head to toe and a ski mask covered his face. The only thing visible was his mouth and eyes.

"Lora get behind me," Kristy whispered.

There was no way Lora was going to let Kristy put herself in danger when she was pregnant. Lora glanced toward Hulk and realized he was incapacitated with something either thrown or sprayed in his face. He was coughing and trying without success to open his eyes.

"Fucker," Hulk wheezed.

"My love, come on. You can escape now." The man held his hand out to Lora as if he'd just done her a favour.

"Escape from what?" Lora didn't recognize her own voice, and she certainly didn't know the man.

"I know these people have been keeping you from me. Now we can be together." He grabbed for Lora's hand, but she stepped back.

"Who are you?" Kristy stepped around her.

"You're one of them." The man growled, and his hand raised slowly.

Lora stepped in front of Kristy as soon as she saw the gun. She wasn't going to let this man kill another person. This was the man she'd been hiding from all this time.

"Don't hurt her." Lora tried to sound firm, but her entire body trembled.

"Hurt her? She's one of your captors." He growled and waved the gun in their direction.

Hulk managed to get to his feet and staggered toward the man. It was as if everything happened in slow motion as the man turned the gun on Hulk and fired. Kristy wailed as Hulk fell back against the door to the pub.

"Stop, please." Lora howled as she lunged toward the man, grabbed his arm, and pushed it up into the air.

"But they've kept us apart, my love." He grabbed Lora's arm harshly, and she winced.

"There's been enough killing." Lora glanced toward Hulk hoping to God he wasn't dead

The large man was motionless on the floor, and she could see the blood seeping through his shirt. She wasn't sure if this guy had killed Hulk, but she wasn't about to let him hurt Kristy too.

"You've saved me." Lora forced herself to smile and tried to sound convincing.

"Yes, my love. I'm your hero." He cupped Lora's cheek, and she tried not to flinch.

She attempted to see if she could recognize the voice, but the adrenaline coursing through her body made it hard to concentrate. He was taller than her, but not by much, and his eyes were dark brown. There was something familiar, but she couldn't put her finger on it.

"Yes. Hero." Lora glanced at Kristy.

Kristy's eyes were focused on Hulk, but when she tried to move toward him, the man stepped in front of her. As a nurse, Kristy would be able to help him until Lora could get the crazy man out of the pub.

"What are you doing?" He growled.

"I want to check on him." Kristy snapped.

"The only thing you're going to do is…" His growl was sinister as he pointed his weapon at Kristy.

"No," Lora shouted and put herself directly in front of Kristy. "You can't hurt her. She's going to have a baby."

Lora couldn't see the expression on the man's face since it was still covered, but his eyes widened. He slowly lowered the gun and a grin crossed his lips.

"Boy or girl?" His tone sounded almost reverent as he spoke to Kristy.

"We… I don't know yet. I'm only six weeks." Kristy grabbed Lora's hand and they both squeezed.

"Well, I guess you'll have to come with us too. I can't leave a poor innocent child to be born with these evil people." He kicked Hulk's foot away from the door and pushed it open a little.

Once he checked outside, he pointed the gun through the door. Lora felt Kristy's grasp tighten again. Probably because she was expecting this asshole to shoot someone else.

"Let me protect you both. Come on, let's get out of here." He cooed.

At first, Lora or Kristy didn't move, and he stared at them. She felt Kristy move, but not toward the exit. That was when he pulled Lora out of the way and saw what Kristy was doing.

She'd pulled her phone out and was trying to message someone without the crazy man finding out. He growled raised his hand and backhanded Kristy across the cheek. She yelled in pain, and her phone dropped to the floor.

"I know these people got you brainwashed and you don't know what you're doing, but I'll help you and my love through this." He grabbed Kristy's arm and pushed her ahead of him.

"Please, don't hurt her," Lora begged.

"As long as she behaves herself she'll be safe." He waved the gun in a motion that told Lora she better follow Kristy.

Before he herded them through the door, he fired his gun through Kristy's phone. He also held his hand out to Lora, and she knew he wanted hers as well. She slipped it out of her back pocket and held it out to him. He tossed it next to Kristy's and shot a bullet through it.

When they got outside, Lora hoped someone had heard the gunshots, but Nick's band were still playing, and the sound traveled all the way up Harbour Street. They were in trouble, because there wasn't another soul around to save them.

Nick, please help us.

He was so excited as he pushed the two women into the back of his van. He hadn't planned on taking the other woman, but she was having a baby, and he had to protect the innocent child. It was hard to contain his glee at the thought of raising a child as his own.

The hardest thing he had to do was secure both women in the back of the vehicle. They were brainwashed, and he knew they might try to escape or do something while he drove them home. He couldn't take that chance, and he'd heal them soon enough.

The one called Kristy was a lot like his love. She was small and beautiful. He wanted to keep her as well, and he hoped his love wouldn't mind sharing him. After all, he had plenty of love for both. Now that he had his love next to him, he wouldn't have to try and replace her with women that didn't even come close to her.

"Where are we going?" Her voice was music to his ears.

"Home, my love." He singsonged. "Home to the place we met and fell in love."

"What's your name?" She asked.

Anger bubbled in the pit of his stomach and he tried to swallow it down. How could she not remember his name? She loved him. He took a deep breath and tried to remember that she'd been with her abductors for almost a year. They'd probably erased any memories of him, but he'd fix that. It was why he kept his face covered. He didn't want to shock her or do any damage by revealing himself too soon to her. After all, she had to be cleansed and healed.

Chapter 26

"I hope everyone had a great time tonight. Please be safe on your way home. We're *Rockin' The Law*." Aaron's voice echoed through the air as soon as they'd finished their final set.

The cheering crowd started to move off, except the members of his family that were moving toward the stage. His heart sank when he didn't see Lora. He frantically scanned the crowd for a glimpse of her or Hulk.

"She went to the pub with Emily and Kristy. They had to use the ladies room." Marina must have seen his panic. "Starting to wish I had gone with them."

"We can stop into Mom and Dad's on the way home. I'm sure the boys are asleep by now and won't ruin our plans." He wiggled his eyebrows.

Marina playfully slapped her husband on the chest, but it was clear she was all in for whatever James had in mind. Nick smiled because for a moment he could see a picture of himself with Lora swollen with his child.

"You guys were great as usual." Stephanie hopped up on the stage and wrapped her arms around John.

She grinned as she whispered something in her husband's ear. John's eyes practically rolled into his head as he snatched her hand. He was halfway up the beach before he called back to everyone.

"Yeah, I'm going home," John shouted as he towed a giggling Stephanie behind him.

Since their house was right across from the beach, it only took seconds for them to make it to their front door. From the look on his brother's face, Nick was pretty sure they weren't going home to sleep.

"I'm so ready to curl up in bed and go to sleep." Billie placed her hands on her back which made her swollen belly jut out further.

"The firefighters are going to put all the equipment in the truck for us. I'll take you home and give you a nice massage." Mike wrapped his arms around her from behind and splayed his hands over her belly.

"I will love you forever if you do that." She sighed and rested her head back against his shoulder.

"I'll get the truck in the morning." Aaron jumped down off the stage and wrapped his arm around the woman he'd picked up at the pub a few nights before. "I've got plans too."

At one time, Nick could see what Aaron found intriguing about the woman, but since he'd met Lora, women like her didn't even turn his head. The only woman he wanted was Lora. Before he could hurry off to meet her at the pub, several phones went off at the same time. Nick, Mike, James, Marina, and Aaron all pulled out their phones.

"Oh my, God. Emily's water broke," Stephanie shouted as she and John came running back to the beach.

"Keith said Lora and Kristy are back at the pub with Hulk. Bull had to drive them to the hospital because Keith had a few beers." John had the phone to his ear.

"Are we all going to the hospital?" Billie grinned.

"Someone should call the Health Science maternity ward and let them know they're about to be invaded by the O'Connor family." One of the firefighters Nick knew from school chuckled.

Ernie Marsh was one of Mike's oldest friends and grew up in Hopedale. He shared an apartment in St. John's with Mike and another friend for a few years. That was until Mike met Billie and moved back to the small town.

"Hey, Nick." Nick turned around to the soft voice behind him.

"Hey, Sunny." He smiled at the young teenager that worked at the grocery store.

"You guys were great tonight." She smiled and nodded at all the band members.

"Thanks." Aaron winked at her.

"I was wondering if one of you guys could do something for me?" The smile faded from her face.

"Sure, what's up?" Nick asked.

"Well, I do house cleaning for Mr. Batten. He lives on Knob Lane." She explained.

"Okay, that's the same road Nick's girlfriend lives on." James nodded.

"I'm worried about him. I was supposed to drop by there last week, and I did, but he didn't answer the door. Which is odd? I tried to call him but there was no answer, and I've dropped by every day since. His curtains are all closed but the lights are on, and I can hear the television. I know sometimes he just ignores me when I knock but…" She sighed. "I'm just worried…." She trailed off.

"I can check on him on my way to the hospital. I need to stop by the pub and pick up Lora." Nick put his hand on her shoulder. "I'll give your grandfather a call when I get some information."

Mr. Lawton the pharmacist was her grandfather, and Nick knew his dad could get in touch with the man if he had to. Nick knew Mr. Batten but didn't know a lot about him.

"Thanks. Mr. Batten has no family that I know of, and he can be a cranky butt, but I've grown fond of him and would hate if something happened to him." Sunshine's eyes filled with tears.

"We've got this." Aaron winked at her. "Let's go make fun of Keith."

"I thought you and me were going back to my place." The blonde whined.

"Sorry Jocelyn, my brother's wife is having her baby." Aaron grinned.

"Seriously, you would rather spend the night at the hospital than in my bed." Jocelyn stepped back with pure shock on her face.

"Not that I'd rather do it, but family is first." Aaron seemed annoyed at her attitude.

"Well, I guess I'm going home alone." She stomped off mumbling to herself.

"Oh well, guess I won't be getting any tonight." Aaron shrugged his shoulders, but if Nick wasn't mistaken, his brother looked almost relieved the woman went off in a huff.

"Maybe there'll be a cute nurse at the hospital." Marina winked at Aaron.

Nick sent a text to Lora to let her know he was on the way to the pub to pick her up. When she didn't respond right away, he figured she was lost in conversation with Kristy. He sent a text to Hulk to let him know.

Since most of the families' vehicles were parked in the pub parking lot, the group strolled up Beach Street and turned on to

Harbour Street. Marina and Billie hurried ahead. Apparently, the babies caused havoc with their bladders.

Mike and Ian were teasing Aaron about losing out on his roll in the hay when loud screams had them all running toward the pub.

Billie staggered out of the door just as the rest of them got to the steps. Her face was ghostly white, and Marina stood against the outside of the door trembling.

"I think… Oh, God…. I think he's dead." Billie bawled as Mike wrapped his arms around her.

"Who?" John shouted.

Nick and Aaron ran up the steps with John and Ian behind them. Aaron yanked open the door. The sight that greeted them made Nick's heart feel like it stopped.

"Fuck," Ian pushed by them and fell to his knees next to Hulk's motionless body.

"Is he…" Nick couldn't finish the statement.

Hulk may not be blood-related to him or his brothers, but he was unquestionably part of the family. Ian held up his hand and pressed his fingers against Hulk's neck.

"I got a pulse, but it's weak." Ian ripped open the front of Hulk's shirt. "he's not breathing. Get a bus here."

John was already on his phone as Sandy moved Marina and Billie away from the doorstep, along with anyone who wasn't police.

As much as Nick complained about it on stage about having to wear his weapon, he was glad to be holding it at that moment. Aaron carefully edged into the diner with Nick close behind. The whole time they searched Nick prayed they'd find Lora and Kristy hiding somewhere inside.

With each shout of a room being clear, his heart sank. Nick made is way to the exit when the blare of the ambulance roared as it pulled in front of the pub. When Cory and Steve exited the pub section and shook their heads, Nick's stomach lurched, and his body trembled.

He moved out of the way of the medical personnel that entered to work on Hulk. Ian continued to help them, but Nick couldn't concentrate on anything they said or did.

"Someone has to call Bull." Marina had her arms wrapped around Stephanie.

"I'll call him." Sandy's voice cracked.

She seemed to be doing her best not to fall apart, but out of the whole family, she was probably closest to the men that worked for Keith and Bull. She'd known them before the business home base was moved back to Newfoundland.

"We'll find them, bro." Aaron squeezed Nick's shoulder as he walked up to him.

"We don't even know who this fucker is," Nick growled.

"When I find this bastard, I'm going to beat him within an inch of his life." Cory stomped around his truck and punched the side of it several times before John stopped him.

"When this is over, you and I are going to have a long talk, but right now get your head out of your ass. We need you to help us find our cousin and future sister-in-law." If anyone outside the family heard John, they'd say he was calm and collected, but Nick knew his brother well, John was about to lose all control.

Nick turned and braced his hands against a truck behind him. He took several deep breaths trying to keep himself from completely losing his own control. Not only was the love of his life missing, but his cousin as well.

"What the fuck happened?" Kurt and his father ran into the parking lot.

"Lora and Kristy are missing and Hulk…" James stopped.

"He was shot." Steve appeared next to James.

"Someone took my daughter?" Kurt growled.

"And Lora." John reminded his uncle.

"What do you know?" Kurt's voice calmed into a deep rumble.

"Only what we just told you," John explained.

Before Nick knew what happened, he was on his knees with his head against the bumper of the truck. It was hard to breathe, and it felt as if someone knocked the wind out of him. He needed to get himself together, but he couldn't control his breathing.

"Here, bro," Ian held a paper bag in front of Nick.

"Wha… don…" Nick gasped.

"You're hyperventilating. Breathe in and out into this bag to get that under control. She needs you, bro." Ian held the bag up to his mouth. "That's it. Slow that breathing down."

Nick felt like a complete idiot as he watched everyone around him. He was a fucking cop for Christ's sake. He needed to get himself together for Lora and Kristy. Losing Lora wasn't an option now that he found her. *No.* This bastard wasn't going to take her away.

He pushed Ian's hand away. Making eye contact with his brother, Nick nodded as they watched the ambulance speed out of the parking lot.

"Let's get to work," Nick shouted when Ian helped him to his feet.

"That's the brother I remember," Ian said as he gave Nick a supportive slap on the back.

He carefully filled the plates with food and counted as he tried to calm his frustration. Getting the two women into the house had been a struggle, and the pregnant one kicked him in the shin.

She wasn't long calming down when he slapped her again. The feel of his hand slapping against her skin aroused him, but he couldn't allow her to do that to him.

His love was more cooperative, but he didn't like the look of fear in her eyes. He tried to soothe her to let her know he wouldn't allow them to take her again, but it didn't help.

Now both women were in his treatment room. They had to be deprogrammed. The first thing was to rid them of all the possessions they had from their captive lives.

He'd let them settle a little before he'd attempt that. After all, one was pregnant, and he would be a father. He grinned as he thought about having a baby to raise. He'd resigned himself that the little girl wasn't an infant, and her room was completed, but now he had to build a nursery for his new child.

Sure, the baby wasn't his by blood, but he'd been blood-related to his father, and that was hell. He was nothing like his overbearing father.

He'd made a few mistakes by trying to replace his love with those other sluts, but that wouldn't happen anymore. He had his love, and someone to give him a child. His life was complete.

He placed the plates of food on a tray with a couple of bottles of water. He needed to go back and clean up his mess at the old man's house. Before he left, he needed to make sure his love and the other were not hungry or thirsty. They'd grow to appreciate his effort.

"I'm coming, my beautiful ladies." He smiled as he pulled on the ski mask and made his way down into the basement.

Chapter 27

"You don't have any idea who this guy is, do you?" Kristy whispered as the man left the room.

"No. I don't recognize his voice, and we can't see his face but there is something familiar." Lora glanced around the room.

"Do you have any idea where we are?" Kristy walked around the small room, but Lora didn't know what she was looking for.

"Not a clue." Lora sighed and wrapped her arms around herself. "Do you think…. Hulk?" Lora shivered.

"I wish I knew." Kristy's voice cracked for the first time since they'd been shoved into the room with pillowcases over their heads.

The crazy bastard said he didn't want them mentally telling people where they were. If it wasn't apparent before that this man was insane, that statement had confirmed it. Lora was scared to death, and Kristy was in danger as well.

"I think he's coming," Kristy whispered as she grabbed Lora's hand and they both sat on one of the beds.

The room was about twelve by twelve and didn't appear to have any windows. There were two single beds on one side of the wall as well as a small fridge in the corner. There were two doors, but one led to a small bathroom with a sink and toilet. The only way out was the door he'd pushed them through. Lora heard several clicks letting her know the entrance was very secure. There was no chance they could break out through there.

"Are you okay?" Lora asked Kristy who was squeezing her hand so tight it started to hurt.

"Me? Sure. I'm locked in a room with you because some crazy ass man who thinks he's saving us. Other than that; I'm just peachy." Kristy was trying to make light of the situation, but Lora found it hard to see any humor.

One click, two clicks and then a third. The door opened, and they heard him call from the opened door.

"My Darlings, I've got some food here to tide you over until I get back. Please stay back from the door. I don't want to have to hurt you, but I will, if I have to." His voice sounded as if he was having a casual conversation with an old friend, and Kristy looked at Lora as if to say '*is this guy for real?*'

He entered the room, and Lora hoped he had lost the ski mask, but he still had his face hidden. He removed his jacket and Lora could now see the man's build.

He was a few inches taller than her, but not as tall as Nick. He wasn't skinny, but he wasn't overweight either. Lora didn't see any visible tattoos or scars on his arms, but she just couldn't shake the feeling that she knew him.

"Now I don't want you to worry. I will be back in the morning. There's enough food here to get you through the night as well as water." He turned and glanced at them. "I would never leave without making sure you are okay."

It looked as if he wanted them to acknowledge what he deemed to be 'taking care' of them. What were they supposed to do? Say thank you for the food and keeping us locked up in a room.

He pulled a bag from his shoulder and tossed it in the middle of the floor. Both Lora and Kristy stared at it as if it would blow up in their faces.

"I've brought you some night time clothes as well as bathroom supplies." He backed toward the door. "I'll see you at lunchtime tomorrow."

"Th…thank you." Lora forced out the words as the bile rose in her throat.

It turned her stomach to thank the man, but she certainly didn't want to piss him off before she and Kristy figured a way out, or Nick found her.

Nick.

Lora swallowed the lump in her throat as she thought about the man she loved. There wasn't a doubt in her mind that he'd move heaven and earth to find them.

"You're very welcome, my love." He smiled as if she'd gave him the biggest gift in the world.

Lora wished she knew who he was. If she could find out why he thought he was saving her, maybe she could reach him in some way.

The door closed behind him, and the three clicks sounded like the loudest noise in the world. Lora didn't have time to panic over it because Kristy jumped to her feet and was knocking softly along the wall, but Lora had no idea why.

"I'm not staying locked in this fucking room until he comes back from God knows where," Kristy whispered as she continued along the wall.

"I don't think we have much choice." Lora stood up and started to do the same thing, but she wasn't sure what Kristy was doing.

"There's no way that a house has a room this size with no window. Even if we are in the basement, there has to be some window here somewhere. This is all new drywall, and you can smell the fresh paint." Kristy glanced around the room.

"Are you saying he built this room to keep us locked away?" Lora's blood ran cold to think this guy planned to keep her prisoner.

"Look at the way this room is laid out. He's been planning this for a while." Kristy turned, and Lora knew at that moment they needed to get out of there and fast.

Lora continued to knock up and down the wall in the same way that Kristy did. It all sounded the same to her, but Kristy seemed to be concentrating as if looking for a specific sound.

"How will you know if there's a window?" Lora asked.

"When my dad renovated the house we grew up in, he was looking for a window they'd boarded up years before. This was how he found it," Kristy whispered.

Before they were halfway around the room music filled the air. Lora loved classical music, so she knew the song. It was *Scarlatti Sonata in D minor*. Most people probably heard the song more than they realized because it was often used as hold music.

"Oh, hell no." Kristy groaned.

It was not that the music was loud, because it was actually at a very soft volume, but the song could be annoying when you heard it over and over.

"Maybe he thinks it will keep us calm." Lora watched Kristy pick up a fork from the tray the man had left on top of the small fridge.

"That music is only going to piss me off." Kristy stood in the middle of the room and slowly turned in a circle.

"Maybe we should check the bathroom." Lora opened the door.

Kristy followed, and they moved around the small room tapping on the wall. Lora was about to give up when Kristy tapped the fork against the wall over the toilet. She did it a second time.

"Bingo," Kristy climbed up on top of the toilet.

"Kristy, you need to be careful." Lora stood behind her and held on to her waist.

"We need to get out of here, and then I'll be careful." Kristy pounded the end of the fork against the sheetrock.

When it didn't do anything but make a dent, she cursed under her breath. She stepped down and proceeded to search the room.

"If we can find something sharp we can cut through the wall, and get the hell out of here." Kristy was frantic.

"I doubt he left us a knife in here, but maybe we could use this." Lora grinned when she found a metal shower rod behind the bathroom door.

"I love you." Kristy kissed Lora's cheek, as both of them grabbed the end of the rod and proceeded to slam it against the wall over the toilet.

For what seemed forever they pounded against the wall until they could get their hands through the opening. they used every bit of strength they had to pull the wall down.

Lora's heart jumped in her chest when she saw the small opening that was most definitely a window. The only issue was someone had boarded it up from the outside. The window itself was gone, but the wood that covered it looked to be secure.

"I wonder how thick that is," Lora said mostly to herself.

"I'm sure if we keep going with the rod we'll get through it." Kristy picked the metal up again and pounded it against the board.

"Maybe you should take a break, Kristy. I'll do this." Lora took the rod from Kristy.

"I'm fine, but we have more weight behind it with both of us." Kristy smiled.

Lora learned a long time ago it was pointless to argue with an O'Connor. Especially the females. Every one of them were stubborn, but the most wonderful people she'd ever met.

A bruise was forming on the left side of Kristy's cheek where the man had slapped her. Bull would kill the man for hurting Kristy, and with the way Lora felt seeing the mark, she'd pay to watch.

The anger gave her the strength she didn't know she had and they pounded the board until they heard a crack. They stopped and looked at each other with huge smiles. With the adrenalin pumping through her body and knowing they were inches from freedom, it gave her all the strength she needed to keep going until the board snapped.

Lora saw the slit, and they jammed the rod into it and used it as a fulcrum to pry half the board out of the way. The creaking of the nails pulling from the window frame was loud, and Lora prayed the guy really left. If he hadn't, there was no way he didn't hear what they were doing.

The wood finally broke from the frame of the window, and they were able to push the second half out of the way. It was a small opening but certainly big enough for both Kristy and Lora to squeeze through the hole. Kristy hugged Lora and pushed her to climb up on the toilet.

"Come on. You first," Kristy said excitedly.

"No Kristy, you first." Lora tried to step back.

"We are not having this argument right now. Get your butt out that window before that fucking doorknob comes back." Kristy shoved her again, and Lora stepped up on the toilet.

It was dark, but she scanned around to make sure nobody was outside waiting. Not that she could see much, but she wiggled through the opening and jumped to her feet. Once she was through, she turned around and helped Kristy climb out.

They both crouched close to the house because Lora still not positive the man wouldn't jump out at them. She grabbed Kristy's hand as she scanned the area.

"Oh my, God," Lora whispered.

"What?" The panic in Kristy's voice was evident.

"This is the house where I grew up." Lora turned her head to look at the house behind them.

"Are you sure?" Kristy followed her gaze.

"Positive." Lora stood slowly.

All the lights in the house were out, and she hoped that meant the guy really left. Lora glanced at her watch. It was a little after one in the morning. She didn't have a phone, and the closest twenty-four-hour gas station was about fifteen minutes down the road.

"Do you know the neighbors?" Kristy asked hopefully.

"I know everyone on this street," Lora whispered.

Even in the darkness, Lora knew how to make her way out of the back garden and between the homes to the front of the house. She kept a tight grip on Kristy's hand as they slowly creeped around the side of the house.

She looked up and down the street hoping to see at least one house with a light but from where she stood all she could see was darkness.

"People in town certainly go to bed early." Kristy's attempt at a joke made Lora smile.

"Not the places I lived after I moved out on my own." Lora tugged Kristy toward the end of the driveway, and they ran by two houses when Lora breathed a sigh of relief.

A man sat on the front step of his house oblivious to anything around him. Including the two women currently running toward his walkway.

"Lora, stop." Kristy pulled her to a halt. "What if he's the guy?"

Lora hadn't thought of it, but she knew the family who lived in the house and grew up with their kids. She stared at the man for a moment and recognized him right away. From the size of him, it wasn't her stalker.

"Roman," Lora shouted as they ran toward him.

"Lora Norris?" Roman Young smiled and stood up.

He was an old friend of her brother and someone she trusted just as much. She didn't realize he'd returned to Newfoundland, but she'd never been so happy to see him.

"Roman, we need your help." Lora broke into tears as she and Kristy met him halfway up the walkway.

"Jesus, what's wrong?" He glanced at Kristy then back to Lora.

"We need to get inside and use your phone." Lora didn't give him a chance to say anything as she pulled Kristy up the steps and yanked open the door.

She knew the house as well as her old home, because she'd been in it thousands of times over the years. Their families spent plenty of time together when they were growing up.

Lora looked around for a phone and when she didn't see one she turned to Roman.

"Your phone?" She sobbed.

"Lora, what the fuck is going on?" He grabbed her by the arms, and she lost it.

"Long story short. Lora was stalked. She moved to get away. He started killing people until he found her. He found her and took us to her old house because he's out of his ever-loving mind and thinks he saved us. Satisfied? I'm Kristy O'Connor by the way. Lora is dating my cousin." Kristy rambled as she wrapped her arms around Lora.

"Okay. That was a lot of information to get in five seconds but here." He pulled his cell phone out of his pocket and put it in Lora's hand.

"Thanks." Lora hiccupped as she tried to steady her hands to call for help.

"You want to tell me where this guy is so I can go kick the shit out of him?" Lora couldn't help but let out a small laugh as he shoved up his sleeves.

"Thanks, but she's about to call in the cavalry." Kristy snorted.

Lora put the phone to her ear and waited to hear the only voice that would let her know everything was going to be fine.

He was pissed. The police had the one entrance to that stupid little town blocked off, and he wasn't able to get to the old bastard's house. They were stopping every car that went in or out.

He really should have taken care of the man before he went through with his plan, but he saw his chance and took it. He was surprised the big ass went down so quickly. He'd heard bear spray was bad when sprayed in the face. He wanted to watch longer to see how long it took for the guy to come back to himself. He couldn't enjoy it because he couldn't take the chance of someone else showing up and preventing his rescue.

He drove by the town entrance several times debating on whether to take the chance and go through the police barricade. He'd been careful up until that moment, and it would be a mistake to press his luck.

There was nothing to lead them to the old man's house. The only one that came there was that annoying teenager and even she'd stopped coming after the third time she got no answer. He was pretty sure the police wouldn't keep the town blocked off too long.

He pulled into the side of the road where he could still see the flashing red and blue lights, but couldn't be seen by the police.

"I'll have to wait until they give up and realize they lost." The sound of several sirens made him sit up straight, but since they all didn't leave, he still wasn't able to enter the town. He made his way back to town and to his love.

Chapter 28

Nick was sure his heart was beating a mile a minute as he waited for the forensic team to go through the pub and the diner. He paced the parking lot and watched his family knowing their expressions probably mirrored his own.

Bull swerved into the parking lot with complete panic written all over his face. Bull had been in love with Kristy for years and they were only a month away from getting married. If anything happened to Kristy, it would destroy Bull. Nick knew how he felt.

"If he hurts her…" Bull's voice cracked. "I'll cut him with razor blades and stick him in a tub of pure alcohol."

"I'll fucking help you." Nick leaned against the side of the building watching the fishing boats bobbing on the water.

"She's pregnant." Bull closed his eyes and rested his head against the brick of the building.

"Really?" Nick turned to look at Bull.

"Yeah, we found out yesterday and wanted to keep it quiet until after the wedding." Bull turned his head to look at Nick. "I don't know what I'll do if anything happens to her."

"I know what you mean. I swear my heart…" Nick's admission was interrupted by the buzzing of his phone.

He pulled it out of his pocket and when he didn't recognize the number was about to let it go to voicemail. Then he thought about Keith at the hospital with Emily and answered.

"Hello," Nick held the phone to his ear and shoved his hand into his pocket.

"Nick? Oh my God, Nick." Lora's trembling voice echoed in his ear, and his heart practically jumped out of his chest.

"Lora, where are you?" He met Bull's wide eyes and held up his hand.

"He took us," Lora whispered.

"Is he there?" Nick put the phone on speaker so that Bull could hear as well.

"We escaped. He took us to the house I grew up in." Lora sniffed. "We got out through a window and ran down the road until we …" Bull stopped her.

"Lora, what's the address?" He practically yelled.

Lora gave him the address quickly, and Bull entered it into his GPS.

"Lora, is Kristy okay?" Bull was unmistakably trying to sound tough, but his voice cracked.

"She's fine," Lora whispered.

"I'm here, Dean." Kristy's voice echoed through the phone.

She was probably one of very few that called Bull by his real name.

"You sure, Kitten?" He asked.

"Yes. Just get your asses out here and get us." Kristy grumbled making both Nick and Bull chuckle.

"That's my girl." Bull laughed.

"Lora, we're coming. Stay on the phone with me until we get there." Nick and Bull ran toward Nick's truck stopping long enough just to let everyone know the situation.

In seconds several large pickup trucks, jeeps, and police cars followed him out of the parking lot. He couldn't wait to pull her into his arms and never let her out of his sight again.

It never took so long to drive into town as it seemed to take them to get to Lora's old neighborhood. Ethan hopped in the truck with Nick because he knew exactly how to get to the house where they would find Lora.

The entire drive into town, Lora and Kristy gave them a play by play of what happened and how they were able to escape. Kristy didn't seem as frightened as Nick expected. She almost seemed pissed that someone would try to lock her away.

Nick pulled his truck in front of the house and shoved it into park. He didn't bother to turn it off or close the door as he and Bull jumped out in front of the house and ran up the walkway. Kristy burst through the door first and ran right into Bull's arms. Lora came through the door and only made it as far as the step when Nick had her wrapped in his embrace.

"Baby, I'm never letting you go again," He whispered as he tucked his face into the crook of her neck.

"I'm not going to complain about that right now." Lora cried and held onto him as if he'd disappear.

"As much as this scene fills my heart with relief, we need to know where this guy is, and who the fuck he is." Cory stood in the center of the walkway.

"I don't know who he is, and as far as I know, he left." Lora turned to look at Cory, but she didn't release her grip on Nick.

"Can you describe him?" John asked from where he was hugging Kristy.

"No, he wore a ski mask." Lora sighed. "Oh... God... he shot... Hulk."

"We know, sweetheart." Nick kissed the top of her head.

"Is Hulk okay?" Kristy's voice trembled.

"As far as we know he's in surgery." John glanced at Nick.

The truth was, things were touch and go with Hulk, but Lora and Kristy were already upset. Giving them bad news would not make it easy to get the information they needed to catch the guy.

Keith had called John to update the family on Hulk. His brother said the bullet had pierced Hulk's lung, and he'd lost a lot of blood. Keith managed to get one of the doctors to keep him informed while Emily was in labor, but there hadn't been any news since then.

The screech of tires drew everyone's attention to the end of the road where a van did a U-turn and sped off.

"I think that's him. He had us in a Van," Kristy shouted.

Police cruisers spun on the road screeching tires as they sped after the van. Nick held Lora tightly against him and stepped into the house where Ethan's friend stood in the doorway.

While some of his fellow officers chased after the suspect, others made their way into Lora's old home and were searching the house for anything to tell them anything concerning the guy.

"Roman, I'm so sorry for taking over your house like this." Lora sighed as the man brought in a pot of coffee.

"Are you kidding? This is the most excitement I've had in my life." He chuckled and refilled Nick's cup.

"You should come to Hopedale. There's never a dull moment." Kristy laughed.

"Know anyone hiring a chef?" He chuckled.

"I just might." Kristy grinned.

"Seriously, I'm glad I couldn't sleep tonight. Since Mom passed away, it's hard to get used to such a quiet house." Roman sat in an old rocking chair.

"I was so sorry to hear about her passing." Ethan cupped Roman's shoulder and squeezed it.

"Thanks. I came back when she got sick and decided I never wanted to leave the province again." Roman leaned back in the chair and wrapped his hand around his mug of coffee.

Nick kept a close eye on Lora as she flinched every time someone came into the house. Kristy must have noticed too because she reached for Lora's hand and held it.

The sun was rising as they pulled into her driveway. Sheila called every hour until they got home and wanted to meet them at the house. Lora talked her into staying at his parent's house. They needed to get some sleep. Ethan stayed with Roman to catch up, but Nick figured Lora's brother was hoping the asshole would return.

The police were questioning several other neighbors through the morning. When they talked to the lady next door, she said a couple told her about six months earlier they'd bought the house. They moved in one day and then disappeared. The next thing the woman knew the man showed up. She'd never seen the couple after.

Lora and Kristy fell asleep in the truck on the way home, and when Nick dropped Bull and his cousin home, the large man carried Kristy into the house.

Nick got out of the truck and opened the door. Lora was curled up on the back seat and only opened her eyes to give him a faint smile.

"Come on, sweetheart. Let's get you tucked into bed." Nick picked her up into his arms and carried her up the steps.

Nick managed to get the door open without putting her down. He knew she felt drained because of the adrenalin rush. Nick had that feeling more times than he could count.

Lora had dust and dirt on her clothes from where she and Kristy practically tore down a wall with their bare hands. Nick was sure she'd want to shower if she was more awake, but she could do that in the morning. At that moment, she needed to sleep.

Nick carried her into the bedroom and helped her strip off the soiled clothes. After he tucked her into bed, she gave him a weak smile and reached for him.

"Sleep," Nick kissed her cheek.

"Come to bed." She yawned.

"I want to check on some things, and I promise I'll come in and hold you when I'm done." He kissed her lips and backed out of the room.

Nick pulled his phone from his pocket and tapped the number for Keith. He'd received a text around four in the morning saying that Emily had an eight pound and three-ounce baby boy they named Patrick Sean O'Connor.

Even though he was a little early, he was healthy and feeding perfectly, but it was hard for Keith to enjoy the birth of his son when one of his dearest friends was fighting for his life.

"Hello," Keith answered the phone on the first ring in a low whisper.

"Hey, bro." Nick pulled a bottle of water from the fridge.

"What's wrong?" Keith's voice quivered.

"Nothing, I just wanted to check on you, Emily and Patrick." The events of the night took away from the family's joy of a new baby.

"We're fine. Em's sleeping and the baby is sleeping soundly in my arms." Nick could hear the pride in his brother's voice.

"Any word on Hulk?" Nick sighed.

"Nothing. His sister and brother got here about an hour ago. They said they'd keep me up to date. As far as I know, they lost him during surgery and had to revive him." Keith sighed. "It's not good, bro."

"He's a tough guy. We need to stay positive and pray." Nick tried to sound convincing, but it was hard when he'd witnessed just how badly Hulk was hurt.

"He banged his head on the metal door handle when he fell, and they're worried about swelling. I don't know, Nick." He could hear Keith blow out a heavy breath. "He's only thirty-one."

"And he's one of the toughest men we know." Nick reminded his brother.

"I know. If you remember the prayers Father Wallace taught us, send one up." Keith sighed.

"I will. Keep me in the loop." Nick was about to end the call when his brother stopped him.

"How's Lora?" He asked.

"Exhausted but she wasn't hurt. The fucker didn't touch either of them." He was more thankful than he ever thought possible.

"Good. That's good." Keith murmured.

"I'm gonna catch some shut-eye." Nick yawned.

"Later, bro. Give that woman of yours a hug for me," Keith said.

"Ditto." Nick ended the call and made his way around the house to make sure all the doors and windows were locked.

He wasn't taking any chances. The police lost the stalker on some side road after a twenty-minute chase through the side streets of St. Johns. They were still searching his house, so he wouldn't be able to go back to the place where he'd planned to keep Lora and Kristy. Nick needed to make sure the house was secure because this guy wasn't getting near Lora ever again.

When Nick entered the bedroom, Lora was curled up on her side, but her eyes were open. She gave him a smile as he made his way to the bed.

"What's wrong?" Nick sat next to her and brushed his knuckle against he cheek.

"Besides the fact that I just escaped from a crazy man who locked me in my childhood home with your cousin?" Lora exhaled.

"You're safe now." Nick cupped her cheek.

"There's just something needling in my head. I'm sure I know who he is, but I can't figure it out." Lora sat up, and the blankets fell from her naked chest.

"You're exhausted. Get some sleep, and we can talk it out later today." Nick smoothed his hand over her head.

"Kristy is one bad ass woman." Lora grinned.

"She grew up with seven male cousins and a father who was a cop." Nick brushed his lips against hers.

"Hmmm." Her eyes fluttered closed as her hands slid around his neck.

"You. Need. To. Sleep." Nick placed a kiss on her lips for each word.

"I want you, Nick. I need you." She opened her eyes as she slid her hands down the front of his chest to the hem of his shirt.

"I want you too but…" She pressed her finger to his lips and shook her head.

"No buts. I need to feel you inside me. I need to feel your skin against mine. Make me forget last night. Just for a while." She tugged his shirt over his head and ran her fingers lightly down the center of his chest to his stomach.

"Baby," Nick groaned and cupped the back of her head. "I need you too, Lora I need inside of you more than I need to breathe."

Lora unbuttoned his jeans as she fumbled to her knees, as Nick stood up and attempted to push them down over his hips, but she pushed his hands away.

"Mine." She growled.

Lora wiggled his jeans and boxers over his hips and down his legs. He kicked them off as soon as they pooled around his ankles.

"You're pretty possessive." Nick chuckled, but he lost the humor when she wrapped her hand around his hard length.

"Your body is so perfect." Lora's voice was reverent, and Nick couldn't help but feel pride in the way the woman he loved worshiped his body with just her eyes.

Nick wrapped his hands around her waist and attempted to push her down to the bed, but she shook her head. Her hand slid painstakingly slow down his length. When she reached the base of his cock, she lowered her head and swirled her tongue around the swollen head several times.

"Fuck, baby. Your tongue feels so fucking good." Nick groaned when her hand tightened around the base of his dick.

Lora teased, licked and sucked only the head but kept her grip tight and unmoving where his cock met his body. Her other hand cupped his balls as she slowly slid her mouth down his hard length taking him into her hot mouth.

"Ahh… Jesus." Nick cupped the back of her head with one hand and used his other to cup her full breast.

Lora hummed as her mouth slipped up and down his length. Nick bit down on his lip to keep from shouting when her teeth graze the underside of his sensitive head.

He had to stop her before he lost all control. He was ready to explode inside her mouth, but he wanted to be inside her sweet folds before that happened.

"Baby, I want to be inside you." Nick pulled back with a gasp.

"I love your taste." She purred.

Nick knew how she felt because he had never tasted anything as good as her wetness. At that moment his mouth watered at the thought of driving his tongue deep into her moist pussy.

"It's my turn to taste." Nick eased her back onto the bed and crawled over her.

Nick ran his tongue over her lower lip, and she nipped at it just before she sucked it. This woman was going to be the death of him. He covered her lips with his and tasted every part of her warm mouth. His tongue swirled against hers as her nails grazed down his spine.

He pulled back from her addictive mouth and kissed his way across her jaw and down to the nape of her neck. Lora raised her hips off the bed as if begging for him to touch her. Nick held himself over her with one hand and slid the other down under her breast. Nick flicked his tongue against the hard nipple once, then sucked it hard into his mouth. Her dark nipples stood out against her creamy skin, and the color reminded him of ripe partridge berries, but she tasted so much better.

"Nick," She gasped, and her nails dug into the top of his back.

"I love these nipples. They are so damn responsive. All I have to do is touch them, and they pop up waiting to be sucked." Nick covered it with his mouth and sucked it again.

As much as he loved her breasts, he wanted to taste her sweet pussy. Nick knelt between her legs and continued to lick, suck and nibble his way down her body to her wettness. He could smell her arousal as his finger slipped between her slit. Her body jerked as his thumb lightly touched her sensitive clit.

"Fucking beautiful," He whispered just before he pushed one finger inside her and swirled his tongue around her swollen nub.

"Nick… God, I need to come." She squirmed under his teasing.

"I'll always give you what you need." He growled as he drove a second finger inside her and sucked her clit into his mouth.

His cock was painfully hard and wanted nothing more than to drive deep inside her, but he loved to see her come undone as he brought her to orgasm with just his fingers and his mouth.

He sucked her clit hard into his mouth as she tightened around his fingers and her body convulsed when her hips thrust off the bed.

"That's it, sweetheart. I love watching you come apart for me." He watched her practically melt into the mattress as she worked to control her breathing.

Nick eased his finger from inside her and rubbed the dampness around her sensitive pussy. She convulsed a couple of times as he slowed his ministrations and eased himself up until he hovered over her.

"My bones are gone." She giggled when he nipped her earlobe.

"I still have a hard bone," Nick growled in her ear.

"Oh my God, that's such a man thing to say." Lora lifted her knees allowing him to settle between her thighs.

"That's because I'm a man that can't wait to bury myself deep inside you," Nick whispered into her ear right before he sucked her earlobe between his lips.

"Ahhh... When you talk like that it makes me so hot." Lora raised her hips, and the tip of his throbbing cock slid between her folds.

"You're playing with fire, sweetheart." He moaned. "I haven't put a condom on yet."

She reached under her pillow and pulled out the gold package. She dangled it in front of his face making him grin. He didn't know when she'd grabbed it out of the drawer, but at the moment, he didn't care.

Nick grabbed it with his teeth and opened it. After he slid it onto his hard length, he moved over her again. For a moment he just stared at her beautiful face and wondered how he got so damn lucky. Nobody was ever going to take her away from him again. With that thought, he guided his thick length to her opening and slowly slid inside.

"So. Fucking. Beautiful." Nick groaned.

Lora squirmed under him as her legs wrapped around his hips and grabbed his ass with her hands. The slight sting of her nails digging into the flesh had him painfully hard.

"Fuck, Nick. I need you to move." Lora pushed her hips up against him, and she squeezed his dick inside.

Nick pulled his hips back and slammed into her. When he did it the second time, she groaned against his ear. He wouldn't be able to last very much longer. He was desperate to feel her come around his dick. Nick snaked his hand between them and pressed his thumb against her swollen clit as continued to pump in and out of her.

Her muscles inside started to clench around him, and her body shuddered under him. He increased the pressure on his thumb as well as his thrusts. As her walls clamped around him, he pushed deep inside and exploded. Her name left his lips in a deep guttural groan.

"Lora,"

How could his love do this to him? He'd saved her, and she ran away. Right back to that cop. He was touching her again. That bastard was fucking his love.

She'd been brainwashed, but he'd underestimated how intense it was. She didn't understand who he was and even if he'd shown her his face, he doubted it would work.

It was time to regroup, but it would be difficult since his home had been breached. It had probably been an error in judgment to bring the other woman. After all, she'd been part of his love's abduction. He'd just got excited about the baby and figured he could at least save the child.

He should have kept his mind on what was important. Saving his love and making sure he got her away from the people that kept them apart.

He stared at the screen as he watched her writhe under the cop, and it made him want to vomit. Cleansing her was going to take a long time, but then she would be clean. Then he could take her as his own.

"I'll have you soon, my love," He whispered to the screen in front of him. "And that cop won't know what hit him."

Chapter 29

Lora rolled over on the bed and reached for him. He wasn't there, and she opened her eyes. The clock at the side of her bed told her it was after three in the afternoon.

After she and Nick made love, he'd held her in his warm arms until she fell asleep. She must have slept pretty soundly because she hadn't even felt Nick slip out of bed. She still couldn't believe what happened the previous night.

Lora turned her head toward the window. It was closed, and she could see it was locked as well. It made her smile. Nick must have made sure all the windows in the house were secured. She hadn't done that in a long time. At least not until she had been in Hopedale for a few months.

Lora threw the blankets back and for some reason had the overwhelming feeling to grab her robe and cover herself. It was weird because the feeling of being watched eerily overwhelmed her. She wrapped the robe around her body and hurried to the bathroom.

She found Nick in the living room when she'd finished her shower and gotten dressed. He was on the phone and Lora didn't like the way his jaw clenched. She wrapped her arms around herself as she waited for Nick to finish his call. For what seemed forever, Nick only listened to whoever was on the other end of the call. When she was about ready to shout at him to tell her something, he nodded.

"Thanks, Keith. Tell his brother and sister we'll keep them in our prayers." Nick took the phone from his ear and blew out a shaky breath.

"Nick, what's going on?" Lora couldn't stop shaking.

"That was Keith." Nick dropped his phone on the coffee table and walked toward her.

"Nick, no. Hulk?" Tears filled her eyes.

"He's not in good shape." She saw Nick swallow hard.

"But he's going to be okay? Right?" Lora prayed he'd give her the answer she wanted to hear but had a feeling he wouldn't.

"He's in critical condition." Nick took her hands in his.

"He'll be okay, Nick. Please tell me that." She swallowed hard.

"From what Keith told me, they had to do another surgery. The crack he got on the head fractured his skull, and there's a lot of swelling." Nick tipped his head back and glanced up at the ceiling, then swallowed.

"Nick," Lora's voice cracked.

"They have him on a ventilator. The next forty-eight hours are critical." Nick explained.

Lora couldn't say another word because the huge knot in her throat wouldn't allow her. Hulk didn't deserve any of this. He was only doing his job. He was fighting for his life because some crazy bastard wanted her.

"We need to stay positive." Nick wrapped his strong arms around her and pulled her into his warm embrace.

Lora rested her head against his chest and blinked back the tears. She wasn't letting this guy hurt one more person she cared about, but Lora had no idea how she could do that.

An hour later, Lora sat on the sofa at Nick's parent's house with Molly, Olivia, Colin and Grace crowded around her as she read them a story. If someone asked her about the book, she wouldn't even be able to tell them the name of the characters. She couldn't concentrate on anything at the moment and the only thing keeping her from falling apart was the way Molly snuggled into her side.

The house was filled to the rafters with Nick's family and extended family as well as the men that worked for Keith. The concern on their faces was evident, but so was the determination. The whole group were hell-bent on finding the man who took her and Kristy, as well as put their friend in such a critical situation.

"I made ya a hot cuppa tea, Lassie." Nanny Betty placed the teacup on the side table next to where Lora sat.

"Thanks, Nan." Lora smiled at Nick's grandmother.

"Doncha worry. My b'ys and girls will figure dis out and our Hulk is gonna be jus' dandy." Lora nodded at the woman, but for the first time since she'd met Nanny Betty, she could see concern in the tiny woman's blue eyes.

"That's right, my darling. He's a strong, lad." Tom wrapped his arm around Nanny Betty's shoulders.

Tom Roberts was a very well-known businessman in Newfoundland and around the world. Although he was technically retired, he still kept his feet wet in all the businesses he started from the beginning.

He was also Nanny Betty's boyfriend, for lack of a better word, and he doted on her. Lora didn't know the whole story, but they'd dated as teenagers and because a series of terrible events they'd been separated. Nanny Betty later married Jack O'Connor and started the amazing family Lora now knew. Jack passed away ten years earlier, and Tom came back into her life six years ago.

According to Alice, Nanny Betty would never admit she and Tom were dating, but with the way they gazed at each other when they thought nobody was watching, it was clear they loved each other.

"Now, lets get dis sleeveen so we can get back to narmal." Lora smiled at Nick's grandmother.

Because she grew up in Newfoundland Lora had no issues understanding her accent or the words Nanny Betty used. Sleeveen was a nice way of calling someone an asshole and narmal was just her accented way of saying the word normal. Nanny Betty's accent could probably be mistaken for Irish to anyone that wasn't familiar with the dialects around the province.

"Excellent idea." Tom kissed the top of Nanny Betty's head, and the couple left Lora with the four young children.

A short while later, Molly crawled into her lap with teary eyes. Lora cupped her daughter's cheeks.

"Sweetie, what's wrong?" Lora met her daughter's gaze.

"Superheroes are not supposed to get hurt." Molly sniffed. "Hulk's a superhero how come he's hurt?"

Lora's heart broke as her daughter snuggled into her neck and sobbed. If Hulk didn't make it, Molly would lose her belief that superheroes existed. Not only that, Lora would have to try and explain his senseless death to her little girl.

"It's okay, Molly. You know what?" Ian's daughter, Lily, sat next to Lora on the couch.

"What?" Molly sat up and looked at the beautiful blue-eyed young girl.

"Hulk has lots of people asking God to make him better." Lily smiled.

"That's right." James oldest son, Mason, sat on the arm of the chair next to his cousin. "Hulk's a tough guy."

It made her heart swell to see how these kids were doing everything to make Molly feel better. Especially since they'd known Hulk a lot longer than Molly did, and were probably worried about the man themselves.

"Just wait, he'll get really tired of being in that hospital bed, turn green and he'll be back here before we know it." James' other son, Danny, flexed his arms and growled as if he was turning into the Hulk himself.

Molly's giggle made Lora smile, and she felt a wave of relief as her little girl ran off with the other kids to the backyard.

She glanced into the large dining room and studied all the men and women gathered around the table. Most were standing, but Sandy and the guy everyone called Smash, sat in front of laptops clicking on the keys. They were doing everything they could to find the guy they now referred to as the unsub. She'd heard the term before on crime shows but didn't know real law enforcement used it.

Of course, they called him other things as well, but since there were children within hearing distance most of them had been holding in those words.

The couch dipped next to her, and Lora turned to see who sat beside her. Her mom smiled as she held the tiny baby. Lora still couldn't believe the hospital allowed Emily to leave with the baby after less than forty hours.

"He's so adorable." Her mother cooed.

Lora couldn't disagree. The little boy was the cutest thing she'd seen since Molly was born. His hair, and he had lots of it, was dark with auburn highlights. His lips pursed as he stretched in her mother's arms and made a little grunt.

"Imagine, he's not even two days old, and he's home with his family." Her mother shook her head. "In my day you were lucky if they let you go home after a week."

"Except for Mike, all mine were born at the hospital, and I remember being so sick of the hospital by the time they sent me home." Kathleen sat on the coffee table in front of Lora and her mom.

"Times sure have changed." Lora looked up at Nick's father. He'd placed his hands on Kathleen's shoulders and bent down to kiss the top of her head.

"Yeah but the more they change, the more they stay the same." Kathleen glanced toward the dining room.

"They'll find this son of a bitch," Sean whispered and winked at Lora.

"I'm so sorry for bringing all this around your family. I…" Lora was stopped when Nick's Aunt Cora touched her shoulder.

"Honey, you are family." Cora smiled and kissed the top of Lora's head.

Those words brought tears to her eyes, and she glanced toward the dining room again to hide them. Nick met her gaze and when he noticed he furrowed his brows as if asking her what was wrong. She smiled and blew him a kiss. Nick seemed to understand that her watery eyes were happy tears.

Lora, Stephanie, Sandy, Kristy, Jess, and Isabelle scurried around the large kitchen in Nick's parents home. After feeding what seemed like a million people, they gathered in the kitchen to clean up.

She was still amazed at how Kathleen, Nanny Betty, Cora, and her mother were able to put enough food together to feed such a large crowd. They used disposable dishes which Nanny Betty had declared a gift from God, but there were still tons of pots, pans and serving platters to be rinsed and squeezed into the dishwasher.

"We talked Mom into keeping the pub closed for the rest of the week," Jess handed another serving dish to Lora.

"I thought she would throw something at me when I mentioned it. Not because she wanted to open or anything but that we would think she would be so inconsiderate of Hulk." Isabelle wiped down the counter.

"I think it's for the best. At least until the foyer is cleaned." Sandy was in the middle of closing a full garbage bag.

"I feel like all this is my fault." Lora sighed as she closed the full dishwasher.

"No, it's not, and don't think for one second any of us think that." Stephanie placed her hands on Lora's shoulders.

"Fuck, no." Sandy tossed a cloth into the sink. "That bastard is why this happened."

"I know, but if I'd left the province like I was going to…" Lora shook her head.

"Then he probably would have killed more women or worse, followed you," Sandy told her. "Look, people like this are crazy. Something in his brains isn't wired the way yours or mine are. They may look and act normal around people, but something could set them off, and it probably wasn't even anything you did or said."

"I know that in here." Lora pointed to her head. "I just wish I knew who it was, so I could figure out why he's so focused on me."

"From what I could figure out when he so sweetly took us for a drive and put us up in his lovely dungeon, he thinks you love him, and he loves you." Kristy reminded her of the things he'd kept saying.

"Is it possible he's an old boyfriend you've forgotten about?" Jess asked.

"I've been over that with the police and Nick. All the guys I've been with were checked out, and they're either married, in other relationships or out of the province. The only one that is unaccounted for is Molly's father, but this guy is not Simon. I saw his arms, and there weren't any tattoos." Lora shook her head. "I just don't know, but there's something familiar about his voice."

"I did notice he never called you by your name." Kristy leaned against the counter next to her. "He just kept saying, my love."

"Yeah, see. That right there is creepy." Isabelle shivered and she wasn't wrong.

For the second night in a row, Molly spent the night out. Stephanie promised the girls princess movies and s'mores. Her mother and Ethan went to town to have dinner at Roman's house. It left her and Nick alone again.

"Have you heard anything on Hulk this evening?" Lora asked Nick when she'd finished her bath.

"Just that there's no change, but he still has brain activity." Nick was on her bed looking at his phone.

Nick's jeans were still on, but unbuttoned. His feet were bare as well, and his legs were crossed at the ankles as his back was propped against the headboard.

"That's good that he hasn't gotten worse, right?" Lora crawled onto the bed and knelt next to him.

"Yeah, it is." Nick dropped his phone and lifted her to straddle his legs.

"Why do I hear a *but* there?" She ran her hand over the top of his head and linked them behind his neck.

"No but. I'm just not going to be able to relax until this fucker is behind bars." Nick rested his forehead against hers.

"I hate what this is doing to everyone." Lora closed her eyes and let out an exasperated breath.

"I hate what it's doing to you. I hate what he could have done to you." Nick cupped her face in his hands, and she opened her eyes.

God, she loved this man, but she hated the worried look in his eyes. She couldn't forget the anguish that was on his face when he'd come to get her at Roman's house.

Before she could sink any more into concern, a loud explosion practically shook the house causing them both to jump. Nick yanked on a t-shirt and shoved his feet into his running shoes at the side of the bed. He grabbed his weapon from the drawer next to the bed. He'd started to keep it there over the last couple of days.

"What was that?" Lora gasped.

"I don't know, but stay behind me and if I tell you to run, go as fast as your legs can carry you." Nick held her hand. "Go right to Ian and Sandy's and call for help."

"Okay," Lora's voice was barely a whisper.

"Promise me, Lora," Nick demanded.

"I promise." Lora met Nick's eyes.

He kept a tight grip on her hand, and held his gun in front of him. Lora heard the explosion, but she wasn't smelling smoke. She was about to point that out to Nick, but a second explosion sounded.

"Jesus," Nick looked out the kitchen window.

Lora glimpsed over his shoulder, and her heart felt like it stopped. Black smoke swirled up over the line of trees into the sky.

"Isn't Mr. Batten's house over that row of trees?" Lora gasped.

"Fuck, Sunny asked us to check on him. Fuck. Lora, call nine, one, one and lock the door as soon as I leave." Nick made her swear to stay in the house and not leave unless she felt like the house was in danger.

In ten minutes sirens blared as fire trucks bounced up the unpaved road toward where Lora saw flames start to shoot up above the trees. She felt useless, and she was terrified for Mr. Batten as well as Nick. He'd run through the line of thick pine trees to get to the elderly man's property. Her hands were clasped in front of her chest as she watched out the window and waiting for Nick to return.

It seemed like hours since Nick disappeared into the woods. The dark smoke made it more difficult to see where he'd run, and flames had started to become visible over the line of trees.

Lora couldn't stay in the house another minute. She needed to know if Nick was okay. As she was about to turn away from the window, he appeared walking slowly toward the house.

Lora ran to the front door and unlocked it while she waited for him to come up the steps. When she yanked it open the sight before her was like a punch in the stomach.

Chapter 30

Nick ran as fast as he could through the dense trees between Lora's place and Mr. Batten's house. Sunshine asked them to check on the man, and with everything that happened with Lora and Hulk, Nick completely forgot. As a third branch hit him in the face, he cursed wishing he'd just ran down the driveway and up the road toward the house.

He broke through the trees to see the entire house engulfed in flames, and his heart dropped. Nick wasn't sure where the explosions came from but from what he could see there was no way he could get into the house to see if Mr. Batten was still inside.

Nick took a step toward the house but stopped when something cold pressed against the back of his neck. He froze when a faint whimper came from behind him.

"Nick," A quiet, quivering voice spoke behind him.

"Turn around cop, and remember if you make one wrong move, the little girl here will pay for your error." A male voice spoke from behind him. "Now put your hands over on top of your head and turn around slowly."

Nick felt his weapon pulled from the back of his jeans where he'd shoved it after he left Lora. He raised his hands slowly as he turned to face the man behind him.

"Sunny?" Nick gasped.

The young girl trembled next to a man Nick didn't recognize. The guy didn't look much older than Sunshine but the look in his eyes said the fucker was crazed. Sunshine's hands were zip-tied in front of her, but it was what was around her neck that made Nick's stomach lurch.

The man held a piece of wood in his hand with what appeared to be a wire attached to it. Kurt would call it a garrote, and it was now digging into Sunshine's slim neck. The blood that was seeping out from under the wire around the young girl's neck made Nick want to lunge at the man.

"Let. Her. Go." Nick growled. "You've got me."

"Officer, I'm not a stupid man. Look at me. You're twice my size and could probably snap my neck with one hand." He grinned down at Sunshine and aimed the gun at her head. It gave Nick the chance to see where the asshole had put his weapon. He'd shoved it into the front of his pants, but Nick couldn't take a chance and risk Sunshine's life.

"What do you want?" Nick's gaze met Sunshine's terrified one.

He'd known this girl since she was born and watched her grow into a sweet young lady. Now her life was being threatened by a crazy asshole that Nick wanted to kill.

"I want you to walk back through that woods to where my love is waiting." He backed up to leave space for Nick to squeeze through the path.

"She's not your love," Nick barked and soon regretted it when Sunshine gagged as the bastard pulled the garrotte tighter.

"Are you sure you want to test me?" The asshole narrowed his eyes.

"Stop," Nick shouted as he eased through the trees.

He prayed Lora saw them before it was too late. Nick walked slow in order to give her time to make a call for help. He just hoped she was watching.

"You're smarter than I thought. Now, move it. I don't want those sirens to find us." He chuckled. "Now keep your hands on your head because this will only take a couple of more twists before it cuts off her air."

Nick's jaw clenched as he made his way slowly back toward Lora's place praying he could give her a signal. The sound of Sunshine's terrified sobs behind him was pure torture.

A sigh of relief whooshed out of him when Lora stood in the window, but before he could give her a warning she disappeared. Hopefully she'd saw what was going on and called the nine, one, one.

Nick moved slowly toward the front door. He even went as far as pretending to trip over his feet to give her more time. When the door opened, his heart sank.

"Nick," She gasped as she noticed the scene behind him.

"My love, I'm back to get you away from these people." Was this man fucking serious?

"It's you?" Lora stepped back into the house as Nick, and Sunshine were led in behind her.

"You know him, Lora?" Nick heard the door close.

She nodded, but looked in a complete state of shock. With the way she shook her head, it was as if she couldn't believe what was in front of her eyes. As if this guy was the last person she expected to see.

"Lora, look at me," Nick shouted to get her attention.

Something slammed against the back of his head, and for a second, he was dazed. He fell to his knees, but it was enough to break Lora out of her bewilderment.

"Leave him alone." Lora shrieked at the man.

Nick attempted to get up but received a kick to the side of his head, and he fell to the floor on his chest. Both Lora and Sunshine screamed as he repeatedly kicked Nick in the chest and face. Nick lifted his arms to protect his head as the man wailed on him with steel toe boots.

"Stop. Please." Lora's voice howled even over the roaring in Nick's ears from the kicks to the head.

"My love, why are you protecting him?" The man's voice calmed, and he stopped his assault.

Nick shook his head several times to keep from passing out. He was dizzy, and his vision was blurred, but he willed the strength to stay conscious. He had to for Lora and Sunshine.

"Because you're going to kill him." Lora's weeping made him push up so he could prop his back against the wall.

"But he's kept us apart." This guy was really out of his fucking mind, but Nick couldn't see him since he stood out of Nick's field of vision

"Nick didn't keep us apart, Sterling." Lora's voice suddenly quieted as if she realized she needed to calm the man she'd just referred to as Sterling.

"Yes, he has," Sterling bellowed.

Nick tried to remember the name from the lists, but his head was spinning from the kicks to the face. He wiped his arm across his eyes where the blood was making it hard to see the situation.

"No, Sterling. I came to Hopedale on my own and..." The man shrieked over Lora's voice, and she stepped back.

"You're. Mine." His voice almost sounded demonic.

Before Nick had time to do anything, something slipped around his neck. When he raised his hands to his throat, he felt the wire against his skin.

"Sterling, don't hurt him. Please." Nick opened his rapidly swelling eye and flinched with pain, but he needed to see Lora wasn't close to this guy.

"Hurt him? I'm going to save you from him." Sterling's voice rumbled next to Nick's ear.

"Lora, get out of here." Nick managed to choke out.

"I'm not leaving you." She pushed Sunshine behind her and Nick felt a wave of relief to see the girl was alive, but neither of the women were safe.

"Now, Lora. Get out of here." Nick croaked when Sterling tightened the wire.

"Leave him alone," Lora begged, and for some reason, her plea must have broken something in Sterling.

The wire around Nick's neck loosened and he gasped in air. Sterling fell to his knees and placed the gun at Nick's head. Nick didn't care about the gun. He kept his focus on Lora.

"You want me to leave him alone? Leave. Him. Alone." Sterling practically screamed in Nick's ear. "You love me. Not him. Me."

"Sterling, we're friends. Nothing more. I enjoyed talking to you at the school, but we were just friends. You were a big help to me with the younger kids and I appreciated it so much." Lora met Nick's gaze, and then her eyes went back to Sterling.

"You said you loved me." He screamed.

"No, I told you I loved your talent. You're an amazing artist and I cared about you, but I never said I loved you that way." Lora stepped toward them.

"Lora," Nick growled a warning.

"It's okay, Nick. Sterling won't hurt me." Lora took another step toward them.

"I'd never hurt you, my love." His voice calmed, but he pushed the barrel of the gun harder against Nick's head.

"I know, and you don't want to hurt Nick either." Lora's voice was soft, but Nick could see the pulse in her neck beating rapidly.

"He touched you." Nick winced when the gun pushed against his swollen eye.

"He was helping me." Lora knelt about two feet away from where Nick sat on the floor and way too close for Nick to feel comfortable.

"You let him inside your body," Sterling growled and pushed Nick's head again.

"No, never." Lora lied.

"You're lying. How could you lie? I saw you. I saw what he did to you and what you did to him." He shrieked.

"Lora, get out of here," Nick whispered.

She shook her head and continued to move closer. Nick was supposed to keep her safe, and he was on the ground with a fucking gun to his head. While the crazy fucker was slowly losing all touch with what little sanity he had.

"I'm not leaving you." She met Nick's eyes.

"Please, baby. I don't want you to see him kill me." Nick's eyes filled with tears as he forced out the words.

"I'm not leaving." A tear rolled down her cheek.

"Stop." Sterling's body shook next to Nick.

"Sterling, please. I'll do anything. Please let him go." Lora begged as the tears streamed down her cheeks and it tore Nick to pieces.

"Why don't you love me?" It was as if something finally clicked in Sterling's head.

"You're my friend, Sterling. You were the first one to hug me after my dad died, but sweetheart, you're twenty years old, and the right woman is out there for you. It's just not me, but I'll always be your friend." Lora didn't make a move toward him, but she continued to talk.

"You need to put the gun down. Please." Lora inched closer and held out a trembling hand.

Nick held his breath as he waited for Sterling to snap and kill them all. Lora wasn't a negotiator, but Nick was in awe of the way she spoke to the guy with a hushed tone. When the gun lowered slowly, it took every ounce of strength for Nick not to grab the guy's hand. It would make things a thousand times worse, and Sterling still had Nick's gun tucked into his pants.

Nick slowly let out the breath he held as Sterling was about to place the gun in Lora's hand. Then things went to hell as the front door opened and two of his brothers walked in with weapons raised followed by three other officers.

"Drop the weapon," John spoke in a calm but authoritative voice.

Sterling stiffened next to him, and Lora's eyes widened just a little as the gun pressed against Nick's head again.

"John, he's not going to hurt Nick. He's going to give me his gun, and Nick's gun as well because he doesn't want to hurt anyone else. Right, Sterling?" Her courage made Nick so proud, but he was terrified something would set Sterling off, and she'd get hurt.

"Is that right, Sterling?" John sounded pleased, but Nick knew it was a tactic to make the subject believe he was doing something right.

"Of course, it's right. We're friends." Lora held her hand out again. "Please, Sterling."

"They'll kill me." Sterling maneuvered until Nick was pulled in front of him like a sheild.

"We won't hurt you as long as you put down your weapons and come with us." James didn't move from where he stood next to John.

"Yeah right. I've seen those shows. As soon as I put down my gun, you'll shoot me in the head," He bellowed over Nick's head.

"No, not unless you shoot first," James stated.

"I'll lower my gun if you do the same." Sterling's body shook, making Nick uneasy.

"I know what you see on television, but I'm sorry we can't do that, Sterling," John explained.

"I want to tell her something." Sterling's body vibrated.

"That's okay, but I'd feel a lot more comfortable if you'd put the gun down." John again tried to get Sterling unarm himself.

"Not until I tell her," Sterling growled.

"Okay, that's fine." Lora held up her hand to John. "What do you want to tell me?"

"You were the only one to ever treat me like a person. The first day you came to the school to help out I was in grade twelve, and you smiled at me as soon as you came into Mr. Norris's office." Sterling stopped and took a deep breath.

"Dad liked you, Sterling." Lora smiled.

"I told my dad I loved you and I was going to marry you. I told him you were mine and he laughed. Can you imagine? The principal of a high school laughed at me, his own son, and told me I was too much of a loser to get a woman like you." Sterling's grip tightened around Nick's neck.

"I'm sorry your dad said that to you." Lora's apology was genuine.

"I sent you gifts. My dad said it was the kind of gifts women wanted. It was the same as the movies he watches. Where women dress in sexy clothes and let the men do things." The gun moved away from Nick's head.

"I see." Lora's voice came out in a shaky whisper.

"He's gonna be pissed. I lied to him." He released his hold on Nick and knelt back.

"What did you lie about?" Lora asked.

"He asked me if I hurt those women. The ones I tried to turn into you, but I told him it wasn't me." Sterling placed both guns on the floor next to Nick.

"Sterling, I need you to put your hands on the back of your head." John sounded pissed.

In twenty minutes, Nick was on a stretcher being pushed into the ambulance with Lora clinging to his hand. Sterling was shoved into the back of a cruiser. His gaze never left Lora.

"It's over." Lora brought his hand up to her lips as they were transported to the hospital.

Nick closed his eyes. The relief of knowing he could stop worrying about her being taken away from him calmed him. They could finally move on with their lives. All he had to do now was make sure Lora knew how much he loved her and that he wanted to spend the rest of his life with her.

Chapter 31

They stood next to where the attendant lowered the urn into the ground. Lora clung to Nick as her heart broke for his family. He was dead, and it was hard to not blame herself.

On the other side of the grave his sister sobbed in the arms of an older man. Lora never got a chance to meet the woman, and now they were at a grave burying her brother.

"May the love of God, and the peace of the Lord Jesus Christ bless and console us and gently wipe every tear from our eyes. In the name of the Father, and of the Son, and of the Holy Spirit." The priest prayed.

Lora still couldn't believe any of this. He didn't deserve to die that way. There was nothing to justify what Sterling did, but he was raised by a father who did nothing but beat down his self-esteem and make him feel unworthy of anyone loving him.

Lora was relieved Clyde was currently the subject of an investigation and fired from the high school for the distribution of pornographic photos to male students. The pictures weren't illegal, but by sending them to kids made him not only sick but a criminal.

Sterling confessed to the murders of all five women, Dulce, as well as the couple who bought Lora's family home. The thing that stunned everyone was he admitted to murdering Molly's father too. She didn't even realize Simon was missing since she hadn't seen him in over a year.

Two weeks passed since Sterling's arrest, and the judge deemed him unfit to stand trial. According to the doctors, he was raised by a verbally abusive father who never showed any affection. Clyde continually humiliated his son to the point that when Lora showed him the tiniest bit of attention, he built a whole imaginary relationship with her. He'd spend the rest of his life in the Waterford Hospital mental health facility.

Lora was relieved that it was over, but the number of people who'd been hurt or killed was tough to get her head around. It was hard to believe that the sweet young man who used to help her when she'd go to the high school to volunteer was the same man that terrorized her for so long.

His father was such a bastard. She never liked Clyde because of the way he treated the teachers, but to know he'd mistreated his son so terribly that Sterling became infatuated with her was unforgivable

"Hi, Lora, Nick," Sunshine's soft voice called from behind them.

"Hey, sweetie. How are you doing?" Lora gave the teenager a huge hug.

"Mom and Dad got me an appointment with a therapist because I've been having nightmares." Sunshine glanced at Nick and gave him a weak smile.

"That's a good thing." Nick touched the young girl's arm.

"I know, and to be honest, it'll probably help me deal with Mr. Batten's death as well." Sunshine looked back to the grave. "I didn't even know he had a sister. He said he had no family."

"I don't think anyone did," Nick told her.

After the police released the name of Albert Batten as the victim of the fire, his sister's husband contacted the police. Albert's brother-in-law told the police that Albert had a falling out with his sister a couple of decades earlier over their father's estate. Albert moved to Hopedale and the siblings never spoke again.

"I can't believe he's gone. He was a cranky old man, but I'm going to miss his gruff complaining." A tear ran down her cheek.

A woman called to Sunshine, and she gave Lora and Nick a quick hug before she hurried off. Hopefully, the young girl would deal with what happened and move on with her life.

"Hey, we're going to see Hulk." Keith stood next to the car.

"He practically begged Keith to come over because his sister is driving him crazy." Emily laughed.

"Do you think he'll mind if I take Molly to see him?" Lora asked.

Ever since Molly found out Hulk was out of the hospital, she'd begged Lora and Nick to take her to see her buddy. She even threw a couple of tantrums when they wouldn't take her right away.

"I'm sure he'd love to see her." Emily got into the car.

"Great. We'll see you there." Nick opened the door for her, and they got into his truck.

An hour later Lora laughed as Hulk tried to explain why he couldn't do his lift trick with Molly. The doctor told him he needed to take it easy and not to exert himself. Molly pouted for a bit but quickly crawled onto his lap when he said he'd let her watch the Disney channel.

Hulk would fully recover, thank, God, but it would take some time, and Lora was happy about that. His sister agreed to stay with him until he was back on his feet, much to Hulk's dismay.

Diana Steel was younger than both her brothers, but Lora found out very quickly the woman didn't let them tell her what to do. She reminded her a lot of the O'Connor girls in her personality. Hulk's brother Clark was the oldest and returned to Gander because he was a firefighter there.

"I still find it so funny that your parents named all of you after their favorite comic book superheroes." Emily chuckled at the story Diana told them about their parent's love of superheroes

"I guess you were destined to be named Hulk." Nick laughed.

"That wasn't where he got that name." Keith snickered.

"I've never heard that story." Diana propped her arms on the chair where she crouched next to her brother.

"And you're not going to." He growled and glared at Keith.

"Oh, come on. I want to know too." Lora leaned forward in her chair.

"Rusty, shut your mouth," Hulk used Keith's nickname with a low warning growl.

"I know how he got the name." Emily grinned mischievously.

"Spill," Diana giggled as she covered her brother's mouth and muted his protests.

"When Keith first hired Bruce, they found an old run-down building for the offices and sleeping quarters." Emily moved to the edge of the sofa where she sat next to an amused Keith.

"Don't you have control over your woman, Rusty?" Hulk groaned.

"How long have you known this family? We don't control any of the women in this family once Nan gets hold of them," Keith laughed.

"Anyway," Emily rolled her eyes, "They were painting the offices and the bedrooms, and there was a slight disagreement between Trunk and Bull about the color of the main room. The guys got a little physical over the whole green versus blue thing."

"For the love of, God." Hulk rolled his eyes. "I was… entertaining a lady friend… in bed… I heard the argument and didn't know what was going on…Fuck… I ran out of the room as naked as the day I was born, bumped into the ladder the idiots left in front of my bedroom door, and I knocked an entire can of green paint over me."

As soon as Hulk finished his embarrassing story everyone in the room broke out into hysterical laughter. Molly glanced around the room, but it wasn't enough to take her attention away from Disney.

"It wasn't funny." Hulk groaned. "The woman took off like a bat out of hell when I walked back into the room."

"Probably because he stomped in the room roaring like a crazy person." Keith laughed

"Oh…what did… Oh my, God. Did she think you were … an alien?" Diana choked as she tried to catch her breath.

"Or she thought he was the Incredible Hulk." Lora held her stomach.

"The truth was she wasn't a really smart woman either." Keith chuckled.

"I'm glad you are all enjoying my humiliation. It took days to get rid of all the paint." Hulk grumbled.

"Yeah, I bet little Hulk didn't enjoy all the scrubbing." Emily giggled.

"I used to think you were a nice lady, Em." Hulk sighed, but when his lips quirked up, Lora could see he wasn't the least bit angry.

"Boy, did I have you fooled." Emily tucked her feet under her bottom and snuggled into her husband.

Lora eased into Nick's side. His laughter vibrated through her body, and she sighed. For the first time in a year, she was relaxed and happy. So very happy.

Lora was glad to be back at her old job as well, but did miss the diner sometimes. Molly started kindergarten, and Lora's mother took over Lora's place at *Jack's Place*. It wasn't that her mother needed to work, but she wanted something to keep her busy. Ethan took a job at the pub as a bartender until he figured out what he was going to do next. Lora was just happy to have her family close to her.

It was the second week of September and Kristy's wedding was the next day. She stood in the middle of the hall at the Hopedale Sailing club making sure all the decorations were perfect.

Kristy hired Lora to decorate the hall for the wedding. Since Lora was an interior decorator, setting up for a wedding was a piece of cake. Plus, Lora got to spend time with the people she'd grown to respect and love.

Alice hobbled toward Lora with a huge smile on her face. The cast was gone, but she was wearing a walking brace for another couple of weeks. She wasn't happy about it, but Pam took her shopping, and she found a great pants suit to wear.

"Lora, this is absolutely beautiful." Alice glanced around the room.

"I had lots of help." Lora motioned to the group of O'Connor women and their friends.

"You always do in this family." Alice chuckled.

By the time she arrived back home, it was just before midnight. Nick and Ethan were still awake and sipping beer while they watched a ball game.

"Hey," Nick tipped his head back to look up at her as she walked behind the couch. Lora bent down and gave him a quick kiss on the lips.

"Hey, I see you guys have had a busy night too." Lora laughed.

"This is tough work making sure we keep up on who will make it to the world series." Ethan pointed his finger toward the television.

"Plus, weren't you the one that told us to scram once all the heavy lifting was done?" Nick raised an eyebrow.

"Yes, I was, and I bet you two are exhausted," Lora said sarcastically.

"You know we could have stayed and helped you decorate." Nick took her fingers in his hand.

"I love you, honey but the ladies and I had a blast." Lora wrapped her arms around his neck. "Plus, I can't honestly see you and your brothers or the other guys, filling vases with flowers." Lora kissed his cheek.

"I'll have you know I do a mean flower arrangement." Nick chuckled.

"Jess is very talented. I only found out tonight that she owns a flower shop. She said she opened it before she joined the academy." Lora was still shocked by the information. "She still owns it and said she goes there when she wants to relax."

"Yeah, we used to say Jess was the only flower child that could kick ass." Nick stood up and pulled her into his arms. "We should call it a night. If there's one thing I've learned over the last six weddings, tomorrow is going to be a long, hectic day."

"I love weddings." Lora glanced at her brother who stared up at her with a wide grin on his face.

"What's that look?" Lora questioned.

"Nothing at all." Ethan smiled.

"Ethan?" Lora warned.

"It's nothing, sis. I better get to bed." Her brother stood up and made his way to the room he'd been staying since he arrived in Hopedale.

"I hate when he does that." Lora groaned.

"How about we forget all about your brother. Molly is all tucked in, and your mother is spending the night at Daphne's house." Nick rested his hands on her hips and backed her slowly toward her bedroom.

"I see, and what did you have in mind, Mr. O'Connor." Lora reached behind her to turn the knob to the bedroom.

"Oh, let's see. How about a hot shower where I fill your shower poof with body wash?" Nick ripped his shirt over his head as he kicked the door closed.

"Yeah? What else?" Lora slipped her shirt over her head and tossed it on the floor.

"I'll take my time and run it down the back of your neck, down your back, and take special care to that sexy ass before I make my way down your legs." Nick rid himself of his track pants and boxer briefs.

"Sounds heavenly." Lora wiggled out of her yoga pants and panties as Nick turned on the shower.

"You *are* my heaven." Nick moaned when her hand wrapped around his erection, and he pulled her against him as they stepped into the shower.

Nick devoured her mouth, and Lora forgot everything else but how it felt to be pressed against him. Skin to skin, body to body. She loved this man with all her heart, and she wanted to be with him for the rest of her life.

Nick treated Molly as if she was his own daughter. Her little girl idolized him, and there was nothing in the world was sexier than a man who loved children. Lora loved him with every beat of her heart. Hopefully one day, she'd be getting ready for her own wedding day.

Chapter 32

Nick took the time to speak to her brother and mother while Lora was out decorating the hall. He'd always been told to speak to the woman's father before he ever proposed, but since Sam Norris passed away, Nick went with asking the two members of her family that were left.

Her mother was thrilled and practically strangled him when she hugged him. Ethan held back a little more. After Sheila left for the night, Nick wanted to know why Ethan was uncomfortable with Nick proposing.

"It's not that I don't think you two belong together. I'm just sad that our father won't be there to give her away." Ethan dropped his head.

"Isn't that where her big brother is supposed to step in?" Nick asked, and Ethan raised his head again.

"Yeah," Ethan held out his hand to Nick. "If you love her as much as she loves you, and you take care of my niece, you have my blessing."

Now he stood at the bar and watched Lora as his father twirled her around the dance floor. She laughed and looked absolutely beautiful in the floral, sleeveless sundress. The pale blue of the dress made the blue in her eyes stand out, and the pink flowers complimented her pale skin.

Nick was waiting for the song to finish so he could introduce Kurt. His uncle was going to sing a song to Kristy and Bull. It was the first time in years that Kurt sang in front of a crowd, but he'd come to Nick and Aaron a couple of days before the wedding to ask their help to pull off the surprise.

The song was called, *I loved her first* by *Heartland*. It was such an appropriate song for a father to sing to his daughter, and Nick was certain there wouldn't be a dry eye in the house when Kurt was done. He'd be surprised if Kurt actually got through the song.

A few minutes later, Nick jumped up on stage and the surprise for Kristy commenced. As he predicted, tears flowed like a river, but Kurt managed to get through the song. There was just one more surprise to pull off, and that one had his heart pounding.

"Thanks for the warning about Dad's surprise." Kristy punched him softly on the shoulder.

"I was sworn to secrecy." Nick laughed.

"It's not fair for your girlfriend to look better than the bride." Nick glanced down at Kristy and smiled.

"You look stunning." Nick wrapped his arm her shoulders and kissed her on the forehead.

It wasn't a lie. He'd never seen his cousin look more radiant than she did in her wedding dress. Nick knew he was one of very few who knew Kristy was also pregnant.

"Thanks, Nick. Are you ready for all this?" Kristy whispered.

"To marry her? One thousand percent." Nick couldn't stop grinning if he tried.

He'd mentioned he wanted to propose to Lora in a conversation with Kristy the week before. She excitedly came up with a plan for him to do it at the wedding when she was supposed to throw the bouquet.

"What if she's not ready?" Nick whispered mostly to himself as he hugged his cousin.

"Are you kidding me? When she sees you down on your knee, she won't be able to say no. I mean, you're proposing to both Lora *and* her daughter." Kristy smiled up at him, and his hand went to the two small boxes in his jacket pocket.

"I hope you're right, Kristy." Nick blew out a breath.

"I just came over to give you the two-minute warning." Kristy laughed. "As soon as that song is over, you're up."

Nick's heart thundered in his chest as he tried to relax but when the Deejay announced that all single women gather in the center of the floor, Nick swallowed and straightened his shoulders. Of course, they were all aware of the plan and made sure they were behind Lora. Isabelle brought Molly to the front as well and placed her next to her mother.

"Okay, are you ready?" Kristy yelled over her shoulder as she gave Nick a wink and he nodded.

"Come on, Kristy," Isabelle shouted.

"Yeah, we're getting old waiting here." Jess laughed.

"One," Kristy lifted the bouquet in the air, "Two," that was his cue.

Nick stalked toward his cousin and snatched the flowers as she held it in the air. They'd been bought especially for this occasion. It wasn't actually Kristy's bouquet. The only one to look surprised was Lora. Nick stopped in front of Molly and pulled a pink rose out of the bundle and handed it to the little girl.

He turned to Lora and held out the rest of the flowers to her. Lora took it reluctantly and glanced around the room at the group of people staring at her and Nick.

"Nick, what are you doing?" Lora leaned toward him and whispered.

"Lora, the first time I saw you at the grocery store something hit me in the chest. I'm guessing it was cupid's arrow. So, I'm not taking any chances with you catching the bouquet and someone else catching the garter." Nick winked at his Aunt Cora.

"Nick," Lora smiled.

"I never thought I'd find someone I could love as much as I love you. You give me more with a smile than anyone I've ever met. You make me want to be a better person because who I am with you is who I really want to be." Nick stole the line for the song he sang for her as he pulled the white box out of his pocket, and dropped to one knee.

"Oh. My. God." Lora's hand cover her lips and her eyes filled with tears.

"Lora, you and Molly are the best thing that ever happened to me. No matter what I say, what I do, there's only one thing in this world that would make me the happiest man on earth." Nick swallowed hard. "If you would agree to be my wife. Lora Norris, will you marry me."

Nick held his breath as Lora stared at him, tears flowing down her cheeks, one hand trembling against her mouth, and the other clutching the flowers to her chest.

"Mommy, are you gonna say yes?" Molly tugged on Lora's dress.

"Yeah, Mommy, are you gonna say yes?" Nick winked, but his heart felt as if it was about to jump out of his chest.

"Yes. yes," Lora whispered and nodded her head frantically as she held out her hand. "My God, yes."

Nick never felt so relieved in his life as he did when he slipped the ring on Lora's slender finger. He jumped to his feet and wrapped his arms around the woman of his dreams. She squealed as he spun her in a circle and covered her mouth with his own.

"Are you sure?" Lora gasped when he finally ended the kiss.

"I'm one hundred percent positive. I just have one more proposal." He placed her back on the floor with another quick kiss to her temple.

Nick knelt back on the floor in front of Molly and took the little girl's hand in his. She smiled shyly at him and he tucked a stray curl behind her ear.

"Molly," Nick looked into the little girl's eyes that were so much like her mom.

"You don't call me Molly." The little girl reminded him, and the group around them laughed.

"You're right. I apologize. Lollipop." Nick cupped Molly's cheek.

"Yes, Nick." She grinned.

"I love your mommy very much, and she agreed to marry me." Nick reached into his pocket. "But I can't marry her unless you tell me it's okay."

"It's okay, Nick." Molly smiled at her mother.

"Do you see this little box here?" Nick held up a small pink box.

"Uh, huh." Molly nodded.

"This is my promise to you, Lollipop. I promise to be the best step-dad I can be, and I'll protect you, wipe your tears, and pick you up when you fall. I'll teach you things and answer any questions you have about life or love. I'm not perfect, and I'm going to make mistakes, but there's one thing you need to know and never forget. I love you from the top of your head to the tips of your toes." Nick smiled when Molly handed her rose to her mother.

"I love you too, Nick." Molly wrapped her little arms around his neck and hugged him.

"I have a question for you, Lollipop." Nick pulled back to see her face.

"What?" She tilted her head and glanced down at the box.

"Molly Lollipop Norris, will you let me be your step-dad and take this necklace, so you always remember how much I love you." Nick opened the box that contained a gold pendant in the shape of a heart with the word's *Daddy's girl* in the center.

"No," Molly shook her head, and Nick's heart sank.

"Molly?" Lora crouched next to her. "I thought you loved Nick.

"I do, Mommy." Molly glanced at her mother then back to Nick.

"But you don't want him to be your step-dad?" Lora looked as heartbroken as Nick felt, and the room was so quiet you could hear a pin drop.

"No," Molly wrapped her arms around Nick. "I want you to be my real dad."

Nick wasn't usually an emotional man, but when Molly revealed her wish, he could hardly keep the tears from spilling out.

"Is that okay, Nick?" Molly pulled back and stared at him.

"Lollipop, that is more than okay." Nick handed the necklace to Molly and Lora helped her put it on.

"Do you know what that says, Molly?" Lora asked as she held up the pendant.

Molly shook her head as she picked up the small heart in her tiny fingers and held it away from her chest.

"It says, Daddy's girl." Lora's voice cracked.

"I am Daddy's girl. Right, Daddy?" Molly threw herself into Nick's arms and hugged him tightly.

"That's right." Nick's voice came out in a croak, but at that moment he didn't care.

"I love you, Nick." Lora wrapped her arms around both him and Molly.

If there were ever a point in a person's life that was considered the happiest, Nick would have put that moment as number one. He was sure there would be more, but it was difficult to believe he could ever be happier than he was at that very moment.

Epilogue

Aaron stood at the top of the stairs and grinned down at Nick as he proposed to Lora. The twinge of jealousy struck again for the hundredth time at being the only one to have love and lose it. Of course, nobody knew how he felt about Bethany.

There wasn't a day that went by in his life that she didn't enter his thoughts. It was stupid, because he hadn't seen her since he was eighteen years old. His last day of high school when she told him she was leaving town. Leaving him the day after he'd took her virginity and she took his.

"When are you going to take the plunge?" Aaron turned toward the older man next to him.

"I don't see that happening anytime soon, Father Wallace." Aaron chuckled.

Father Wallace was the principal of Holy Cross Catholic School, and a dear family friend. The school went from Kindergarten to grade twelve, and separated into three buildings. Elementary, junior high and high school.

"Oh, I don't know about that, Mr. O'Connor." Father Wallace winked.

"I'd make a wager, but I'd be afraid you'd send me to detention." Aaron chuckled.

Father Wallace narrowed his eyes and then let out a hearty laugh. He was one of those priests that you felt comfortable with, and sincerely cared about his students. Aaron always looked up to the man.

"I've actually been meaning to call you." Father Wallace turned to face him.

"Why? What's up?" Aaron turned toward the father.

"Holy Cross has its one-hundredth birthday coming up next September. We're planning a huge celebration, and I was wondering if we could count on you to help." Father Wallace asked.

"What could I help with?" Aaron volunteered at the school a couple of times a month, and he enjoyed helping with the music program.

"Besides the entertainment? We need someone to help with contacts." Father Wallace pulled a card from his inside pocket.

"The entertainment is no trouble. Everyone in our band went to Holy Cross, but the contacts, I'm not sure what you mean." Aaron sipped his beer.

"That's our secretary's number at the school. She has the list of students and most of them we have current information, but there are a lot who left the province." The sadness in Father Wallace's voice was undeniable.

"You want me to see if I can find the ones you don't have information for." It finally clicked what the priest was asking.

"Yes," The priest smiled and held out his hand.

"I think I can manage to do that." Aaron shook the father's hand.

"I was also hoping to ask if you knew how to get in touch with Bethany Donnelly as well." He'd thought about that name every day, but to hear it out loud was like a punch in the gut.

"No. No. I haven't talked to Bethany since the last day of high school." Aaron turned back to the railing and stared down at the people dancing below.

"Oh, I thought you two were great friends in school." Father Wallace copied Aaron's stance.

"We were, but you know. You grow up and go your own ways." Aaron lied.

"Oh. Well, I do appreciate that you can help us out. It's a big milestone for the school. I'd like to see as many old students attending as possible." He slapped Aaron on the shoulder. "It's good to see how great all you boys turned out."

"A little worried about us, were you, Father?" Aaron chuckled.

"Not for a minute." The priest walked away leaving Aaron as alone as he felt inside.

He always tried to keep everyone from seeing just how isolated he felt. Aaron lost the only woman he ever loved twelve years earlier, but he didn't know what he'd done.

He still remembered that day as if it was yesterday. She'd walked toward him on the beach where all the graduates were having a bonfire. School was out, and they were celebrating. He watched her walk toward him, and he smiled from ear to ear. Aaron reached for her when she got close to him, but she stepped back so he couldn't touch her.

She told him she was leaving Newfoundland to go live with her sister in Ontario and wouldn't be coming back. Aaron was so dumbfounded that she was almost halfway across the beach before he ran after her. Bethany told him to leave her alone and said she never wanted to see or hear from him again.

She'd been his first, and nobody ever came close to how it felt to be with her. He knew what his brothers meant when they said being with the women they loved was different than anybody else.

Nick was the only one who knew how devastated he was when Bethany left, but he didn't grasp just how long it took Aaron to get over her. Probably because he still wasn't, and he doubted he ever would

.

About the Author

What does someone say to describe themselves? You could start with giving what others say about you. Scratch that. It doesn't really matter what others think about you. It matters what you think of yourself. So here we go.

First of all, I'm a wife and mother. I'm also a grandmother. That alone would fulfil any woman's life and to be honest it does. But.....

I'm also a writer. Someone who loves to tell stories of love, suspense, heartache and of course happily ever after. For most of my life, I've written those stories for myself. A type of therapy, I suppose. I love the characters I create. They become part of who I am because there's part of me in them.

So.... Now that you know this about me. I hope when you read my books, you fall in love with them.

You should also know that I'm a Newfoundlander. What is that you ask? Well we're a proud people who live on an island, off the east coast of Canada. Some people believe Canada ends with Nova Scotia. It doesn't. If you keep going east, there is a beautiful island full of amazing people and magnificent scenery. That is where my stories are set because let's face it. The best stories always come from the places you know and love.

If there is anything else you would like to know about me. Ask me!

Coming Soon

O'CONNOR BROTHERS

Book 7

Available October 29, 2018

She broke his heart but now she's in danger.

Can he protect her and his heart?

O'Connor Brother Series

Read about the sexy O'Connor Brothers

In Books 1, 2, 3, 4, 5 & 6

Available on

Amazon and

Kindle Unlimited.

Also Available

Dangerous Therapy

Book 1

Officer John O'Connor is giving up on life after a terrible accident. His family are at their wits end when he refuses any kind of therapy. The only thing keeping him sane is his dreams of a beautiful woman he pulled in for a traffic violation months before.

Physical Therapist Stephanie Kelly is healing from a broken heart. When she is hired by Nightingale's personal care and physical therapy, she's ecstatic, but she's shocked when her boss asks her to take on a new patient. Shocked because the patient is her boss's nephew and he's not exactly keen on therapy. He's also the cop who's been heating up her dreams.

As Stephanie helps John get back on his feet, they grow closer, but someone is out to hurt Stephanie, or worse. After multiple attempts on her life, John's family tries to figure out who's after the woman he loves and stop them before it's too late.

Dangerous Abduction

Book 2

Widower James O'Connor has been fighting his growing attraction to his brother's sister-in-law for four long years, but when someone breaks into her home, destroying everything she owns, James takes her and her young son into his home. The break-in wasn't random. Marina and her son are in danger, and James swears to protect them, but can he keep them safe?

Marina Kelly dedicates her life to caring for her sweet little boy, Danny. Since she broke free from her abusive husband, she's sworn off men, but when James O'Connor keeps entering her thoughts and her dreams, it takes everything she has to keep her feelings hidden. Now, her sister and parents are out of the province, and she's in danger, Marina has no choice but to accept James's help and try to hide her attraction and growing feelings.

The attraction between them impossible to resist. Only her ex's family secret may tear it all apart. Can Marina and James unravel the family's hidden mystery without losing each other?

Dangerous Secrets

Book 3

Ian O'Connor has everything going for him. He's got the O'Connor drop dead good looks, an incredible body and to top it off he's a doctor. Why wouldn't anyone want the man but none of that was the reason Sandy Churchill was head over heels in love with the man. After he had stood her up for their first official date, she was weary of taking another chance. When she ends up in the hospital because she turned her back on a criminal determined to get away from her, Ian admits that he loves her and wants another chance. A secret from his past throws Sandy into a tailspin, but she has a secret that she's hiding from everyone.

Ian's on cloud nine when he finally takes a leap of faith and tells the woman he's loved for four years how he feels and wants a chance to make up for his screw up. They have two weeks of bliss, but a murder and secrets come back to haunt him. Sandy's reaction tells him there's another reason why she's avoiding him. She's hiding something, but he has no idea what and to make matters worse there's danger coming from her past that could hurt the people he loves the most.

Dangerous Beauty

Book 4

When you come from a privileged family, you're expected to follow a particular path in life. Unless you're Emily Bradshaw. Defying her father, Emily turned down a full scholarship to Dalhousie University. Instead, she followed her dream and opened her own salon in the small town of Hopedale with her friend. She's happy. Then her mother vanishes. Her father receives threatening messages and hires Newfoundland Security Services to protect his children. Emily doesn't like the idea, especially when the man that walks into her salon dressed in a black leather jacket makes her weak in the knees. Emily knows she's in danger but not the kind her father is worried about.

Keith O'Connor isn't expecting his newest security job to be anything out of the ordinary. Then he walks into Snippy Gals, a beauty salon in Hopedale. Keith gets the shock of his life when an auburn haired beauty turns to face him. Emily is defiant, sassy, and her sexy curves have him in a complete spin. Fighting his feelings for her becomes almost impossible, but when Emily's mother is found, a family secret is revealed turning Emily's life upside down. Can Keith help her cope and keep her out of the clutches of a vengeful stranger?

Dangerous Silence

Book 5

Mike O'Connor's reputation earned him the name Mr. Homerun, but after two hours with Billie, he's ready to change all that. There's one problem. She disappears before he can find out her last name.

Billie Carter had little choice but to leave when she received a desperate text from her friend. Peggy and her daughter have no family, both are deaf, and Billie wants to protect them from an abusive man.

When Peggy is brutally murdered, Billie is determined to protect Chloe. Like a dream come true, Mike walks through her door to help. They soon learn that the little girl is not the only one in danger, and it may take more than Mike to keep them safe.

O'Connor Girls

Book 1

Available on

Amazon and

Kindle Unlimited

Hidden Betrayal

Book 1

Kristy O'Connor never hid the fact that she wanted Dean 'Bull' Nash. He's kept her at arm's length since they met but he's pushed her away for the last time.

Dean loves Kristy more than he could ever tell her. He wants her desperately, but his family secrets could destroy them both.

When he can't stay away from her any longer, murder and a shocking betrayal shake them to their core. Can their new relationship survive?

Rhonda Brewer

Keep up to date on all things new.

Follow me on

Facebook

Twitter

Instagram

Sign up for my newsletter and never miss another release!

http://www.rhondabrewerauthor.com/talk-to-me